UNINVITED

CAROL RAYYAN

ISBN: 0692228063
ISBN-13: 978-0692228067

ACKNOWLEDGMENTS

There are so many angels who helped me finish this book. I love you and I thank God every day for blessing me with you all.

To my sister Laura Scoggins, thank you for encouraging me to get back into writing. Seeing you publish your book *Eavy* made me feel like I could achieve anything.

To my sister Michelle Khbeis and the rest of my fabulous test audience; Kristina Sarris, Nicole Rayyan and Joanna Ziadeh, thank you for reading every version of this story and being unable to put it down. You made me feel like a writer from the beginning.

To my Mom, Dad and sister Diana, thank you for your love and support.

To my friend and editor Noah Ross for pushing me to think outside of the box and make this story come to life. You are a literary genius.

And finally, to my amazing husband, Isa. You always believed in me and kept pushing me to follow my dreams when I wanted to give up. You are my heart, soul and the love of my life. You are my everything.

PROLOGUE:
DEATH KNOCKS

"Selena! Time for dinner," Honoria shouted out the window. Her soft hair fell from the loose bun on her head and she wiped her hands on the front of her apron.

A moment later a beautiful girl with bright blue eyes came bounding in the house. Her long black hair flew behind her like a cape.

"Oh my gosh mom, you should have seen it. Max ate a worm! He just ate it!" Selena's face was a mixture of awe and disgust.

"That's nice, dear. Please don't ever do that," Honoria said, laughing at her daughter's excitement. "William, are you coming?"

"Yep, I'm here. Sorry I had to finish up a few things." William Arturro was a tall, lean man with dark hair and brown eyes, in stark contrast to his wife's light brown hair and blue eyes. He leaned down to kiss his daughter on the top of her head. "What's this I hear about a worm?" He asked as he sat down at the table.

Selena, excited to broach the subject again, described the situation in detail over dinner.

"You had to ask, didn't you?" Honoria looked lovingly at her husband. He shrugged his shoulders and smiled, enhancing the wrinkles around his eyes.

"What are we going to do about the glow? I imagine with all the excitement, it's there, right?" William asked in hushed tones. Honoria's eyes dropped to the table and she nodded. That had been worrying her for years, ever since she saw it. The concern sat like a stone in her stomach now. William clasped his wife's hand and gave it a reassuring squeeze.

After dinner, they cleaned the table and washed the dishes, and William went to tuck Selena into bed.

"Would you like a bedtime story tonight?" William asked his daughter, who looked small tucked under the plush, tulip-patterned comforter.

"Nope. My life is already an adventure." Selena bolted up in bed. "Worms dad! He ate a worm!" Selena still couldn't let the moment go. Her father chuckled, gently tucking her back in bed. He kissed her cheek, turned off the lights, and went back downstairs.

"They're late," Honoria said, pacing anxiously around the living room.

"Relax, they'll be here."

A few minutes later, the doorbell rang, interrupting Honoria's pacing. She redirected her path to open the door.

"Hello, Mrs. Arturro," a kind looking woman said in the doorway. Her short, gray curls encircled her soft, round face giving her a grandmotherly appearance. A boy and a girl stood on either side of her.

"Please come in," Honoria said, holding the door open wider for them.

"Well, what do we have here?" William asked, tousling the girls' hair, and making her laugh. He reached for the boy who was approaching his teens, if not already there, but the boy stiffly shifted out of the way.

"I will make this a quick visit," The woman started, looking through the window at the darkness spreading across the sky. "This young lady here has shown amazing potential already. She has the ability of telekinesis and can create a sphere shield. The boy can control certain elements and has already developed the ability to teleport. They are the right age and will be a perfect match."

Honoria and William exchanged a glance, then Honoria's gaze wandered around the room. The ticking of the old grandfather clock marked the passing of seconds.

The woman shifted her weight from one foot to the other.

"Are you sure you two are up for this?" Honoria asked earnestly. "It's a big responsibility."

"We are well aware," The boy said, his chin up, eyes blazing with a determination that looked more suited to one twice his age. The young girl smiled eagerly.

"Oh yes! I can't wait," she exclaimed.

"You two are very brave. Thank you." Honoria hugged each in turn, and then her husband did the same. The woman nodded.

"We should leave now. Know that everything will be all right. It's just a precaution." She took the children and bustled them out the door.

"It'll be fine," William said, hugging his wife.

"I hope so. My stomach is in knots just thinking about it," Honoria said, burying her head in her husband's chest.

Upstairs Selena looked out her window to see the three visitors leave. The boy looked up at the window, as if he sensed he was being watched. His eyes met Selena's and they stared for a moment at one another before he turned back and hurried to catch up to the woman.

"Selena!" William called from downstairs. "Wake up, honey. Breakfast is ready."

Selena groggily stumbled down the stairs to the smell of pancakes.

"Good morning, baby girl," Honoria said, placing a few stacks on a plate.

William laughed, "She will never be a morning person." He sat at the table, one leg crossed over the other as he read the paper.

"Oh sure she will. She'll be a go-getter, you'll see." Honoria smiled sweetly at her daughter and placed the plate on the table. William sipped at his coffee, shaking his head. Selena dropped her weight into the chair and looked up at her mom.

"No, mornings suck mom." Selena lifted her fork in anticipation of tasting the sweet fluffiness of her mother's special pancake recipe. William choked on his coffee, and Honoria raised her eyebrows.

"You'd never think she was only ten." William laughed.

Selena shrugged her shoulders and scarfed down her food.

"I think I want to go back to bed." Selena slid off the chair.

"Oh no you don't. You've had plenty of sleep. Go and play or something," Honoria said.

"Mom!" Selena dragged the word out into three syllables. "It's Saturday."

"If you don't go out, you won't get to see things like boys eating worms," William chimed in. Selena's eyes widened.

"Okay!" She rushed up the stairs to get dressed.

"That girl has a thirst for adventure." Honoria removed her daughter's empty plate.

That night Selena woke to a shrieking, wailing noise. She jerked up and saw smoke in her room.

"Mom!" She called, crawling out of bed. In a flash her mother was there.

"Selena, go downstairs and across the street right now. I have to get your father, and we will meet you there. Go!" Honoria's voice was full of panic. Selena obeyed immediately. Her small bare feet slapped against the hard wood floor and Honoria let out a sigh of relief when she heard the front door open and close.

She ran to her husband's room. "William!" She shook him. "Oh please, William, wake up!" She checked for his pulse. Nothing. Her heart sank, and her stomach rolled with nausea. She swallowed back a sob. The carbon monoxide had gotten to him, her heightened senses allowed her to smell it now. Why hadn't she noticed it before? It wouldn't affect her or Selena that quickly, but William couldn't take it. She ran for the stairs, tears streaming down her face. It tortured her soul to leave him but she had to get to Selena, she had to protect her daughter.

As she reached the top of the stairs a figure appeared and stood in her way.

"Who are you?" She asked, anger and venom in her tone, but not fear. The figure didn't answer. Honoria looked around at the flames licking the banister and eating through the walls. She had no time for this. She flicked her fingers and the figure flew across the hall away from the stairs. She ran down almost slipping in her haste.

She was only a few feet from the door when something grabbed her leg, and she fell on her face. She turned to see that someone had hold of her. She moved her arms frantic-cally, but the smoke was in her lungs weakening her, and she was losing consciousness.

She reached for the door, tried to drag her body toward it, but she couldn't move. The figure had her pinned down by her feet. She kept trying to free herself, but the more she moved, the more smoke she inhaled. The fire reached her, burning her flesh and she screamed until the smoke engulfed her. She couldn't breathe. She coughed reflexively, trying to clear her lungs of the soot that coated them. Her skin seared as she writhed in agony.

I love you Selena, I'm so sorry, she thought. Then everything went black.

1.JUST ANOTHER DAY

"Honey, I'm home!" I said as I entered my empty ground floor apartment. I'm not crazy, not that I know of anyway; it just seems to fill the silent void I usually enter when I come home. I threw my keys into a porcelain bowl I dedicated to them on my kitchen table. Another day of meaningless interviews finally ended. I used to have a job, I am not lazy, I was just unhappy. I used to be a bartender at a strip club, until I couldn't tolerate the guys grabbing my ass and calling me baby anymore. It was for the best; the smell of cigarettes and alcohol started seeping into my clothes and eventually my apartment, but I should have thought twice before I quit. It would have saved me the grief of tapping into my savings to pay my rent while I found another miserable waste of time job.

I went to the bathroom and washed my face. The cool water washed the feeling of corporate sludge off. I looked at my reflection and ran my fingers through my straight black hair that fell down to my waste. My sapphire blue eyes weren't as bright as usual, but I blamed the stress of job hunting. On my way home from this last interview I decided I was going to take a break from it and just focus on myself. Maybe I would take a trip, or go shopping – whichever was cheaper. I ran my tongue over my straight teeth, which thankfully came that way naturally and wiped the gloss of my mouth. I un-tucked the white dress shirt I wore in an attempt to make myself look professional, and started un-buttoning it. After working at a strip club, I learned quickly that the better shape a girl is in, the better the tips, so I kept my body slim but lean – which worked well for my 5'5" height. I had curves in all the right places but I was toned enough to make sure guys knew I could take care of myself. I flipped the bathroom light off as I left the small room and changed into shorts and a tank. The Arizona summer was too hot to wear dress shirts all day.

Finally relaxing I sat in front of my T.V. and turned it on. Flipping through the channels in a daze I went over my interview that day. The guy, Mr. Heffernan, all but laughed at me when he read my resume. I couldn't believe how rude he was. Why even call me in for an interview? Probably to laugh at me, I guessed. I felt my blood pressure rise and tried to breathe. The sound of my pictures clattering against my wall brought me back to the present. I often wondered what my neighbors were up to that would make the items in my apartment shake. Whatever it was, it was happening more often lately, and it was getting annoying. I wasn't entirely sure I even wanted to know.

The rest of the night past uneventfully like most of my time recently. I really needed to find something productive to do. As I crawled into bed I decided, tomorrow I would start doing more active things.

The next day I woke to the sun shining brightly into my room, the light making the inside of my eyelids turn red. I wasn't surprised to find my sheets crumpled into a ball at the foot of my bed; the summer heat here made bedding useless. Remembering my promise to do something productive I got out of bed and got ready. Thirty minutes later I was out the door.

Getting into my metallic blue mustang GT, I cursed having leather seats, not that I had a choice. It was inevitable; every time I sat in it, I burned my butt on the seat and my hands on the steering wheel. It didn't help that I was wearing a short sundress. Pressing down the clutch, I turned the key in the ignition and felt the familiar roar of the engine around me. I blasted my air conditioning and regretted it immediately. The hot stale engine air blew in my face, making me turn down the dial a notch and roll down my windows. I put the car in first gear and pulled out of the parking lot. I wasn't sure where I was headed but just the drive alone and watching the palm trees disappear as I passed them was comforting. After a few minutes I rolled up my window and turned up the A.C. The cool air was heavenly, but I was already starting to stick to my seat. Changing gears, I lost myself in the feel of the 300 horse power engine carrying me farther and farther away. Before I knew it I found myself pulling into the parking lot of Sam's Hair Salon.

Jumping out of the car, I adjusted my blue dress, and peeled the fabric away from my sweaty back. As I walked into the salon I pulled my sunglasses up and on my head. It didn't take me long to find Alexis among the stylists. Her lone pink streak in her pixie cut blond hair stood out considerably. Her small pointed nose, which matched her pixie look, was raised as she assessed the hair of the woman sitting in front of her, taking care to calculate each snip. Alexis didn't notice me until I was three steps away from her, and when she finally saw me she did a double take. Her brown eyes widened, her eyelash extensions almost reached her eyebrows, and she stopped mid cut.

"Hey, Selena! What are you doing here?" She whispered the last part in case Beth, her boss, was around.

"I just thought I would drop in and say 'hi', you know, stuff like that," I said awkwardly.

"Wow, you must be bored. You know, some of us do work. I don't need Beth breathing down my neck today. I go on break in fifteen. Can you wait till then?"

I nodded and went to sit in the waiting area. I didn't blame Lexi, Beth was pretty scary when she wanted to be, and Lexi's 5'2" 115 pound frame didn't seem like she could take Beth's 5'10" 150 pound mass of anger.

I sat cross legged, flipping through an extremely outdated magazine when Lexi finally came over. We decided to walk to the coffee shop next door to talk. After ordering our over-priced latte's, we found a table to sit at in the back of the room.

"So you really had nothing better to do than crash my workplace?" Lexi asked, gracefully shimmying into the metal-backed seat.

"I…sure I do, I just thought *you* could use a nice break. I'm plenty busy, but I was thinking of my friend. I guess it was a mistake to care about how your day was going." I dramatically pouted.

Lexi rolled her eyes. "Right, I'm sorry. Thanks." She seeped sarcasm.

"Okay fine, I had nothing better to do. I needed my friend and to kill some time. Sue me."

"You are so dramatic Selena. Find a hobby or something. Stop moping."

My jaw dropped open. "I am not moping!" I hissed.

"Sure you are. You remember when you finished your criminology degree and couldn't get a job? You sulked for over a month before you found that bartending job."

"So?" I folded my arms across my chest. I was missing the point that Lexi was annoyingly trying to make. She sipped at her latte and gave me *the look.* That don't play dumb look.

"Fine, I'm moping. As my best friend it is your duty to cheer me up. And…go!" I smiled, waiting anxiously for her to accomplish this impossible task.

"Alright, fine. I'll show you just how good a friend I am." She removed the plastic lid off her coffee and hid it under the table. A moment later she bent her head down into her lap and when she popped her head back up her mouth looked stuffed with something. Lexi smiled, revealing that the plastic cap had been molded into an impossibly realistic set of pointed teeth. I raised my eyebrows in wonder and Lexi stuck her tongue through the plastic veneers. Laughter bubbled in my chest but I refused to give Lexi the satisfaction. I suppressed my smile.

"Is that all you got?"

Lexi's face contorted into one of irritation.

"Fine," she said over her mouth full but it came out as "frime." She bent her head down again, but went completely under the table this time. The few patrons around us looked over in curiosity, making me feel uncomfortable.

"You okay down there?" I asked, putting humor in my tone so the others would know there was no emergency.

When she came back up I bit my lip to not laugh. Lexi had somehow twisted the plastic of the lid in her hair. She had five separate sections sticking up all around her head, her hair twisted around the plastic in each chunk. She looked like she stuck her finger in a socket and then she smiled, the spiked plastic teeth still in place, her tongue poking through the sharp points. I couldn't hold it in this time, I laughed until my cheeks hurt and my eyes watered. Lexi wriggled her eyebrows adding to the effect and I buckled over trying to catch my breath. When I was finally able to compose myself, Lexi had taken out her accessories.

"How did you do that?" I asked, wiping my eyes. That lid must have been bigger than I thought.

Lexi shrugged her shoulders. "What can I say? I'm gifted." She beamed.

"Well, you passed. I'm all cheered up." I chuckled.

"Good. So, how's the job hunting going?" Lexi asked, veering the subject back to the serious matter at hand.

"Damn it Lexi, you were so close to being cool."

Lexi gave me the look again.

I rolled my eyes and huffed. "It's…fine. I have decided to take a break. I feel like doing something fun. Do you have any ideas?"

Lexi thought about it for half a minute, knowing very well that I was changing the subject back to the fun stuff.

"There's always something fun in Old Town. Let's go out dancing tonight!" The light in her eyes seemed to glow and her enthusiasm was contagious.

"Okay, meet me at my place around ten; that should give us plenty of time to get ready."

We finalized some more details and then I left Lexi to get back to her work. Walking back to my car I contemplated what to do next. It was still early and I had a lot of time to kill before tonight. How ironic, I hated working, yet it seemed to be the one thing that kept me sane and busy. After brainstorming, I decided to work on my tan.

I drove home and changed into my bikini, threw a beach dress on top and headed to the pool by my apartment. Since it was mid-day Friday, no one was there and I loved the solitude. For the next 4 hours I tanned, swam, and read a self-help book on acing interviews, by the pool. It wasn't a fun book to read obviously, but it made me feel less guilty about swimming instead of job hunting. I would much rather read a fantasy book like *The Princess Bride* but I had to be a little responsible. It was a great afternoon.

Once the sun started to sink behind the buildings, I gathered my things and went home. After showering I decided to watch some movies in an attempt to pass the remainder of the day.

Finally there was a knock on my door and the excitement returned. I opened the door to find Lexi standing there with a bag of outfits I was sure she was going to model for me.

"Hey! You won't believe what I found in my closet while fishing for clothes." She barged past me with her bag and made her way to my room. It wasn't a far walk; my place was pretty small; standard kitchen, living room, bedroom and bathroom. Lexi dramatically threw her sack on my bed and started rifling through it.

"Aha!" She said as she found the object she was digging for. As she handed it to me I couldn't help but chuckle. It was a book we had when we were teenagers. A best friend memoire if you will. Skimming through it I laughed at how naïve and silly we were, talking about boys and boy bands. Ah, the life of a thirteen year old. Wait, thirteen? My stomach did a small flip and I moaned as I threw myself face down on the bed. After a moment of silence, of which I was sure Lexi was staring at me with confusion, I lifted my head to look at her. I was right; she squinted her brown eyes, pulling her eye brows together in worry. Then her face smoothed out in curiosity. I let my head fall back into my bed and said, "When did we get so old?" into my mattress.

"Uh, what? I don't speak muffled bedding."

I lifted my head and suppressed a smile. "I said, 'when did we get so old?'"

Lexi's mouth dropped open slightly. "Speak for yourself! I am two months younger than you, so you're old, not me," she said with a smile I knew all too well.

"Ugh! We're twenty-five Lex, still living the single life, renting instead of buying, doing stuff teenagers do. Don't you think we need to start being...I don't know, grown-ups?" Even as the words rolled off my tongue, I had a bad taste in my mouth. I honestly still felt like I was fifteen, just with ten years of experience. Lexi laughed and sat beside me.

"You just turned twenty-five last month. I'm still twenty-four thank you. You know, I honestly don't think real grown-ups feel grown up. Does that make sense?" She laughed.

"Not really, but I get it." Yeah figure that one out. I had no idea where my head was lately. Deciding to change the subject from my impending doom of oldness, I started rifling through Lexi's clothes. That was enough of a cue for her to start trying on different outfits. While she modeled one outfit after another, I straightened my hair, and did my make-up. Finally she found an outfit she looked and felt hot in. She wore a white, off-the-shoulder ruffled shirt that showed just a minimum amount of her midriff and white short shorts. She completed her outfit with gold jewelry, and white beach shoes that strapped around her ankle and lower calf. Her short pixie hair was spiked and she looked great. Now it was my turn, but it didn't take me half as long to find an outfit as Lexi.

Finally settling on a gold tank, black short shorts and black stilettos, I checked my reflection in the mirror. I let my hair hang down my back and wore some simple gold jewelry. Lexi stepped beside me and I marveled at our contrast. She had creamy skin, light hair and a white outfit, whereas I was tan, dark haired and wearing mainly black. I knew she was sharing the same thought, and we chuckled. Grabbing our necessities, we left my apartment and headed to Old Town.

2. NIGHT HIKE

We could hear the cacophony of music warring from the numerous clubs as soon as we turned onto 7th Avenue. I parked my car as close to the club as I could, but parking in Old Town was a nightmare. We walked down the sidewalk and toward the line to get into *Majestic*, which was thankfully short, since it was just Eleven o'clock. We leaned against the wall of the building, being last in line, when a bouncer walked up to us. He was dark skinned and quite large actually, not so much fat but husky, at least 6" and 230 pounds of bulk.

Walking towards us, his eyes travelled up from our stilettos, to our short shorts, our chests (staying there a moment too long) and then finally up toward our eyes. He nodded his approval and signaled for us to follow him with a wave of his hand. Not wanting to disobey the big intimidating man, we followed. He led us to the V.I.P. line and said, "Two fine ladies such as yourselves should never wait in line." His smile showed perfectly straight, white teeth, and he walked away, no doubt looking for other 'fine ladies'.

Thirty seconds later we were in the heart of the noise. Didn't even have to pay cover – God, sometimes it is fantastic being a woman. We walked up to the bar and each got a B52 shot. After gulping the smooth liquid in one straight motion, we started scouting the area. We weren't really looking to meet anyone, just see what the crowd was like. The short line outside was deceiving, the club was full of people. Most of them in our age range, mid-twenties to early forties.

Mid-twenties, ugh.

After a few minutes at the bar we decided to walk around. There were two floors to this club, the first floor had a live band that covered songs from Journey to Ke$ha, and the upstairs had your typical Top 40.

Not liking the 80's song *Whip it!* the band was currently playing, we decided to check out the scene upstairs. Walking onto that floor we were engulfed by more loud music, smoke and lights. Rather than yell to talk to each other, we decided not to talk at all.

So, we danced, and danced, and danced.

Numerous men had the courage to openly watch us, but very few actually talked to us or tried to dance with us. And with good reason too; a lot of these guys were creepers, kind of leering at us. Some actually licking their lips at us, so any one of those goobers who tried to approach us were quickly shot down. Lexi and I didn't need men grinding up on us to have a good time; we had a system. If we liked the guy, we danced normally, if not, we signaled to the other for help, and the guy was sent away. Lexi and I perfected the signal years before; it was to wink twice and pretend to wipe dirt off our shoulder. When I saw Lexi give the signal, I would take her hand, spin her around like a ballerina and turn so I was standing between her and the unwanted male dancer. Worked every time.

Somewhere during one of our rejection dances, I turned to see a man leaning casually against the bar, scoping out the dance floor. He was probably 6'2", and had a muscular but lean build. The color of his hair and eyes were hard to see from across the floor, being obscured by the smoky air. There was something about this guy though, he wasn't like the others. He had an air of confidence around him and…something else, something I couldn't place, but it made it obvious that he was in a different league than all the other men here. No leering…unless I was the one doing it. He turned my way and our eyes met. I had a weird sense of all the noise dimming around me, everyone fading in the background except him. Not wanting to look creepy I broke eye contact and turned back to Lexi. I was surprised to see that she had stopped dancing and was staring at the same man.

"There's something about that guy, isn't there?" I asked, breaking Lexi's stare. She blinked and looked at me.

"Yeah, definitely," was all she said, and then started to dance again, looking distracted. I shrugged my shoulders and got back into the groove. I was so curious about that guy though, and no matter how hard I tried, my mind kept wandering back to him. I turned around again to see if he was still there. He was, and he was looking straight at me. I turned my attention back to Lexi in an attempt to look aloof. It lasted about five seconds. I turned to the bar again, but he was gone.

My heart sank a little. All these yahoos here trying to rub up on us, yet the one decent looking guy in this place leaves. Oh well, nothing a drink can't fix. I grabbed Lexi and we went to get another shot. I felt every sweet drop roll over my tongue and work its way into my system. Okay, that sounds bad I know, but I really needed it at that moment. Being fuelled by the alcohol, Lexi and I danced for a while. Finally needing a break, we walked around until we reached a lounge area. We found a vacant couch and sat down resting our throbbing feet.

"I hate heels!" I yelled over the music, taking my shoes off and rubbing the balls of my feet. "Whoever created high heels did not have women's feet in mind." Lexi laughed and then looked down at her hands. "Are you okay?" I asked her, hoping she could hear me over the music. She looked up, smiled slightly and nodded.

"I think I'm just tired. Want to head out?" She asked. I checked the time on my cell; it was already past 1:30 am. I nodded and we weaved our way downstairs and out of the club.

The quiet of the street was sudden and welcome. As we walked back to the car we saw a girl in a very small leopard print dress, trying to hold herself up against a larger man. She was so drunk her ankles looked like they were made of rubber. She lost her balance repeatedly until she fell on the ground and just lay there. I got a clear view of her panties, though I guess I should be grateful she was wearing any at all. I shook my head and kept walking as the man tried to pull her off the ground while she protested to moving. Now that was a sight to see.

I dropped Lexi off at home and gave her a hug good-bye after helping her with her bag. She only lived a block away from me, so she had walked to my place earlier. I wondered what she must have looked like walking down the street with her bag of clothes.

Finally getting home myself I washed up and got into bed. The comforter enveloped me, making me sink further into my mattress. The silence was deafening, causing an irritating hum in my music damaged ears.

I fell asleep and had a dream about being in a room with many doors, each with a different picture on it. It was as if the door I chose, determined the story I would be in. I found myself in a version of Jack and the Beanstalk, watching a tree grow all the way up and disappear in the clouds. Then my dream suddenly shifted into one of a mysterious man. I was in a field, the burnt yellow grass cropped short. Surrounding the field was a ring of large Oak and Maple trees. It was night, the stars shone in the moonless sky. The man stood across the clearing, leaning against a tree. His hair was dark brown, falling in choppy layers around his face. It was a little longer in the front than the back, and his eyes were an odd mix of dark green and yellow. His chiseled jaw was clenched, his muscular arms folded tightly across his chest as he stared at me.

I felt a sense of recognition as I stared into his eyes. Shyly I walked across the field towards him, but before I got half way there the earth crumbled beneath my feet. I ran in the direction I came from, trying to escape the gaping blackness that tried to engulf me. My feet were milliseconds faster than the ground dropping to nothing below them. I looked back where the man had been. He was staring at me now, all guards down, his face a mask of shock. Just then, he vanished right before my eyes.

I woke up breathing heavy, the lamp on my night stand wobbled slightly on its base. I steadied it and shook my head not wanting to think about my neighbors. Instead I was trying to understand what I had just dreamed. I had no idea what any of it meant, but one thing I did know; the man in my dream was the one I had seen at the bar.

"Tell me what he looked like again?" Lexi asked over the phone.

"Really, you are making way to big a deal out of this," I retorted. I called Lexi that morning to tell her about my dream. I was still in bed, I hadn't even showered yet. I just woke up and called her. I don't know why, maybe because the dream left me feeling uncomfortable; Scared and intrigued at the same time. I explained the mysterious man for the third time to her.

"Did you recognize him from somewhere?" She asked. I let out a sigh.

"Yeah, well, I don't know. I—don't laugh, but I think it was the guy from the bar last night." Lexi paused a moment before responding.

"Did you really get that good of a look at him? I could hardly see him across the room."

"I know, that's the weird part. I guess my subconscious just filled in the details I couldn't see before. It's not like that's how he looks in real life, but it just felt like he was so real! Like he was really there." There was a silence over the phone as Lexi processed this, and thought of what to say next.

"Well dreams are weird like that I guess. Listen, it's no big deal like you said. Don't think too much about it. I need to do some stuff. I'll talk to you later?"

"Yeah. Sure."

We signed off and the line disconnected. I felt a little disappointed that Lexi couldn't give me any answers, but really, what did I think she was going to do? It was just a dream after all. Pressing the end button on my cordless I lay back in bed and pulled the covers over my head.

I stayed under the sheets until the heat of my breath (and the smell of it) threatened to suffocate me. I had to get up, brush, and do something to get my mind off the dream.

A few days passed uneventfully. I talked to Lexi a few times but they were all brief conversations, none of which were about my dream. Although I didn't speak of him, that guy from the bar often came to mind, and I couldn't shake it. Feeling restless one night, I decided to go hiking since the sun had long gone down, cooling the desert air. Putting a few water bottles in my back pack and grabbing a flashlight, I left my apartment and headed for the trail. I had my hair tied in a high ponytail, the end of it softly brushing against the middle of my back. I wore shorts, a t-shirt and my runners. Although the sun was down, it was still pretty warm outside.

I got to the trail and stretched, loosening my joints and muscles. I took out my flashlight and started the short hike. It wasn't the safest idea, walking alone at night with snakes and potentially coyotes hiding in the dark, but I just had to get out and do something. I knew this trail well, but I kept alert as I skimmed the ground in front of me with the light. The dirt path was lined sporadically with small bushes and cacti, but the almost moonless night hid most of them from my view.

I had been walking about half an hour when I heard it: a soft rustle ahead of me and to my right. I quickly swung my light to the direction of the noise, squinting in an attempt to see further into the dark. I thanked the heavens that I had been studying karate for a few years.

My heart rate sped up to the point that I could hear its fast pace in my ears. The wind around me started to blow with an unusual fierceness, whipping my ponytail around and swirling dirt into my face. Holding the light still, I willed the shadows to reveal their secrets to me. Just then I saw a figure stand up and then crouch down behind a bush. I moved my light to try and see, but they moved just out of sight.

"Who's there?" I shouted, glad that my voice didn't betray my fear. I contemplated running back to my car, but the thought of possibly being chased unnerved me. If there was someone here that would try to hurt me, I would face them, not run. "I don't have patience for these games." The edge in my voice revealed my anger. Having made a mental and potentially stupid decision, I walked toward the bush that hid my stalker. The wind was still blowing ferociously.

As I got closer, the creeper decided they couldn't really hide anymore and stood straight up, the shadow loomed almost a foot above me. I am not sure why, but I stepped forward, and punched where I thought I would hit face. I was dead on, hitting a nose. I heard a grunt and saw the shadow's hand fly up to its nose. I was about to turn and high-tail it back to my car when the light caught the face that was attached to the punched nose.

There in the superficial glow of my flashlight, stood the man from the bar. My breath caught in my throat as I saw that his dark shaggy hair and green eyes specked with yellow, mirrored the image I had of him in my dream. The expression on his face looked angry but not aggressive, he blinked repeatedly as his eyes watered, and his nose was red.

Although there seemed to be shock in his eyes, his jaw was clenched and his arms moved to fists by his side, probably mad that I had the courage to confront him. I must not have hurt him much if he was standing tall, the need to put pressure on his nose gone. Just as suddenly as it started, the wind died down. My breathing was quick and shallow as I contemplated what to do with this situation. I almost apologized, but thought better of it. He deserved it for lurking around at night like that.

"Who are you? What do you want?" I decided to ask the obvious questions. He seemed to relax a little and let out a long sigh of defeat.

"Tristan," he said shortly.

"Okay. Are you going to try to kill me or something?" Tristan flinched at my question. I was re-thinking running to my car. My curiosity was the only thing keeping me rooted to the spot, well that and probably fear. I didn't want to let this guy out of my sight.

"Of course not!" He yelled, as if I was supposed to know that just because someone hid in the bushes, didn't mean they would hurt you. He let out another long sigh. "I know this will sound weird--"

"No weirder than you hiding in a bush," I interrupted.

"I am actually here to protect you." I'm sure my face was an ugly mask of confusion. "You have no idea how important you are yet, but you will," he said, sending me further down the confusion path.

"What are you talking about?" I almost screamed, the wind starting to stir slightly at my feet, the trees rustling softly around me. Looking around at the moving trees, he seemed to be thinking of an answer. Finally he met my gaze, and I felt an eerie sense of calm. The wind died down again, obviously deciding there was nothing here to stick around for.

"You are in danger. There are things out there that can hurt you. I am here to make sure that doesn't happen," he explained.

"Listen, I know this trail through and through. I know there are snakes but I will avoid them. I Promise." I added. I had no idea why I felt like I had to justify my night hike to this guy, or why I was even talking to him. All I can say is that I just couldn't bring myself to leave. Tristan was shaking his head in frustration.

"You think I care about snakes? I know you can take care of snakes with a snap of your fingers. There are bigger and badder things you need to worry about."

"Like...coyotes?" I could've sworn his mouth twitched, almost in a smile, but just as quickly, it was gone. "How long have you been following me? Why do you care?" Tristan's face fell slightly at my last question.

"We need you," he said softly, never breaking eye contact. I was afraid to even blink. He ran his fingers through his hair, pushing it back from his face. My flashlight put a sparkle in his intense eyes. "This isn't how this was supposed to happen." Shaking his head he tensed again, clenching his jaw as if to force himself to say no more. He looked around, probably to see if anyone else was crazy enough to go hiking at this time of night. Suddenly, in a puff of white light, he vanished - right in front of my eyes!

"I must be losing it," I said to the space Tristan had just been in. I looked around to see where he had gone, expecting him to pop out behind me somehow. I couldn't stay there to find out. My fear and confusion spiked. I started to run. I ran faster than I ever had before back toward my car. As I ran, the rough wind came back with vengeance, encircling me, sweeping up the dirt from my path and obscuring my vision.

My breathing became ragged and my heart was racing wildly. I had never been that scared in my life. A bright light flashed from the heavens. Looking up I saw lightning crackle across the sky, threatening to split it apart. Following just after was a thunder clap so loud I had to cover my ears. My feet hit the ground harder and faster. Trying to be cautious not to run into a cactus, I maneuvered quickly down the well-worn path. I rounded the bend around a cholla giving it a wide berth – I didn't need those things jumping on me – as my car came into view.

Finally approaching my car I pulled the keys out of my bag and unlocked the door with the remote while still running. Reaching my salvation, I threw open the door; the wind at my back almost threw it off its hinges. I hustled inside slamming the door closed, silencing the noise of the wind and thunder.

Trying to catch my breath I locked the door and leaned my head back on the head rest. A strong gust of wind shook the car, throwing me into action again. I started the engine and peeled out of the parking spot. Finally calming down, I looked in my rearview mirror, but the dust seemed to have settled and there was no sign of lightning or rain. That was when I vowed never again to go night hiking alone...or at all for that matter.

3. KARATE CHOPPED

I had finally stopped shaking by the time I got home. I had also managed to get myself to believe that my eyes had played tricks on me. There was no way people could just disappear. I threw my bag on the floor and took a shower. I allowed the hot water to beat down on my hair and back as I replayed the night in my head. So many questions ran through my mind. Tristan said 'we need you.' Who's we? And why do they need me? Why am I important? Had he been following me at the club too?

After twenty minutes of exhausting my brain, I realized there was no way I could get the answers to my questions. Tristan must be crazy; that was the only solution.

I finished up, dried off and put on a fresh tank and shorts to sleep in. Lying in bed, I couldn't help but feel paranoid. I was worried that he had somehow managed to follow me home, and thoughts of being murdered in my sleep haunted me. Sleep eluded me for a few hours, but finally I succumbed to a restless night.

The next morning came all too soon, and I felt like a piece of meat that was punctured one too many times and left to marinate in a tub of mud. My eyelids felt weighed down, but I couldn't fall back asleep. I flopped out of bed, washed up and called Lexi. After telling her what had happened the night before, she started… well… freaking out.

"Oh my God! Are you okay?" She asked in one breath.

"Yeah, just confused. He said he was protecting me. It was the weirdest thing, Lex. I could have sworn he just, poof, disappeared in a puff of white smoke."

"Protecting… White…? Okay, we need to talk, in person. I'm on my way to work right now. Can you meet me there in about forty minutes?"

"Sure," I responded, curious to know what she couldn't tell me over the phone; probably that I needed to go to a psych ward. I hung up and got ready in twenty minutes flat. I made coffee to kill some time and sipped at it anxiously before giving up and leaving to meet with Lexi. Ten minutes after that I pulled into the parking lot, got out of my car and walked toward the salon.

The familiar chirping of my phone invaded the silence of the shopping center. I stopped walking and opened my purse to grab my phone before the caller lost interest. Seeing Lexi's name come up on my call display, I debated answering since I was about to see her, then shrugged and pressed the 'talk' button.

"I'm just about to walk in," I said instead of my usual greeting.

"I was worried you might be close. I won't be able to take my break just yet."

"No problem, take your time. I'll just wait for you to finish." I hung up the phone and heard someone clear their throat behind me. I turned around to see a man standing there, holding a pen. He was just less than 6 feet tall, and had a fit, solid build. He had brown eyes and hair kept short and neat.

"You dropped this," he said, holding my gaze as he handed my pen back.

"Thanks," I said, still staring at his deep brown eyes. Realizing I was staring, I blinked and tried to look away. He chuckled softly.

"I hope I see you around," he said smiling, then turned and walked away.

Wow.

I collected myself again and headed inside the salon. Lexi smiled as I walked in and sat in the waiting area again. She rolled her eyes behind her current client, annoyed that she couldn't finish yet. I smiled back, hoping to reassure her it was fine, and started my usual perusal of her magazines.

Lexi finally finished with her client and waved me over. I stood quickly and followed her to the back room. It was very small with enough room for a vending machine on one wall, a water cooler glugging in the corner beside it, a mini fridge against the opposite wall next to an outdated microwave on a rickety wooden stand, and a table with three chairs around it in the center. I took one seat as Lexi sat down across the table from me, clasped her hands together and just looked at me.

"Alright Lex, what's going on?" I asked, resisting the urge to squirm in my chair from anticipation. Lexi let out a breath.

"There's something you need to know, but I am just not sure how to say it," she started, further piquing my curiosity.

"Just say it. It's me; there's nothing you can't tell me." I made eye contact to reassure her that I was being sincere.

"Okay. Uh…" She paused, collecting her thoughts. "Things aren't exactly as they seem." She paused again, closing her eyes and rubbing her eyebrows with her left hand. "You probably won't believe me, but--" Beth chose that particular moment to walk in the back room startling Lexi.

"I need you up front. A wedding party decided to just walk in without an appointment. We need all the hands we can get right now," an annoyed Beth announced before leaving as abruptly as she entered.

"Crap. I'm sorry, I need to go. We'll talk about this later, okay?" Lexi stood and headed toward the door.

"Hey wait! You can't just start saying that stuff and leave before telling me the rest!" I fumed.

"I know. I'm sorry, but what I have to tell you will take some time, and I just don't have it right now. I promise I will tell you later." She gave me a quick hug and was out the door before I could protest again.

I followed Lexi to the front of the salon trying not to trip on my lower lip that protruded in a pout. I passed the group of excited bridesmaids all removing the elastics and clips from their hair in preparation to be beautified. I tried not to glare at them for inconveniencing me as I walked out. Walking to my car, a part of me hoped to see the pen rescuer again. Then I found myself daydreaming about Tristan, the intensity of his eyes burned in my memory.

He may have been crazy but he sure knew how to leave an impression. I had a sudden desire to see him and ask him all the questions that had been evading me. Instead I got into my car and pushed all thoughts of men aside.

"One," my sensei said, walking around the class, and observing our stances.

"Ayah!" We all said in unison, throwing out our right fists into the air in front of us.

"Two."

"Ayah!" A left handed punch this time. We had been practicing our katas for the past twenty minutes. After executing a few more punch and block combinations, sensei Li called us together to sit cross-legged on the floor. The dojo was a large open room with hardwood floors and white walls. Scattered along the white walls were championship banners and pictures of the winners over the past fifteen years.

"You will now pair up and practice your defensive and offensive attacks. First person to get three hits advances." He then proceeded to pair us up with a point of his finger. I got paired up with Lucy. I was actually excited to fight her because, well, I hated her.

She often talked bad about me behind my back to my other classmates. One time she told my class that I had slept with her boyfriend. Luckily our classmate Luke knew better and squelched the rumors before they got too out of hand. Even so, the rest of my classmates turned against me for a while. She even went to the extreme of telling my then boyfriend the same thing. Needless to say, the ass broke up with me right after.

I honestly didn't think I had done anything to make her despise me so much.

Lucy was shorter than me, maybe 5'1", and had a husky build. She had medium length red-brown hair, big brown eyes and full lips. If I didn't hate her so much I would think she was pretty. As it was, beauty truly does come from the inside, so she was quite hideous.

We stood in front of each other, each staring the other down. She raised her upper lip in a sneer. "Well, this will be easy," she snarled. I smiled. It was on.

I bowed toward her, and without raising my head, I knew she was doing the same. We might have been catty, but we still had honor. Facing each other, we started to spar. Lucy came out strong, trying to get a few quick punches in before I could block her, but I was familiar with her fighting technique. I blocked easily, and countered with a quick but hard punch to the stomach. She grunted, but showed no other sign that I had hit her: One point for me.

We circled each other, never losing eye contact. Lucy came at me again, I tried to block, but I was a split second too slow. Her fist slammed into my shoulder, but I barely felt it: One point for Lucy. I was watching her every move, anticipating what she would do next. I feigned a punch, making her flinch and block, but instead I swept her leg. She went down, hard. Ha-ha: Two points for me.

One more and I would own her. She stood up, her face red with anger as she huffed toward me. Getting back into her stance, she tried to calm her breathing to think clearly, like we had been taught. For the next minute, neither of us made a move, each watching warily.

Finally she came in for the punch but left herself open. I moved away from her fist and did a double kick into her stomach, and once she buckled over, I threw an uppercut into her face. I was surprised to see her fly backward, landing on her back. Then I saw blood streaming from her nose.

Crap.

My heart picked up a beat. I know I didn't like the girl, but I didn't want to hospitalize her either.

"Stop!" My sensei called, getting the entire class's attention. Apparently he had been watching Lucy and I. He went to Lucy where she still lay on the ground and checked to make sure she wasn't seriously hurt. He ordered Monika, a sweet, tiny blonde girl, to get a towel from the other room. She ran off and returned faster than I thought was possible. Sensei Li put the towel to Lucy's face and helped her sit up. Finally noticing her surroundings, Lucy tightened her grip on the towel placed on her face, stood up and stormed off toward the change rooms.

"What was that?" Sensei asked me, his almond shaped eyes seeking the truth.

"I honestly didn't mean to hurt her. I just saw an opening and went for it. I'm sorry." I bowed down hoping to show empathy. I heard him sigh.

"Alright everyone, get back to your sparring." Obediently everyone went back to work. Sensei Li looked around to make sure everyone had fallen back into their fights before speaking. "I know you didn't mean to, but you are much stronger than you realize. You must gauge your opponent and only do what is necessary to defuse their attacks." I nodded in agreement. "Go get changed." Sensing his disappointment, I lowered my head and headed to the locker rooms. "Selena," he called after me. I turned to see him trying to suppress a smile. "Good work." He turned back to observing his other students. I smiled to myself and went to change.

I decided not to shower there. I grabbed my clothes, and laced up my shoes.

"What do you want now?" Lucy asked angrily. She had just come out of the shower, her towel wrapped tightly around her. Her nose had stopped bleeding.

"Just changing," I said curtly. She clenched her jaw and stood watching. I don't think her lack of clothing would have stopped her from fighting me. Her fear did though. "Look, I didn't mean to hit you so hard." That was as close to an apology as I could get. I really did want to hit her, and hard too, but my conscience got the better of me, making me feel guilty for doing so. I grabbed my stuff and walked away.

Driving home, I rolled down my windows, letting the warm air blow my hair around. I blared the music, sang along, and felt the best I had in months.

4. BOYS WILL BE BOYS

That evening, after changing out of my Gi and shower-ing, I decided to go for a walk. Feeling the night air against my face was rejuvenating. I felt empowered as I remem-bered finally hurting Lucy, and feeling the remainder of my adrenaline course through me.

"If beauty were time, you would be eternity."

I spun to see a man standing nearby. He met my shocked gaze, his brown eyes laughing. I was completely caught off guard.

"You're the guy from the parking lot, right? You gave me my pen." I was trying to figure out the odds of running into him again, and so far away from the place we met.

"I prefer Darien, as opposed to 'the guy from the parking lot'. Not as creepy," he said, still smiling. I laughed nervously.

"I'm Selena." I held out my hand, but instead of shaking it, he lifted it to his lips and kissed it softly. Huh. I guess gentlemen were not completely extinct.

"There's a coffee shop a few blocks away. Come on." He walked a few steps and then waited for me to follow. There was no fear of rejection in his voice, just complete confidence that I would go with him. I did. We walked for fifteen minutes before getting to that coffee shop "a few blocks away."

"So, do you usually meet random women on the streets?" I asked before thinking. I cringed as I thought of what I had implied, then I almost started laughing. He chuckled quietly. I couldn't hold it in anymore, and a laugh bubbled out of me. He turned to look at me.

"You have a nice laugh. It's sincere."

"Thanks," I replied. I personally thought my laugh was loud, but I couldn't deny that it was sincere.

"What do you do for work, Darien? Do you work or live around here?"

"You ask a lot of questions. Did you want to be a journalist when you were a kid?" He teased, not sounding angry, but not answering my questions either.

"No, I didn't want to be a journalist. I did want to get into forensic science though."

"Let me guess, you started watching CSI and thought, huh, I want to do that."

"That's totally irrelevant." Crap, how did he know?

Darien laughed. "You come across as more of a cheerleader than a science type."

My jaw dropped. "And you would base this on…?"

"Your looks of course; you're a beautiful woman, nice, small body type, I could probably carry seven of you."

"I take personal offense to being called a cheerleader. And I seriously doubt you'd be strong enough to carry me." I walked a few paces faster in a huff. Before I could take my next step my feet were off the ground.

I let out a yelp.

Darien had lifted me clear off my feet, one arm under my knees, the other supporting my back. I instinctively wrapped my arms around his neck.

"See? Light as a feather." Darien's warm breath caressed my hair.

"Okay, you made your point." I squirmed to get free, and Darien gently set me back on my feet.

"So you're not a CSI agent, or a cheerleader, what do you do?" He asked.

I took a moment to gather my wits before speaking.

"I'm in between jobs at the moment," I answered, not really wanting to get into the details of not being able to find a job, or knowing what job I really wanted to get. We walked into the shop, ordered our coffees and found a table away from the other patrons. As we walked by the tables, some of the women turned their heads to Darien. One in particular had stopped her fork mid-way between her plate and her mouth which hung open unattractively. Her green eyes widened as she took in Darien's appearance, and her date turned to see what had stolen his girlfriend's attention. After seeing Darien, the man rolled his eyes, shook his head and returned to his sandwich.

I studied Darien and found I couldn't blame them; His lightly tanned skin glowed in the light, enhancing his chiseled jaw line, and subtle, yet masculine cheekbones. His suit was pressed, and he had an air of confidence around him that no one could miss. For some reason, whenever I saw or even thought of Darien, I was reminded of Tristan. I couldn't figure it out. Tristan was crazy after all.

"Do you have any family here?" Darien asked after a moment of silence. I shook my head and sipped my coffee.

"My parents died when I was ten. I spent the next eight years in and out of foster homes, and when I turned eighteen I got a job and my own place."

"How did your parents die?" He asked quietly; as if afraid that raising his voice would make the question hurt more. I took another sip of my coffee and stared into the mug.

"There was a fire," I started, suddenly remembering the fierce heat of the flames that engulfed my house. I heard an echo of my mother's screams in the distance. I shivered. I hadn't talked about that night since the police questioned me about it fifteen years ago.

I thought twice about confiding the darkest night of my life to this stranger. He looked up and met my eyes. His eyebrows pulled together, giving him a sad dog look.

I shook my head, "Some other time."

His face flashed disappointment, but then it changed to his regular carefree expression. He sat back, resting against the chair.

"Any brothers or sisters?" He asked casually.

"Nope, just me. But I have a best friend, Lexi, that I consider my sister."

"How did you meet?"

"It was kind of cool actually. Right after my parents died, she just kind of showed up. I met her outside the foster home. I felt like she was a gift from God, sent to help me through it all. Anytime I needed someone to talk to, she would just be there." Darien looked up from his coffee. "I don't have any other family that I know of. So…" I let the sentence hang, not really sure what more he wanted to know. Or what I was willing to tell him. "What about you? Do you have any brothers or sisters?" I asked, trying to imagine how beautiful his siblings would be if they were anything like him.

"No."

Getting answers out of this guy was like pulling teeth. Of course, it piqued my curiosity about his story. He was keeping me reeled in. This guy was good.

"What's your favorite band?" Darien asked.

Caught off guard with the sudden change of discussion, I took a moment to ponder his question. Really how does anyone decide which band they liked the best? So I named a few.

"Aqua, Backstreet Boys, N'Sync." I shrugged my shoulders. Darien's eyebrow shot up and it took all my restraint to keep a straight face.

"Did you fall out of the '90's?" He asked in shock.

"Oh, come on, it was late '90's, early 2000's." I rolled my eyes.

Darien was quiet for a beat, then said, "You're joking, right?"

I looked at him evenly, "I really am."

Darien studied my face and finally realized I was joking. He let out a sigh of relief. We both laughed.

"Seriously, I like so many bands and different types of music, I couldn't pick one."

And so our mundane conversations kept evolving. We had a debate about X-Men, trying to imagine ourselves with superhuman powers, and discussing the pros and cons of exposing the race. Thankfully this subject took up over an hour and we did not need to refer back to our personal stories to fill the silence.

Darien walked me home as we finished our debate.

"It all comes back to peace. There is no reason why people can't live in harmony. They just need to get past their prejudices," I argued.

"That's the problem though. Humans are so ignorant they would never be able to accept someone for being different, especially on a mutant level," he said in rebuttal. The way he said 'humans' sounded funny, like he was disgusted with his own race. I laughed it off as we got to my front door.

"Let's just agree to disagree." I smiled, hoping to defuse the argument.

"Deal," he said, smiling back. His eyes bored into mine as he took a step closer to me. He trailed his fingers down my arm, making the hair there stand on end. I held my breath in anticipation. Leaning in, our faces were an inch apart, his eyes never left mine.

"I had a great time tonight," I said, breaking the tension. "Thanks." I unlocked my door, slipped in and closed it behind me without giving Darien a second glance. Holy crap that was hard. I wanted to kiss him, but as long as he was being all dark and mysterious, I wouldn't give in.

I waited a little while and then peered through my curtains. Darien was still standing outside my door. He pulled his cell out of his pocket and started clicking away at a text. I wondered if it was about me, and if so, if it was good or bad. He sent his message and put the phone back in his pocket. Giving my front door a final look, he turned and left, his back to me as he walked away.

I realized then that I hadn't given him my number, or vice versa. Though I'm sure he would have asked if I hadn't shut the door in his face. Oh well, he knew where to find me. Suddenly, the thought of him knowing where I lived unnerved me. Probably because he knew more about me than I knew about him, and he was just so closed off.

At least he didn't claim that I was important and needed to be protected. The image of Tristan's yellow flecked, green eyes popped in my mind. I shook it off and got ready for bed. I couldn't fall asleep right away, and images of Darien and Tristan were both in my head, refusing to leave me alone. I am not sure what time I fell asleep, but when I finally did, I dreamed of the two men.

I was back in the field; Tristan was again standing across the clearing. He didn't lean against a tree this time, but instead stood tense, an expression of worry and anger on his face. I thought he was glaring at me, but then a shadow moved to my right. Suddenly Darien stood next to me, and a smile crossed his face as he made a show of putting his arm around my shoulder. Part of me wanted to rest in his embrace, but the other part wanted to run to Tristan and the feeling of safety he offered.

I moved away from Darien's arm and slowly walked toward Tristan. As I took a few steps away from Darien, Tristan's face changed into one of curiosity and… was that pride? The ground opened into a gaping hole of blackness willing to suck in anything along its path. I had no choice but to go back toward Darien, a smile spreading across his face as Tristan yelled something I couldn't make out. I woke up breathing heavily.

I reached across my nightstand and steadied my shaking lamp before turning it on. These dreams were weirding me out. I decided to read for a little bit, just to get my mind off my dream. It worked; thirty minutes later I fell asleep, and this time I didn't dream.

"Hey Lexi, we never did get to finish that weird conversation. Give me a call back when you get this. I'm dying to know what you were going to tell me. Okay, bye." I left the message and hung up, walking into my kitchen to get some coffee.

I sat at the table, lost in thought. My mind wandered back to my dreams. A noise outside my door brought me back to the present. I looked out the window, but no one was there. I went back to my coffee, trying to make a plan for my day. I decided to swim while I figured out what to do with the rest of my time.

The heat was building outside and just hitting the 112 degree mark. I put my gold bikini on and a pair of jean shorts. It was a short walk to the pool, so I figured I could get away without wearing a shirt.

Grabbing my bag and towel, I headed out of my apartment. I opened my door to find a small envelope topped with a red rose lying on the ground. My name was neatly handwritten on it. I locked my door, picked up the envelope and opened it on my way to the pool. I smelled the rose and put it in my bag. I took out the small piece of paper and read the scrawl:

> Since you didn't give me a chance to
> tell you yesterday, I had a good
> time too. I would be honored if you
> would join me for dinner tonight. I'll
> pick you up at 6:30.
> Darien

Well, that was a surprise. I put the paper back in the envelope and put it in the bag with the rose. I did have fun with him last night, but for some reason I felt unnerved. I remembered my dream and wondered if the uneasiness I was feeling was remnants of it. I had no way of calling him or contacting him to let him down; he was going to show up at my place no matter what. I sighed as I got to the pool and put my things down.

The sun beating down on me during that short walk was enough to make me slip my shorts off immediately and jump into the water. The cool water lapped against my skin, making me shiver for an instant before I adjusted to the new temperature. I treaded water for a minute and then started swimming laps. It wasn't ideal doing the front stroke in a bikini, but I didn't have a one piece.

There were a few kids at the pool today, which was a little annoying, but seeing me swim laps, they moved to the other side of the pool.

It felt good to work my muscles and pull my body through the water. I did a few laps and then switched to the back stroke. Looking up at the sky, the sun almost blinded me. When I reached the other end of the pool, a figure stood by the ledge. Recognition hit my gut and I stopped mid stroke and stood in the shallow water. Tristan knelt by the pool, and I looked at him quizzically.

"What are you doing here?" I asked, my heart skipping a beat, though I wasn't sure if it was from fear or some-thing else.

"We need to talk. Can you come out for a minute?" He asked. He offered his hand, and I allowed him to help me out of the water. I was glad I was wearing my nice, gold bikini; it brought out my tan. Petty I know, but Tristan brought out the flirt in me.

Tristan grabbed my towel as I wrung out my hair. He handed it to me, trying not to stare openly at my lack of clothing. I used the towel to dry my hair, and then threw it on the arm of a tanning bench before lying on my back. If he was going to talk, I was going to tan. I positioned myself to show all my curves and let my hair fall in wet strands around me. Tristan glanced at the way I was lying and turned away to get a chair. As he placed it next to my bench I noticed him looking at my body, but only for a second, and he sadly didn't do it again.

"So, what do you want?" I asked, turning my head to face the sun.

"I didn't mean to scare you the other day. I can only imagine what you thought of me, and I assure you, I would never hurt you."

I turned to face him again, the sun glinting in his eyes.

"Yeah that was super creepy, and so is this actually."

"I'm sorry, I'm really not doing this right, but I needed to talk to you. I know Lexi tried to talk to you as well."

"How do you know Lexi?" My mind raced trying to put the pieces together.

"It's... not an easy story to tell, and I don't know that you would believe me right now anyway."

"Try me," I challenged.

"I will, just not right now. There are more important things." He swept his hair from his face with his hand. Seeing him up close and in the light, he was really very handsome. His dark eyelashes accentuated the color of his eyes, his chiseled jaw was set and his lips, which were just the right amount of full, were pressed in a hard line. He wore a white t-shirt, and loose fitting jeans. He must have been boiling in this heat, but he wasn't sweating.

"How old are you?" I surprised us both by asking.

"28. Why?" He retorted.

"I don't know," I said, feeling my face flush. What the hell was that? I couldn't seem to control my mouth, so I just clamped it shut.

Tristan looked confused, but then shook his head. "Listen," he said, changing the subject. "I came here because there's something you need to know."

"Okay…"

"I know you met a guy named Darien, and I came here to tell you that…" He let the sentence hang as he thought of the right words.

"That…?" I prodded, getting frustrated. How did he know about Darien? What was this guy up to?

"I know you won't understand this yet, and you think I have no right to interfere, but it's just… he's bad news. I can't explain how I know this, but you shouldn't see him again."

I scoffed at his order. "You're damn right you can't interfere."

"Look I get how crazy this all sounds, but I'm trying to keep you safe, and Darien is not safe."

"Who *are* you?" I asked, the anger evident in my tone. Tristan flinched briefly. "I don't know you, and I don't owe you anything except maybe another punch in the face." I didn't wait for his response. I stood up and sauntered off.

I jumped back into the pool and started doing laps to let off some steam. What kind of jerk thinks he can give me orders, especially when he doesn't even know me? How did he know about Darien? Again I was left with more questions than answers when it came to Tristan. He was so weird. But still, in the pit of my stomach, I knew I felt drawn to him. Ugh! I hated my taste in men. I looked back to the bench I had been sitting on. My towel was laid out flat on the bench to dry, but Tristan was gone.

Darien showed up right on time. I obviously hadn't taken Tristan's advice to stay away from him. In fact his warning may have just pushed me closer to Darien.

"Wow," he said as I opened the door. I wore a black cocktail dress, and my hair was loose down my back, but I had curled some at the ends.

"Same to you," I said taking in his black dress shirt and suit. He smiled crookedly at me, and I held the door open for him to come inside.

"So what's the plan for tonight?" I took the single red rose Darien held out to me and inhaled its beautiful perfume.

"Dinner and a movie?"

"Are you asking me or telling me?" I laughed.

"Telling you."

"My kind of date. Let's go." I locked the door and followed Darien to the parking lot. "BMW M3. Nice. I would have pegged you for a Camaro kind of guy," I joked. Darien frowned slightly at my comment.

"Camaros? Come on." He opened the passenger side door and I sat down on the smooth leather seat. Thankfully it was evening, so I didn't have to worry about maneuvering my short dress to cover any bare skin that could get scorched from the sun heated leather.

Darien got into the driver's side. When he started his car, I almost laughed.

"What?" Darien asked when he saw my expression.

"Nothing I'm just used to the loudness of my Mustang. This sounds so… foreign," I teased.

Darien laughed. "It is." He set the car in first gear and peeled onto the road. I fussed with the radio until I found a song I liked. Surprisingly Darien didn't object to me playing around with his car.

"So where are you from?" I asked after a few minutes.

"How do you know I'm not from here?" He retorted.

"You talk different than people from Arizona."

"What? How do people in Arizona talk?"

"I don't know… normal?" I laughed.

Darien laughed too. "What does that mean?"

"I don't know. Never mind," I said smiling and looked out the window. I saw a Camaro in my side-view mirror and laughed. "See, that's what I see you driving."

Darien narrowed his eyes at his rearview mirror and clenched his jaw, but didn't say anything. Guy must really hate Camaros.

We drove in silence for another few minutes before Darien said, "We're here," and pulled into the parking lot of a restaurant I didn't even know existed.

"Where are we?" I asked. I knew we were close to my apartment, but how could I not know this place was here?

"I thought you were from here. Don't you know what's in the area?" Darien teased.

"Funny," I said as I opened my car door.

"Wait. I'll do that." He jumped out of the car and opened my door for me.

"Thanks." I wasn't used to this kind of treatment, but I could learn.

We walked into the restaurant and my breath caught. It was gorgeous but in a simple, elegant way, not flashy or showy. There were chandeliers that hung delicately from the ceiling, their crystals dangling like stars above our heads. There were wrought iron designs on the walls with leaves weaved through. It reminded me of something I would see in Italy.

The waiter led us up a side stairway and onto a terrace. We sat at a table for two, right next to the rail. A small candle centerpiece flickered, creating moving shadows on the white linen table cloth.

"This place is amazing." My eyes roamed the terrace and then the view of the mountains beside us.

"I thought you would like it." Darien smiled. My heart leaped a little.

We ordered our dinner – chicken fettuccini Alfredo for me and Darien got the mushroom linguini – and then we fell into silence.

"So I know this is a question guys are supposed to ask before they take a girl on a date, but are you seeing anyone right now?" There was a mischievous glint in Darien's eyes that I couldn't decipher.

"No," I answered honestly, but Tristan popped in my head uninvited. I shook it off. "How about you?"

"I'm looking at her." He smiled again.

"Smooth, really, does that work on a lot of women?" I teased.

Darien shrugged, "You'd be surprised," he admitted.

"You're not supposed to say that!" I laughed. "You're supposed to keep up your charade and say 'I wouldn't know, you're the only one I've said it to' or something equally cheesy." Darien and I laughed.

Our food came quickly, which was fantastic because I was starving.

"What's the worst pick-up line you've heard?" Darien asked.

"You mean aside from the one you used on me the other day?"

Darien chuckled, "Yes, aside from that one, though I thought it was pretty good."

"Uh-huh." I ran through the numerous bad one-liners and picked one. "You look cold. Want to use me as a blanket?" I tried to say it with a straight face but failed at the end, almost laughing.

"Wow, that is actually really bad." Darien laughed. I nibbled on my fettuccini.

"What about you? What bad ones have you heard, or said even?"

Darien thought about the question while he took a few bites of his pasta, and then he put his fork down.

"I was so enchanted by your beauty that I ran into that wall over there." He pointed to a wall beside me. "So I am going to need your name and number for insurance purposes."

I cracked up. "Oh man! That one is actually… not horrible."

"Okay here's a bad one; Smoking is hazardous to your health... and baby, you're killing me," Darien said dramatically.

"That's terrible. You just know those have worked on some women." I laughed, "Wait was that one you heard or one you used?" I asked.

Darien laughed, "Definitely heard. I don't use pick-up lines."

"You just did!"

"Nah that doesn't count, it was just a statement."

"Uh-huh. And the one from when we met?"

"Again, more of an observation."

"You sure change your story a lot," I teased.

We laughed and talked while we ate dinner, never really touching on any serious conversations. We joked some more about pick-up lines and the things some women were so willing to believe.

After dinner we went to see a re-release of Rocky. We joked about how much prettier Rocky gets throughout the series, when as a fighter, he should get uglier.

"I had a great time tonight," I said as Darien walked me to my apartment.

"I did too. Can I see you again sometime?"

I thought about it for a moment, and again Tristan popped into my head telling me I shouldn't. Naturally I said, "Sure," and smiled.

"How about tomorrow? Same time?" Darien asked. We were standing in front of my apartment door now, the scene awfully familiar.

"Don't you have anything better to do?" I teased. I was surprised by his availability. Most guys didn't call for a week after a date never mind set one up for the next day.

"There's nothing I'd rather be doing," he said as he took a step closer to me. I laughed.

"That's a pick-up line in my book." I unlocked my door. "I'll see you tomorrow." I gave him a quick kiss on the cheek and went inside.

5. DATING JUST ISN'T WHAT
IT USED TO BE

There was a knock on my door just as I was finishing getting ready. I looked myself over once more in the mirror before answering. A tight, red, sleeveless dress hugged my curves down to my knees, and my hair hung loose down my back. I opened the door to find Darien standing there in a black suit, and carrying a dozen red roses. I smiled taking the roses from him. It was a drastic upgrade from the single rose he gave me the night before. He looked me up and down before walking in.

"You look great," he said, standing just inside the doorway.

"Thanks. These roses are beautiful." I placed them in a vase as I spoke. Roses are the most romantic flower, but they are also overdone. My favorites are tulips, beautifully simple and underrated. I set the roses on my table, and admired them for a moment before leaving.

The car ride was quiet for the most part, neither of us really knowing what to talk about. We arrived at the restaurant around seven and were seated right away. It was a high-end steakhouse, and glancing around, I was glad I was wearing a dress.

The waiter pulled my chair out for me, which surprised me. I hadn't ever had that kind of service before. As I sat, he went over the wine list and specials and left us to decide what we wanted. A few silent minutes later, our waiter returned. I ordered the sirloin, and Darien ordered the Prime Rib, with a bottle of merlot. It all felt kind of weird; like I didn't belong there. I just wanted to grab a burger, Dr. Pepper and fries. It was uncomfortably silent for a minute, until finally, Darien spoke.

"Have you ever been here before?"

"No. I usually eat where meals are $7.50 or less." I smiled.

"You did well last night," he joked.

"True, it's just it was more... down to earth last night." I took in my surroundings and the oil paintings on the walls. It felt regal.

"Well, you'll enjoy this. The steaks all come out on a plate that's 200 degrees, so make sure you don't burn yourself. You can hear it sizzle from across the room." My stomach twisted with hunger.

"That sounds amazing." I suddenly couldn't wait to try this scalding hot piece of meat. "So Darien, how old are you?"

"You know, it's not polite to ask a person their age."

"It's not polite to ask a *woman* her age." I laughed. "You're fair game."

"Alright, alright, I'm 28," he finally answered. Huh, what are the odds…? Darien interrupted my thought. "How old are you?"

"Didn't you hear what I just said about asking a woman her age?"

"Yes, yes. Well I would guess you're 24. Am I right?"

"Close enough." Our waiter came out, and as promised, the sizzling meat could be heard tables away. He placed our hot plates in front of us, and I did my best not to touch it, though once or twice a spit of butter would jump off the plate and sting my hand. I decided to wait a minute so I wouldn't burn my mouth with my food.

Eventually we gave in and ate. The meat melted in my mouth. I had never tasted anything so good.

"So I remembered another pick-up line," Darien said.

"Shoot," I prodded.

"Okay, do you know what I did last night? I looked up at the stars, and matched each one with a reason why I love you." He looked up from his plate and gazed into my eyes. I shifted uncomfortably.

"No way anyone uses that as a pick-up line," I said, trying to lighten the mood.

"Why not?" Darien asked over a mouthful of food.

"Because no one says they love someone they just met." I chuckled, thinking of the idea.

"That's not true." Again Darien's eyes pierced through me.

"Can I get you some more wine?" The waiter asked, breaking the tension. Darien's jaw clenched and unclenched. I took the opportunity to break eye contact, and stared at my plate instead.

"No, and next time you decide to barge into our conversation I'll dock your tip, understand?" Darien stared the waiter down.

"Yes, sir. I'm very sorry, sir." The waiter bowed slightly and quickly retreated.

"What was that?" I asked

"I don't like being interrupted." Darien smoldered.

"Not like we were talking about anything important. Just pick-up lines, right?" I offered, needing the clarification for myself.

"Yeah, sure." Darien went back to his food.

"You never did tell me what you do for a living?" I asked after swallowing a piece of the buttery meat.

"I didn't, did I?" He sipped his wine. After a few moments, he went back to his food.

"Hello?" I asked, shocked that he had completely disregarded my question. It wasn't even that personal, not like I was asking for his social security number. He looked up at me and smiled, motioning to his mouth that he couldn't talk because he was chewing. I shook my head.

"You are unbelievable," I said.

"What did I do?" He asked over a mouthful of food.

"Oh, so you can speak," I taunted.

Darien smiled, and chewed silently.

I finished my plate and waited. I didn't bother to ask any more questions, knowing he wouldn't answer them. It was extremely annoying, no matter how good looking he was. The waiter returned with our bill and I didn't offer to pay. Not trying to be rude, but I was unemployed and couldn't afford that place. He left a wad of twenties on the table and we left. I suddenly couldn't wait to go home. Last night was fun, but tonight was different. Darien was even more closed off if that's possible, and we spent most of the night in silence.

We got into Darien's car, and I buckled up. I leaned my head on the seat behind me. I felt sleepy from the amount of food I ate, but I knew it would pass soon. Darien got in the driver's side and pulled out of the lot.

"What's your deal?" I asked, annoyed.

"What do you mean?"

"Why don't you ever answer my questions? You practically ignored me, and I just don't get it. Why ask me out at all?" I clenched my jaw to stop myself from rambling.

"You do ask a lot of questions. I would like to show you something."

"No, I'm good. Just take me home." I didn't miss the fact that he had just avoided answering me again. I was disappointed with the way this night was turning out. Darien seemed to have potential, or maybe I was just distracted by his looks. Could I really be that shallow? Whatever the case, I was having doubts that this relationship was going anywhere. We drove for another fifteen minutes in silence, and then I noticed that we were merging onto the 202. "Where are you going?" I asked, worry creeping into my voice.

"You need to stop stressing so much."

"Please, just take me home," I said through clenched teeth.

"Sorry, I can't do that. I may never get this opportunity again." Somewhere in the back of my mind I heard Tristan telling me to stay away from Darien. I mentally told him to shut up.

"Opportunity for what?"

"You really have no idea how important you are, do you?" Great, there comes that important stuff again.

"Are you here to protect me too?" I asked sarcastically. Darien twitched, but stayed silent as he drove farther away from my home. I tensed, trying to keep track of my surroundings and the direction we were heading in. I looked at my side mirror and saw another Camaro behind us. There seemed to be an overpopulation of those lately. I wondered what would happen if I flailed my arms outside the window. Would the driver behind us help me or think I was crazy? Not sure what I was going to do, I silently clicked my seat belt open just in case. Darien finally got off the freeway and stopped at a red light.

I decided this may be the only chance I would get, so I threw open the door and jumped. My palms scraped the ground, but my foot got caught on something. I turned to see that Darien had grabbed my ankle and was snarling at me. I kicked at his hand with my free foot until he let go and I fell out of the car. I started running as fast as I could. Behind me I heard tires screeching to a halt. I wondered if a car would hit Darien, but when I didn't hear a crash, my hopes plummeted.

My heart raced as I ran off the road. I headed to the curb and into the row of trees lining the street. They stood well over twelve feet tall and I was surprised at the large area they covered. The wind blew around me, and I grabbed a tree to keep my balance. I cursed my high heels and slipped them off as I hid behind the tree.

"Selena! Come back, I won't hurt you." I heard Darien yell into the dark night. I ran through the trees and toward the other side to an intersecting street. I knew better than to stay within the trees where no one would be able to hear or see me. Just before I reached the clearing of the intersecting street, a heavy weight pulled me down. Darien had grabbed my feet, knocking me on my back. He moved over my body so that I was pinned down with his weight. I tried struggling and then punching, but I couldn't land any shots with him so close. I elbowed him, grazing the side of his face. He grunted, shifted his body, and I wriggled free. I got to my feet and started to run before Darien grabbed me again and tackled me down. He grabbed my wrists in one hand and held them pinned over my head. Every which way I tried to move I failed.

"Stupid bitch, stay still," he snarled into my hair. I whimpered, trying to think of what I could do to get out of this situation. Karate taught me a lot, but being this scared, I couldn't think of any of it. The wind swirled fiercely around us, whipping dirt and debris into our faces. Darien laughed, and it sent shivers down my spine.

"Is that the best you can do?" He yelled over the torrent. My heart pounded so hard I thought it would jump out of my chest. Lightning crackled across the sky, and a loud booming thunder followed.

Was this how I was going to die? I refused to let myself be a victim. I focused all my strength and tried to lift my leg to knee him wherever I could, but Darien was too heavy. I pulled at my wrists, hoping to get one hand loose, but Darien had them in a death grip. I growled out of frustration. A streak of lightning charged out of the sky and hit the tree just above Darien's head. He flinched, but didn't loosen his grip.

"Oh come on! You are supposed to be big and bad. Where is your power? You are pathetic!" Darien yelled, laughing. Rage filled me, and I could feel my wrists heating to an uncomfortable temperature where Darien held them. His smile vanished as he tried to maintain his hold over me. Suddenly, Darien flew off me with a force that sent him slamming into the trunk of a large tree.

I crawled away, got to my feet and ran. I turned and saw that Darien was laughing and looking past me. When I faced forward, I saw Tristan standing a few feet ahead of me. His hands were outstretched in front of him. As he moved his palms up, Darien was lifted into the air. Tristan quickly lowered his arms, and Darien slammed against the ground. I shook my head. I couldn't have seen that. It must be the shock making me see things.

"Tristan. How nice of you to join us," Darien yelled from the ground. The lightning had disappeared, but the wind still blew.

"Darien, as always, you are a disappointment." Tristan turned to face me. "Come with me. We have to get out of here." I didn't think twice. I ran with Tristan beside me. All of a sudden, Tristan flew through the air and landed on his side a few feet away. I ran faster to him, but he was on his feet before I could get there.

"You didn't think you could get away that easy, did you?" Darien asked, walking toward us. He flicked his wrist and Tristan stumbled backward. Tristan dusted off his jeans and faced Darien with a look so fierce I thought it would freeze him in place. Tristan raised his arms, and the wind that was blowing around us funneled and spun toward Darien. Darien crossed his arms over his chest and then swept them open, breaking the cyclone of wind.

Tristan flicked his fingers, and a heavy branch fell forcefully on Darien's head. Darien fell and didn't move. I considered going to check if he was alive, but before I could move Tristan took my hand. The heat from his fingers comforted my cold hands, and I realized I was shaking. I looked up at him and our eyes locked for a moment before he turned away, and we ran again.

"Where are you going?" I panted.

"Come on, my car's just over here." He pulled me along by my hand and led me to the street and a Camaro shining in the moonlight. Another Camaro, ugh! Then I realized he must have been the one following us. In one swift motion, he swung open the car door, pushed me inside, and closed my door. He was behind the wheel in no time. The purring of his engine snapped me out of my daze, and before I knew it, he peeled out onto the street.

"What the hell just happened? Did you really just-" I couldn't finish my sentence, it all just sounded so crazy.

"Yes, I have the ability to move objects with my mind, as does Darien."

I shook my head. This wasn't happening. This stuff only happened in the movies, right? After driving for a few minutes, Tristan pulled over. He turned to face me, concern all over his face. "Are you alright?" He asked, gently lifting my chin to check for any scrapes. As soon as he saw I was okay, he let go.

"I'm just a little shaken up. I don't understand what happened."

Tristan ran his fingers through his hair and let out a sigh.

"I know this will all sound crazy, but try to be open minded." He looked into my eyes, waiting for me to agree. I nodded my head. "Twenty-six years ago there was a prophecy that a child would soon be born who would change society as we know it. A year after the prophecy, you were born."

"So... what? You think the prophecy is about me?" No, that couldn't be right.

"I do," Tristan answered shortly.

"Based on what?"

"The prophecy described a girl with hair black as night and eyes as blue as the ocean. She would have powers that no one person has ever had. In her 25th year, she will stop the dark ones from conquering all the good people in our world."

"What are dark ones? And what makes you think this prophecy is about me? There must have been a million black-haired, blue-eyed girls born that year," I asked, trying to absorb all of this strange information and keep my agreement to be open minded.

"Darien is one of the dark ones. He has an army of followers who want to destroy all the good people of our kind. We are not sure why, but since he found out about you, he has been trying to hurt you or even kill you. As for how I know the prophecy is about you, well aside from the dark hair and light eyes, you glow." He scrunched up his face after he said the words. I had been about to ask what he meant by 'our kind,' but once he mentioned glowing, I got side tracked.

"I glow?" I was having a really hard time with this prophecy, good versus evil, I glow stuff. I looked down at my arms to see if I was glowing.

"Well…" he started, struggling for the right words. "Everyone has an aura. Our kind are the only ones who can really see it though. We all glow in one way or another, but because you have so much power, you really glow." He shook his head, obviously frustrated that he wasn't explaining this right. "Have you ever noticed how some things shake when you get scared or upset? Or how you can control the weather?" He asked so casually it was as if he was asking my name. I was starting to lose my composure.

"I—No," I stammered, shaking my head. "Can you please just take me home? My head is starting to hurt."

Tristan nodded and pulled back onto the road. We drove the rest of the way in silence. I was trying to process everything I had just seen and heard and I was having a hard time. All the times I thought my neighbors were responsible for the things shaking in my apartment flashed through my mind. Then the first time I talked to Tristan at the trail, how the weather was uncharacteristically wild then and tonight. I chided myself for actually crediting Tristan's story with a shred of possibility. There was no way I could have been responsible for those things. It must be some kind of trick.

Tristan reached over and covered my clasped hands with one of his own. I had been shaking, but once he touched me, my hands steadied. Just as quickly, he removed his warm hand and placed it back on the steering wheel. He pulled in front of my apartment, and I unbuckled my seat belt. "How do you always know where to find me?" I asked, exhaustion in my voice.

"I told you. I am here to protect you, so I always know where you are. I don't mean for that to make you uncomfortable. I hope it's more reassuring that I am always looking out for you. I'll sit outside your place tonight if you like?"

My heart skipped a beat, but I nodded. I opened the car door and got out. As I turned to close the door, I leaned my head back into the car.

"Thanks, for saving me." I attempted a smile, closed the door and went home. Once inside, I locked my door behind me, checked to make sure all my windows were still locked and showered. After cleaning all the dirt out of my hair I got a glass of water from the kitchen. I had stopped shaking, but I was still scared. I wondered if Darien would try to break in and kill me, truly believing that I was the one this stupid prophecy was about. I, on the other hand, was having serious doubts that I had any powers. Then again, I couldn't help but wonder… I looked at the roses on my table and wiggled my fingers. They stood completely still, the perfume a tainted reminder of the night's events. I shook my head at my silliness, threw the roses out and went to bed.

I stayed up most of the night, and even though Tristan said he would be watching, I couldn't settle my nerves. Then again, maybe my nerves were shot because I knew he was watching.

6. SPECIAL DELIVERY

I felt like I had just closed my eyes, when a loud banging noise slammed me awake. I jerked up and checked the clock; 7:00 am. I couldn't have been sleeping more than a few hours. Suddenly, memories of the night before came rushing back and my body tensed. I crept out of bed and went to the closet for my baseball bat. Holding the bat like Babe Ruth, I tiptoed to the door. Another loud bang caused me to jump back.

"Selena, open up! I know you're in there. We have to talk!" It was Lexi. I let out a breath I hadn't realized I was holding and lowered the bat. I opened the door to find Lexi standing in the doorway, hand poised to knock again. When she saw me, relief flooded her face and she grabbed me into a fierce hug. "Oh my God, I am so glad you're okay!" She exclaimed, still holding me tight. Did she know what happened to me last night?

"I can't breathe," I wheezed.

"Oh, sorry." Lexi let me go and came inside, eyeing the bat curiously. I closed and locked the door behind her, and leaned the bat against the wall. "How are you doing?" She asked, pacing my small living room.

"Oh, just peachy! Considering I could have been caught up in a freaking man made tornado last night!"

"Yeah, I know about that."

"What? How?"

"I saw Tristan, and he explained everything." I had forgotten Tristan was keeping watch outside. She must have bumped into him. "Look, we do need to finish that conversation."

I nodded and we sat next to each other on the couch. "Tristan is telling you the truth."

Okay, that I was not expecting.

"How do you know-?"

"I have known Tristan for a long time. He just lectured me for choosing to go to work over telling you what I'm about to, so that was fun." She took a breath before continuing. "Look Selena, I'm sorry I haven't been honest with you. I have been protecting you too."

"What?"

"I was sent after your parents died to keep an eye out for you."

"Keep an eye – you were only ten! What could you have done?"

"My parents looked out for us, but mainly it was my responsibility and honor to protect you. I had certain abilities at ten that most adults would dream of." She lifted her finger, and with it, my coffee table levitated. I let out a string of expletives I'd rather not repeat.

"Not you too! What are you people?"

"We - and by 'we' I mean you too- come from a long and powerful line of witches. We can all move objects with our mind, among many other things, and some of us can do more powerful magic as well. Tristan, for example, can teleport to pretty much anywhere. It's really cool – actually you've seen it. That night on the trail when you said he disappeared in a ray of white light. I didn't know who you were talking about until you mentioned that. Anyways," she continued on excitedly, not realizing my reaction to all of this.

"I can create a sphere shield which was why I was chosen to protect you. All of us can do a lot of things other than that, but you – well you can do everything. You can move things with your mind, disappear, create sphere shields and even control the weather! The cool thing is our powers don't stop changing and increasing."

"A sphere shield?" I asked breathlessly. Was I getting dizzy?

"Yeah, it's like a force field." Finally looking at my face, she realized the shock I was feeling. "Oh, I'm sorry, honey. I know this must all be so much to take in. Maybe this will help." She handed me a manila envelope with my name written across the front.

I opened it and took out a folded sheet of paper. As I read, my hands began to shake.

Selena honey,

If you are reading this then something has happened to your father and I, and you have recently turned 25. Oh my baby girl, I wish I could be with you through this, but I can't. I am assuming Alexis has given this to you, as I instructed. She was chosen to watch over you when you were just a child. I know this sounds strange, but what I mean is that she was assigned to you as soon as we were aware of what her powers were, so that she could look out for you, and on the day when I was no longer there, she would step in. Trust her. She is a wonderful girl, so much spirit.

I almost started laughing. My mother didn't know the half of it.

You must understand who you are. You were chosen to bring peace to our people. Yes, I was like you, and although your father knew of my powers, he was human. From the moment you were born you could move things around. Since you were showing your abilities at such an early age we had to bind your powers. We bound them for your protection so that no one would be able to find you. We couldn't take a chance that you would draw too much attention, and we knew you would be protected until you could use them again. The binding spell was to wear off on your 25th birthday, so I'm sure strange things have been happening to you. Don't worry, you will learn to control them. As Alexis has probably told you, the prophecy stated that you will need to use your powers in your 25th year. I hope you are adjusting to them well, and if not I'm sure Alexis will show you how. I arranged to have her give this letter to you on this specific day. The prophecy foretold that you would be 'awakened' on the 21st of June, 2014. If Lexi followed my instructions, today should be the 22nd. I was hoping that by receiving this letter after your awakening you would be able to understand it and accept it easier.

You may have already met Tristan, he was also assigned to protect you. If you have not met him yet, don't worry, I am sure he is watching nearby. Even though he is young he shows so much potential. I am sure that by the time you read this, his abilities will be extraordinary.

Your father and I love you so very much, and no matter what, we are very proud of you.

Love you always, xoxoxo
Mom
P.S. I have left you my ring, in hopes that it brings you comfort during hard times, as it has done for me.

I wiped at the tears that threatened to spill over. My mom was… whatever I was. What was I? A witch? Lexi put an arm around my shoulders. I opened the envelope and saw the ring in the corner. I flipped the envelope over so the tiny ring fell in my palm. It was silver with an emerald cut sapphire in the center and a small diamond baguette on each side. The band was carved with intricate designs that I couldn't make out exactly; they looked like an entwining of swirling lines and stars. I remember my mom wearing it when I was a kid, and how she would gaze at the stone and get lost in her thoughts. It was beautiful. I put it on the ring finger of my right hand where my mom used to wear it, and it fit perfectly.

"I have been dying to tell you! For years I came so close to telling you everything, but you didn't have your powers yet, so I figured you would never believe me. I was right too. If you hadn't seen Tristan and Darien fight, would you have believed any of this?"

I shook my head.

"I'm still not sure that I do," I said quietly. "Is that what the prophecy meant by awakening? Watching Tristan and Darien use their powers?"

Lexi nodded. It made sense. The only way I could accept this was to see it for myself. "So if you are my protector too, where were you last night?"

Lexi's face fell. "I'm so sorry, Selena. I wasn't there for you when you needed me. Tristan convinced me that you would be fine under his watch. He was right, but I didn't want to leave you. I went to see if I could find someone to tell me what Darien was up to, but it was a complete waste of time." Her eyes filled with tears, and she shook her head.

I leaned over to hug her, and Lexi's face finally brightened to its regular expression. I twisted the ring on my finger and admired it again. My heart sank as I thought of my parents. I missed them terribly, and it took all my effort not to cry just then.

"I'm still kind of confused. You said you didn't know about Tristan until I told you he vanished before me, but you saw him at the bar, you must have known who he was. He is a protector too, right?"

"I haven't seen Tristan in years; he always watched over you, I knew that, but I hadn't actually seen him. Not until today. When I saw him at the bar I couldn't get a good look at his face to be sure who he was, I could just tell by his aura that he was gifted too. When you described him in your dream it sounded like it could be him, but since you had never seen him before, I wasn't sure how much credibility your dream offered. How did you know what he looked like anyway?" She asked, turning the questioning back to me.

"I honestly have no idea. All I know is that I feel so drawn to him." Even when I thought he was crazy, which I still haven't cleared him of yet, I still wanted to talk to him or be around him.

"It could be a protector thing. Maybe a part of you knows he's trying to keep you safe, so you're drawn to that. Self-preservation and all."

I shrugged. I was sure what I was feeling was more than that.

"What would have happened if we didn't get along? Would you have still protected me?"

"Yeah, I would have had to. I just got lucky you weren't a psycho." Lexi wiggled her eyebrows.

"How do you know I'm not?" I tried to look as menacing as I could.

Lexi just laughed.

Well that didn't work.

I fidgeted with my ring before I asked, "What happens now?" I was scared to know the answer.

Lexi smiled. "Now we train."

7. PRACTICE, PRACTICE, PRACTICE

This was the weirdest training I had ever done. I was used to physical lessons, learning how to use my body as a weapon, but what Lexi was teaching me was how to use my mind.

"Focus, Selena. Channel all your energy and move whatever you want to move." She swept her hand in front of her, causing one of the tennis balls to fly off the table. I sighed in frustration. I had been trying to get this down for half an hour, and she made it look so easy. I took a deep breath, looked at another tennis ball on the table and willed it to move.

It didn't.

I squinted my eyes.

Nothing.

I flailed my arms around, but that damn ball stayed put.

"Watch it!" Lexi said dodging my swinging arm.

"Sorry," I mumbled. "This is so frustrating!" I clenched my fists. The tennis ball rolled away.

"Hmm, looks like you need to hone in on your anger. That may be the only way to get started, and then once you get used to it, you can control it at will." Lexi rubbed her chin in thought.

This was nuts. I tried to focus on my anger and the fear I had experienced before, but I was too distracted. It was all still so new and unbelievable. Lexi sighed beside me.

"Come over here," she said, sitting down on the couch and patting the cushion next to her. I flopped down beside her and crossed my arms over my chest.

"This isn't working," I huffed.

"I know, we need to think of a different strategy. You need to work on your mental abilities as well as your physical. I will train with you every morning to try and get you to gain control over your powers. From what Tristan told me, they are already quite impressive. Not everyone can manifest the elements, and you have already created a sand storm and lightning."

"Tristan created a little tornado," I corrected Lexi.

"Yes, Tristan is very strong, and his physical fighting abilities are just as good as his magic. That's why he is going to train you how to fight after our morning sessions."

"He what?" I asked. My heart started beating oddly. There was a knock on the door that snapped me out of my emotions. I stood up and checked the peephole. Standing outside, as if on cue, was Tristan. I swallowed hard, and ran my fingers through my hair. Damn it, why didn't I change out of my pajamas? What was wrong with me? I shook it off and opened the door.

"Hi," Tristan said, smiling. I couldn't help but smile back. Damn my willpower. He looked great as always, wearing jeans and a black short-sleeved dress shirt that showed off his muscular arms.

"Come in."

Tristan walked past me and I locked the door behind him.

"Perfect timing!" Lexi cheered. I'll say, I thought. "I was just telling Selena that you will be training her on her fighting technique."

Tristan nodded. "We should start right away. Are you done training with Lexi?"

"No. I am not even close. I can't seem to get this at all."

"You can't expect to get it right away," Lexi giggled.

"Well if I am supposedly the chosen one, shouldn't I?"

Lexi looked at Tristan who shrugged his shoulders. I clenched my jaw, my frustration rising. The tennis balls started bouncing around.

"It seems to be happening much easier now, just by practicing. You don't even need to get that angry or scared; just a little frustration will get it going," Lexi said.

Tristan laughed. "Wait until you see what she does when she is really scared."

I pictured the lightning and wind storm. I felt my face flush. Part of me felt proud that I could control the weather like that, but the other part of me was embarrassed that my emotions were so easy to read just by what happened around me. "She even made me come out of hiding."

"What do you mean?" Lexi asked.

"I was hiding behind the bush to keep an eye out for her and she willed me to show myself. You think I would have let her see me otherwise?" Tristan almost laughed.

"Cool," Lexi said. I stopped and remembered willing the shadows to reveal their secrets – I guess they listened. Huh.

"Come on," Tristan said. "You need to get your mind off this and just let it happen naturally like you have been. When you try to force it, it just doesn't work the way you want it to. Some physical training might clear your mind enough to help you concentrate."

I nodded. "Let me change."

I went to my room as casually as possible, but once I got there and closed the door, I was running around trying to make myself look good without taking too long. I slipped out of my grubby clothes and put on black fitted shorts and a black tank. I threw my hair up in a high pony-tail, slapped on some deodorant and perfume, and put as little amount of lip gloss as I could to look good without looking like I was wearing make-up.

Satisfied that this was the best I was going to look in two minutes, I walked out of my room slowly, as if I hadn't just been running ragged. Lexi's back was to me, but Tristan had a clear view. He did a quick double take, and then looked back to Lexi as if he hadn't noticed me at all.

"Alright, let's do this. Where do you want to go?" I asked, trying to think of any gyms nearby.

"My place," he said, standing up and walking toward the door.

"Huh? How is that going to work?" I asked.

"Will you just come on?" He asked impatiently. Jeez. Lexi stood up realizing that she would have to leave too. We gathered our things, and I locked up behind us. I was still paranoid that Darien would find his way back here again. Although he could probably break the lock with his powers, I felt like I should at least try to secure my home. Lexi hugged me goodbye and then walked to her car and drove off.

"Where's your car?" I asked, remembering his sleek black Camaro. "Or did you want me to drive? I have a Mustang," I said smugly. Tristan smiled and shook his head. I was hoping to start a debate, but it didn't seem to faze him.

"I live a block away, we can walk."

I internally complained about walking in the heat.

"Lexi lives a block away too, but she drove. Do you know why?" Without waiting for his response I continued, "Because she understands the importance of air conditioning," I said sarcastically. Tristan chuckled softly. Okay so I outwardly complained about walking in the heat.

"You need to toughen up. Consider this your first lesson."

"Hey, is living close to me a requirement to protect me?"

Tristan shrugged. "It definitely helps."

The walk went by mercifully fast. I was standing in front of a white bungalow with a red roof and wooden door. In the middle of the walkway was a fountain. There was nothing fancy about it, but seeing the water trickle down the porcelain steps was comforting. We walked in and I was grateful Tristan hadn't taken his heat lesson so far as to not have air conditioning in his house.

I looked around and saw that Tristan's furnishings were not simple like I would have predicted, but practically non-existent; he had a small kitchen table for two, a couch that was pushed up against one wall of his living room, and some exercise equipment, but the rest was bare. I now understood why he wanted to train here; there was a lot of empty space. I stood in the middle of the open room and looked at Tristan.

"What now?" I asked.

"I will teach you, to the best of my ability, every which way you can use your body to defend yourself and harm others. You in return, have to give me 150% effort. Agreed?"

He was so serious. I nodded. I needed to know how to fight against creeps like Darien. "Alright, show me what you got. No powers of course, we will introduce that once you can channel them."

"So what? You want me to throw a few punches in the air or something? Or should I show you my katas?"

Tristan rolled his eyes. "No, you will fight me."

My stomach dropped and my heart raced. No good could come of this. I eyed him up and down, trying to assess his strength, and regretted it. I pushed my attraction aside.

"Don't you want to change?" I asked.

"I don't expect to sweat today."

My mouth dropped. How rude! "You know, I have been studying karate."

"Yes, well, we'll see where that gets you."

My anger flashed, but I kept it in check and tried to focus. I stood in my defense stance, and Tristan circled me. I turned to keep him in my line of vision. I struck out with a punch, but he caught my fist and pushed it down. I tried to counter with a round-house kick, but he was faster and he pushed my leg away as if it were a toy. I tried to feint a punch and then leg sweep, but he hardly flinched at my punch and easily side-stepped my leg.

"You won't be up against weak humans. The ones you will have to defend yourself against, like Darien, are much stronger and faster than humans. You won't be able to knock them back with just an uppercut." I thought of my fight with Lucy. Had he seen that too? Just how much time did he spend watching me? Looking at his empty house I realized he wasn't spending much time here, unless he was training.

Tristan let out a lightning fast punch toward my stomach but stopped just as it grazed the front of my shirt, not actually wanting to hit me. Then he grabbed my arm, twisting it so he was behind me. It didn't hurt, but his body was pressed up against my back and I could feel the heat humming between us. He let me go an instant later.

"Again."

I tried, I really did. I used every single attack I could think of, but he found a way to dodge or block each one. When he came at me, I tried to block, but I was too slow. My frustration at my lack of strength grew, the shutters shook slightly in response, and before I knew what I was doing I tackled him. He didn't see it coming, I'm not sure how he missed it to be honest, but I think he was just expecting me to maintain our stand-up fighting. I knocked him so he landed on his back, my legs were on each side of his body straddling him. I had one hand pushed down on his chest and I poised my other arm up in a mock punch, showing him that I could punch him in the face if I wanted to.

He looked amused, almost tempting me to try. I knew he would block it, so I just left it hanging there. He let his hands fall, resting them on my upper thighs. We were both breathing a little heavily, me more than him. Tristan smiled, but then faltered. He cleared his throat as he realized the position we were in, bringing my attention to it as well. Heat rushed to my face and we both looked away. I stood up and offered Tristan a hand. He took it and pulled himself up, letting go immediately.

"That's enough for today. Good start." He walked away, leaving me alone in the empty room. I let myself out and walked back home.

The next day, it started all over again. Lexi came over and brought little dolls with pictures of Lucy taped on their face. I smirked. If there was anything that could get me mad, it was Lucy. I didn't bother asking how she managed to get a picture of Lucy; that's the convenience of living in the digital age. The thought of Lucy having an online dating profile made my stomach turn though. She set the three of them lined up in a row, making them sit up on the edge of the table.

"Okay, I want you to focus on moving the first one any way you can. Just make sure you move the first one only. Got it?" Lexi asked.

I nodded my head and stood up, facing my miniature arch nemesis. I remembered all the times she had back-stabbed me, all the rumors she had spread, every lie she told to my face and behind my back. I thought of all the things I wish I had said, and all the times I wish I had confronted her. My anger was equal towards Lucy as towards myself for my weakness.

I felt electricity course through my fingers, and I rubbed them against my thumbs subconsciously. I took a deep breath, and stared, focusing all the anger and resentment toward that one little, stupid doll. I could feel my power coursing through my veins. It was the first time I had actually felt it, and it was invigorating. There was a sense of familiarity to it, like finding a favorite book you hadn't read in years. Only problem was the doll didn't move. I let out a sigh and looked at Lexi. She stared at me wide eyed.

"What?" I asked with a little too much edge in my voice.

"You're, well, you're glowing. It's crazy!"

I rolled my eyes. "Will you quit talking about this whole glowing business?" I asked hotly. "Obviously it doesn't mean anything! I can't even make the damn doll move!"

"Well, maybe the binding spell is still wearing off. That's why you can only move things in spurts, and in cases of emergency when you get angry or scared." This was all feeling so repetitive. Even Lexi couldn't find any new explanations to this madness. I threw myself down on the couch in a fit.

"I hate this crap. I don't even know why I'm trying; I don't care what happens to Darien. I think I should just go back to my boring existence."

"How can you say that? You are the only one who can stop him and his followers. You have abilities the rest of us could only dream of. You have been given this gift, destined to be the best. You cannot turn away from it. I will not let you." The intensity in Lexi's voice made it impossible to argue. I let out a long sigh.

"Whatever." I stood up again and faced the dolls. I concentrated for a few more minutes without any success, when a knock on the door snapped me out of it.

"I'll get it," Lexi said, "You keep working on that doll." She went to the door and I refocused my attention on the Lucies. I studied the picture taped on the doll. I focused on the big brown eyes and red-brown hair. I imagined punching her, and relived the satisfaction of it. My fingers twitched and I was deep in thought.

"You're trying too hard." A man's voice broke my reverie. I turned quickly to see Tristan standing just behind me. His dark hair fell over his green eyes that glowed with knowledge. He was wearing a black t-shirt and black cargo shorts that reached his knees. I was glad I hadn't been caught in my pajamas again. I was feeling good in my jean shorts and white t-shirt. "You need to relax and just let it come naturally. I think I told you that yesterday. You're training will be much easier if you listen to me."

I scowled at him.

"Aren't you a little early?" Lexi asked Tristan.

"I figured I would come by and see what kind of progress Selena was making. Apparently I'm not missing much."

Ouch.

I hung my head and walked to my room. I closed my door quietly and sat on my bed. I tried to stay calm, but my anger festered inside me, growing like a flesh-eating virus through my body and across my skin. I could take criticism, but after failing all morning, being shot down by Tristan hurt too much. I couldn't handle it. Not today. My hands started to shake. So did the objects in my apartment. It was a low rumble, but everything shook. My bedroom door swung open to reveal Lexi's excited face.

"Are you seeing this? That is all you, babe!" Lexi was laughing. I got angrier.

"What good is this if I can't control it? All it does is let everyone know what I'm feeling." I stood up and stormed past her. I walked toward Tristan, who had gotten himself comfortable on my couch. "Are you happy now?" I asked through clenched teeth. He smiled.

I lost it.

I tried to contain my complete irritation and anger, but it only caused me to shake more. I didn't want to get this angry, and I wasn't sure why I was. I only knew that I couldn't calm down. Maybe Tristan had more of an effect on my emotions than I liked to admit. The sepia pictures of my parents - some of the few remnants I was able to salvage from the fire - shook so fiercely on the wall they fell and shattered on the floor. The lamps shook, causing them to flicker off and on. Lexi came into the room, watching in amazement. I raised my arms and the Lucy dolls flew across the room.

I looked at Tristan and saw that he was no longer smiling. His expression was a mix of fear and pride. Seeing his face like that reminded me of my dream, snapped me out of my anger and made me realize my overreaction. I calmed down, and everything went still.

I felt so humiliated. I couldn't believe I had let my feelings take over so much, and I couldn't believe what I was capable of. I lowered my arms, felt my heart rate return to normal and turned to see the damage in my apartment. Aside from a few broken picture frames, everything else was in place.

Lexi and Tristan were both staring at me, and I just wanted to crawl into a hole and hide until they left. I didn't want to kick them out, so I decided to leave instead. I grabbed my keys and walked out the door. The heat engulfed me immediately, and I welcomed the warmth. I headed straight for my Mustang, and felt a small rush of relief when I saw it shimmering in the sunlight.

"Selena," Tristan called after me. I felt my face flush. I didn't want him to see me like this anymore. He caught up to me and grabbed my arm to stop me from reaching my car. "What's wrong?" He asked, staring straight into my eyes. I couldn't find my words at first. I shook my head, and the effects of Tristan's gaze off.

"I'm not cut out for this. I can't control my powers. I get mad, everyone can tell, and I ruin my apartment, but I can't seem to make a stupid doll move when I want it to." I clenched my fists and looked away. "This is all just a stupid mistake. There is no way I am the girl in that prophecy." I wrenched my arm free of Tristan's grip and got to my car. He stared at me for a moment. Maybe he realized there was no point in arguing with me just then.

"Huh, so here is the infamous Mustang." He circled to the front of the car and eyed it. "My Camaro's hotter." He smiled a half smile, setting my heart beating faster. I had to get a grip already. The change in conversation was welcomed, and relieved my stress a little.

"Please. Camaros disappeared for years. If it wasn't for *Transformers* they wouldn't be that big a deal," I argued.

"Really? Well Mustangs that aren't GT or higher are ponies."

"Well it's a good thing mine is a GT."

Tristan laughed. "Feel like releasing some steam?" He asked. My mind wandered to the many meanings of that question. Then I decided, whatever way he meant it, I could use an outlet. I nodded. "Come on." He held out his hand for me to take, but then thought better of it, letting it fall to his side. He started walking and I followed, not knowing where I was going, and not really caring.

Before I knew it, I was standing in front of a familiar fountain. We were at Tristan's house again. We walked in and Tristan gestured to the weights in his living room. I slumped and sighed. I guess this was one way to blow off some steam. I picked up the ten pounders and attempted a couple sets of arm curls. It didn't take long for my muscles to protest. I was active for the most part, but I didn't lift weights often.

"I was thinking," I started, wanting a break from the weights. "When I was in the car with Darien, he told me that he wouldn't take me home because he may never get this opportunity again. Would you happen to know what he meant by that?"

Tristan's jaw clenched, probably at the memory of that night.

"We are still trying to figure out what he wants with you."

I flinched, feeling like a used toy, the owner deciding whether or not to throw me out. "I think he meant that he wouldn't get you alone and vulnerable like that again and the next time you meet, he won't stand a chance against you."

He looked at the ten pound dumbbells at my feet, and turned his head at an angle. "You're only using the ten pounders?" He asked, surprise in his tone. I gritted my teeth.

"What the hell, Tristan? Why do you say things like that to me? Do you think it makes me feel good that I'm weak?" I stood up and was inches from his face.

"You need to stop playing around. You are stronger than you think. You need to put in that 150% you agreed to. You are only as weak as you believe yourself to be. Stop crying about your lack of skill and do something about it."

"You don't think I'm trying? It's only been two days; what do you want from me?" We stood glaring at each other.

"I want you to be the strong, powerful witch you were destined to be. It kills me to see you quit so easily when things don't go your way."

I looked down. He was right. I expected things to just happen, but I needed to work for it.

"I just can't seem to make my body do what I want it to," I said, lowering my voice, still looking at my feet.

"Once you can fully access your powers, your strength and speed will increase too, to the point where you could, *maybe,* beat me one day." I looked up and he gave me that half smile that made my heart skip a beat. "You already experienced a taste of it when you fought Lucy. No normal uppercut could send someone airborne."

So he had been watching me. Weird. I suddenly felt proud and slightly self-conscious. I nodded.

"What do I do until then?"

"Just keep trying. It never hurts to learn the skill of fighting before you can apply the strength to back up your attacks. Keep doing arm curls, I will work out over there." He nodded his head to a bench press I hadn't noticed before.

"Even though they're only ten pounds?" I asked sarcastically.

"Unless you want to try the twenties?" He challenged.

I scowled and turned my attention back toward my dumbbells. I eyed the twenties and lifted one tentatively to see how sore my arms already were. I did a curl, then another, and I looked up to see Tristan pull his t-shirt off over his head. I almost dropped the weight. His body was tan and lean with muscle. I subconsciously counted his abs and then did a double-take. He had eight of them, and there seemed to be no fat on his superhuman body.

Tristan lay on the leather cushioned bench and took a deep breath. He wrapped his hands on either end of the bar and lifted it. He made it look effortless, so much so that I thought my eyes were tricking me when I saw he was lifting 400 pounds. I guess Tristan was right; once you have access to your powers, your strength is unmatched by any human.

After a few minutes, Tristan put the bar back on the brackets and took a break. I hadn't realized I had been gawking, open mouthed, until he looked at me. I shook my head and turned back to my dinky dumbbells. No wonder he thought I was weak. I felt my face flush slightly with embarrassment.

We worked out in silence for another two hours, rotating between running, squats, push-ups, crunches and weight lifting until I was pretty tired. I didn't want to admit to Tristan that I wanted to rest. After all, he had been working out with me, doing much more exerting things, and he barely broke a sweat. I was finishing another rep of push-ups when I looked at Tristan and saw that he was staring at me. Not in a creepy gawky way like I had been looking at him earlier, but with concern. He seemed to be assessing my physical strength. I sat up, looked him in the eye, and lifted my chin, trying to show no weakness.

"You did well today. We will pick up where we left off tomorrow."

"I'm okay. I can keep going," I said, internally hoping he would call my bluff.

"I'm sure you can, but you did enough for today. Go home and get some rest."

I nodded and got to my feet. I felt my muscles protest even with that small movement, but I didn't let it show. I walked straight and steady until I closed his front door behind me. Only then did I allow myself to limp. I took a few wobbly steps and turned to look at Tristan's house. He was looking out the window at me, a smile on his face as he shook his head.

Damn it.

I went home, took a shower and then fell into a deep sleep.

The next few weeks were quite repetitive and excruciatingly painful. Tristan refused to let me take a day off training, saying that I needed to learn to work through the pain and build up my endurance. I wanted to punch him in the face, but figured I would keep that anger in reserve for the next time we sparred. I hadn't made any new progress with Lexi, which was maddening. Lexi had come over every day before her shift started and we would train, but I still wasn't getting better. I really needed the bind to wear off soon or I was going to blow up my apartment with my anger.

There was a knock on the door, and Lexi, who had just come by for another training session, answered it.

"Hey," she greeted Tristan at the door, aviator glasses on the bridge of his nose, brown hair stylishly messy as usual.

"Hey, how's it going today?" Tristan asked, removing his sunglasses as he came inside. I realized that he hadn't been giving me too hard a time about my slow progress since I rocked my apartment. Maybe I really scared him.

"It's going. Still nothing new," I said quietly.

"You'll get there," he reassured.

Lexi and Tristan moved to the living room, and stared at each other as if having a silent conversation, while I tried yet again, to move objects with my mind. I focused on the tennis balls, trying to move them, roll them, anything, but it wasn't working.

Selena, I heard someone whisper.

"Yeah?" I automatically responded. I looked up to see who had called me. Tristan and Lexi were looking at me with confused looks on their faces.

"Yeah, what?" Tristan asked.

"You called me?"

Selena, I haven't forgotten you. I heard the whispered voice again, but I was looking at Tristan and Lexi and neither of their mouths so much as twitched.

"How are you doing that?" I asked.

"Doing what?" Lexi retorted.

Ah, Selena I've missed you. I will come for you.

"Who-?" I started to ask, but a loud thud against my front door interrupted my sentence. The three of us jerked in response. I walked to the door, but before I could reach it, Tristan cut me off.

"Let me check it out." He looked me in the eye and didn't move until he knew I wouldn't get in his way. I took a step back to reassure him. Tristan walked to the door and Lexi stood beside it in case anyone tried to get in. Another thud sounded, making me jump. Tristan peeked through the blinds covering the window in the door to see who was there, and I stood behind him trying to see as well. No one was there, but when Tristan opened the blinds completely I saw a red streak smeared down the window.

Something black came flying toward the door, but I couldn't make out what it was until it got closer. I saw the red eyes come into focus first, their brightness unnerving and unnatural. Then I saw the rodent-like body and the scaled wings unfurling as they flapped toward my door.

Selena, this is for you. I heard the whisper, so close to my ear that I turned to see who was standing there, but I was alone. The bat flew right into the window with such force it exploded on impact, leaving a trail of blood as the remains slid down the window. Then I saw another bat, and another, until it was a swarm of them, all flying toward me. One splat after another made my door shake. A crack in the window formed from the pressure, the blood of the bats started to seep through the fissures. The noise grew thunderous as one after the other they came. The rattling of my lamps added to the noise as they shook with my increasing fear. Tristan stepped back and stood directly in front of me, shielding me from the gruesome image.

"Lexi, recast the shield spell you put on the apartment," Tristan said. "Something must have broken it."

Lexi stood straight and closed her eyes. She raised her hands so her palms faced my front door and whispered an incantation under her breath. I saw a faint light shine from her hands and hit the door. The light spread as it hit the flat surface and continued until the walls of the entire apartment were covered in the faint glow. Once the light sealed the unit, it vanished and the noise stopped. I looked around Tristan's towering form and saw that the bats were still coming, but instead of hitting my door they hit an invisible barrier.

Every time they hit, a blue light retracted, resealing the shield spell. Tristan stepped forward and I followed. I looked down and saw that I had grabbed the back of his shirt, and held it in a death grip. The number of bats dwindled until finally, the bats stopped coming all together.

"What was that?" I asked, my breathing heavy and uneven from my fear.

"Looks like a rabid spell," Tristan answered, his back still facing me.

"What is a rabid spell?" I asked. Really, they should know by now that I need explanations and definitions.

"It's where the spell caster sends an animal as an attack, so it multiplies and becomes infected as though rabid," Lexi explained.

Ew.

I let go of Tristan's shirt and saw I had left wrinkles where my damp hands were. I tried to smooth them out and realized he might think I was feeling him up, just as he turned around.

"Sorry, I wrinkled your shirt," I said, looking down. I looked at Lexi from the corner of my eye and saw her try to repress her laughter. This was embarrassing.

"That's not important. What did you hear before? When you said someone called you."

"I heard someone call my name. I think it was a man's voice, but it was so soft I couldn't tell for sure. It said it hadn't forgotten me and that this," I gestured toward the door, "was for me." Tristan's jaw clenched.

"Darien," he said, and Lexi nodded her head. I looked at Tristan, wanting more of an explanation. "Darien was speaking to you telepathically, so Lexi and I didn't hear what you heard. He's sending a message, and he's trying to scare you."

"Well, it worked. I'm freaked out right now," I almost shouted.

"Are you okay?" He asked.

"Yeah, just a little shaken up. I'll be fine." I took a deep breath to steady my nerves, and the shaking lamps steadied with me.

"Good, I need to take care of something," Tristan said. "Will you be okay here with Lexi?"

"Yeah, of course," I answered.

Lexi shot him a haughty look, "Why wouldn't she be?"

"Just checking," Tristan said. He swung the front door open before stepping over the bats and walking away.

Lexi looked after Tristan as he left, and then she saw all the carcasses at my front door. She looked out to make sure no one was watching, and then she swept her hands across the ground and up my door. In a flash everything was clean and my door was repaired. I stood open-mouthed as Lexi closed the door and turned to face me.

"You should sit down," she said motioning to the couch. I sat down.

"You can do that? You can clean stuff too?" I asked in awe.

"Only when it pertains to spells, it will undo the damage it caused. I can't clean your apartment. That would be cool though."

I nodded. "Are you telepathic too?" I asked.

"Yeah, and you will be too once you get your powers."
She smiled.

"There were a few times when you and Tristan looked at each other like you guys were communicating. Are you doing the telepathic thing?"

"Yeah, we tend to discuss you at those times."

"Oh, really nice! That's so rude, like talking in a different language in front of someone."

Lexi laughed. "Oh, don't take it so personally. We need to agree on certain things when it comes to your protection and it's just easier to discuss it right away as it comes up. It also keeps you shielded from the fights we have, giving the illusion that we are working and deciding things together. I know it's a lame explanation, but Tristan just thinks it's better that way."

"Ugh. I feel so left out."

"Don't, I'm telling you, once you access your powers you will make our heads explode with the force of your mental voice." She laughed, hard. She was kidding, right?

"What was it that you were whispering for that spell?" I asked, curious to know if I could learn to seal my apartment.

"Oh, there are no specific magical words or anything. We just have to state what we want to do, and magic does the rest. Most of the time you can just think it. The only time you need an actual incantation is when you perform a ritual. You'll learn that later though."

"So, if I want to make a million dollars--"

"You can't make money appear from thin air – it has to come from somewhere and that's stealing. You start to get into dark magic when you do those things."

"So is that what Darien works with, dark magic like those bats?"

"Yeah, each person decides how they want to use their magic. It's like… what stops you from stealing or killing?"

"I know it's wrong."

"Exactly. There are good people and bad people, just as there are good and bad witches. We choose how we use our magic, and most of us use it for good." She smiled.

I nodded my head, but what I thought was *a million dollars sounds good to me*.

"Do you guys have police, or some authority that keeps you in check?"

"Sure," Lexi thought a moment. "They're called The Charge, but they don't wear badges or anything like that. They do go after witches who break the law and bring them to court."

"Cool… Witch court. I'd like to see that."

"Something tells me you will."

"I can wait. I've seen enough lately."

8. CRYSTALS, SHOPS AND THINGAMABOBS

"Guys, I need a break," I said, coming out of my room one morning. Tristan and Lexi were sitting at my kitchen table like I knew they'd be. Ever since Darien sent the bats, Tristan had been on a mission to train me and make sure I could protect myself. The last few days I was pushed and forced to train eight to ten hours a day, exhausting me to the point where 7:00 pm became my new bed time.

"No," Tristan said.

"What do you mean?" I placed my hands on my hips and tried to glare at him.

"I mean, no," he said, eyes scanning the newspaper. Lexi looked at Tristan, and a moment later he looked back. They stared at each other, having a silent conversation. I resisted the urge to growl, then I resisted the urge to laugh. Lexi squinted and ground her teeth, apparently having so heated an argument she had to stop herself from yelling out loud. Tristan on the other hand, merely stared back, looking almost uninterested. I guess he was winning the debate.

"Fine, I guess I don't deserve a break," I pouted. "I'll go wash up and change for training." I started to leave the room when I felt a pressure pulling and twisting me. "Oh, my God," I whispered when I found myself in the bathroom. "I think I just teleported," I yelled.

"Uh, yeah," I heard Lexi call from outside the bathroom door. I looked at my reflection and smiled. Cool.

"How do I control the teleporting?" I asked, as I walked back to them. I was only slightly scared, which was weird. I would have thought I would freak out about teleporting on my own. Instead I was only worried about spontaneously disappearing.

"I'm not sure," Tristan said. "I always had to concentrate very hard to get myself going. Were you concentrating on going to the bathroom?"

I shook my head. "No, I just thought about going there, and then poof!" I smiled. Tristan frowned.

"That's a lot of power," he said, worry creasing his handsome face.

"Okay, no big deal," Lexi started, "Selena will need to learn how to control her strength, that's all. She will have to assess how much power or thought is needed to cast a spell and tone it down, or up accordingly."

"I can barely do anything at all," I said. "How can I learn to control something I don't fully have yet?"

"Well you can start by controlling the powers you do have," Lexi said, "like teleporting."

"This is crazy," I said.

"You have no idea." Lexi wagged her eyebrows, while Tristan shook his head.

"Alright," he said, "try it again."

I focused on the bathroom again, but nothing happened.

"Damn."

"Just believe you can do it," Tristan said.

I rolled my eyes, took a deep breath and focused, believing that I had the ability to teleport. I felt a stirring in my stomach as the magic coursed through me, and before I could take another breath, I was in the bathroom. I laughed as I walked back to Lexi and Tristan.

"Awesome!" Lexi said, smiling ear-to-ear.

Tristan nodded, "Now, normally with teleporting, you need to know exactly where you're going. Your case isn't exactly normal, but regardless, make sure you don't try to teleport to a place you've never been."

"Why? What will happen?" The slight fear I felt began to grow.

"You hit a barrier, and it could hurt," Tristan answered.

"Can I get trapped in a mountain or something?"

"No, you either teleport, or you don't. We'll work on this some more. In the meantime, you can have today off." He turned and walked out the door. Again.

Okay.

"You know what?" Lexi said after a moment, "We should get out of here and do something fun." Her eyes twinkled.

"What did you have in mind?"

Half an hour later we were on our way to Sedona. It was almost a two hour drive, and the distance was liberating.

"So, are you enjoying this little getaway from physical training?" Lexi asked.

"Yes, my body really needed a break - even if it's only one day."

"Tristan is a good instructor though, right?"

My stomach dropped at the sound of his name.

"Yeah, he pushes me a lot, which is good, you know? He shows me that I can keep going long after my body yells at me to stop." I chuckled.

"And he's really easy on the eyes too, so that must make training a bit more fun." She looked at my face, still trying to get information out of me. I really didn't want Lexi to know how I felt about Tristan, it was embarrassing.

"Sure, if you like that brooding, tough guy type." Which I did. Lexi laughed.

"You're telling me, after all the time you have spent training with him, you haven't been checking him out?"

Ugh, the trick question. If I said no, she would know I was lying, and if I said yes she would get me to admit I thought he was good-looking. I stared out my window, pretending to admire the view.

"Selena," Lexi pressed.

"Yesno," I said, slurring the two words together.

"Huh?" Lexi asked confused.

"What's that over there?" I asked, pointing to nothing just to distract her from the current conversation.

"I don't see anything--" Lexi started, then she looked back at me. "Are you kidding me? Why won't you just tell me what you think of Tristan? I can't believe you're trying to change the subject with that sad ploy." Lexi laughed. She knew me too well.

"Because, I just don't know what to think. Yes, he's hot, but he's my teacher, so what's the point of thinking about it at all?"

"You make it sound like he's an old professor, and you're in high school. He's only three years older than you."

"It doesn't matter; it's the principle."

"The principal? You had a crush on your principal?" Were we actually having this conversation? I couldn't help but burst out laughing.

"No!" I said in between gasps. "It's the principle, the ethics, rules, whatever." Lexi started laughing when she realized what I meant.

"Oh man, I need more sleep I think. Anyways, all I'm saying is it doesn't hurt to have a crush and it doesn't hurt to tell your best friend about it."

I shrugged. I knew Lexi was right, but I didn't want to confront the subject at all.

"Well there's nothing to tell so... unless... do *you* like him?" I asked, afraid of the answer. Lexi looked at me.

"He is ridiculously gorgeous, but I have known him my whole life. He's like a brother, and as a fellow protector, I just can't see him as anything other than that." She returned her attention to the road. I was surprised at how relieved I felt. It would have really bothered me if Lexi liked Tristan. But why? My emotions frustrated me; I needed to be stronger than this.

The rest of the drive Lexi and I had our windows rolled down and the music blaring, leaving all our magical worries behind.

We finally found a parking space in the shopping district of Sedona. There were shops pressed side-by-side on both sides of the road. The mid-day sun shone brightly, but since we were two hours from Phoenix, it was significantly cooler.

Lexi and I walked through the small stores, studying the crystals and charms. Many stores advertised psychic palm and tarot readings, others advertised specials on their books and crystals. We perused through the stores, but nothing caught my eye.

"Are the store owners witches?" I asked as we walked into another store.

"Not that I've seen yet."

"How can you tell?"

"Their auras. Remember when I told you that when I saw Tristan at the bar, I could tell he was a witch by his aura?"

I nodded.

"Well, humans have auras too, but they are significantly diminished."

I thought about Lexi's words, wishing I could see what she saw.

"Let's get lunch at The Hideout," Lexi suggested, weaving her way out of the store. My stomach growled in response.

We walked past the shops and onto a more populated road, crossing a bridge and a few other stores on the outskirts before we reached the restaurant. It was a wooden, two-storey structure with seating inside and out on the terrace. We walked up the stairs to the second floor and took a seat on the balcony, overlooking the lush trees and a small creek that ran alongside us.

A young man approached us with two glasses of lemon water, as soon as we were settled. His face was serene and his blue eyes gleamed in the sunlight.

We both ordered Philly cheesesteak sandwiches with side salads.

"God, it is so peaceful here," I said, once our waiter left.

"I know. I love Sedona. There's something in the air here that makes you feel so calm." Lexi gazed out at the red-rock mountains in the distance.

We took a quiet moment to enjoy the day until the waiter returned. He placed our meals on the vinyl, red and white checkered table cloth in front of us, with a smile.

"Anything else I can get you?" He asked.

"No, thank you," Lexi responded, before turning to her sandwich. We ate in silence. The melted cheese and delicious tender meat hit the spot.

"There's one more store I want to hit before we leave, if that's okay?" I asked Lexi.

"Sure," she said over a mouthful of food.

A short while later, we paid our bill and left. Bellies full, I was glad to be walking to digest faster. After fifteen minutes, we reached our destination; a purple shop, shaped like a small house...or it could have actually been a small house, I wasn't sure. The door chimed as we walked in and the scent of incense greeted us.

The shop had four separate rooms, each with a different selection of items. One had crystals, another pentacles, cauldrons and other witchy things, the one next to that had Buddhist items and the last had books and psychic readers.

"You have an amazing aura," a woman said behind me. I turned to see a small, blonde woman squinting at me. She was maybe half a foot shorter than me, and she wore a ring on each finger. "I've never seen anything like it," she carried on.

"Thank you," I said, not really sure what the proper response was.

The woman smiled, but turned serious as she continued to squint. I felt Lexi walk up behind me.

"There is darkness coming," the woman said, "a danger that you must confront. Be warned, you cannot do it alone. You will need others. There will be pain in your future...a lot of pain. Be strong." The woman averted her gaze and darted to another room.

"What?" Lexi asked.

"I… have no idea," I said slowly. I turned to leave the creepy shop when the woman returned.

"Please, take this." She handed me a small, smooth stone. It had a silver shimmer to it, but darker. "It's hematite, to ward off negativity," the woman explained. I studied the smooth stone and felt its weight before placing it in my purse.

"Thank you," I said. We left the shop and I looked back at the woman. She stood where I left her, shook her head as if to clear it and walked to the back room.

"That was weird," Lexi said, as we began the hike to our car.

"Yeah," I mumbled, reaching into my purse to take out the stone. It shone in the sunlight, and I felt a sense of comfort. I shook my head and kept walking.

"Do humans have psychic powers? Or was she a witch?" I asked.

"She was definitely human," Lexi answered. "Through meditation and practice, some more sensitive humans are able to develop a small portion of psychic ability. Not like witches though, and it is rare."

"What makes witches different from humans? Why are we able to use magic and they can't?"

"Well, witches have an extra chromosome that allows us to connect with the energy around us. It's like," Lexi paused thinking of the right words. "Think of it as humans having an extra layer, or a veil, that prevents them from accessing the elements and magic around them. That extra chromosome gives us a direct line, an ability to manifest energy into our will."

"Wow." I smiled.

Sometime later, we finally reached the car, and I was grateful for the rest; so much for giving my body a break.

I settled in the passenger seat, stone in hand, but as soon as I reached for the seatbelt, the stone flew from my palm and stuck onto the metal tab.

"Huh," I said, prying the stone off the buckle. "It's magnetic. Cool."

Lexi smiled, but shook her head, "Let me see that."

I gave her the stone and she held it for a moment.

"What are you doing?" I asked.

"Just sensing if there are any magical attributes infused in it," she answered, eyes closed.

"And...?"

She opened her eyes, "I don't sense anything, just a stone. It was a nice gesture though." She started the car and we left the peaceful city of Sedona behind us.

"What are we doing here?" I asked two hours later, looking at the familiar fountain in the center of the yard. The setting sun reflected pinks and oranges off the water, making it look like a waterfall of rainbows trickling down each tier.

"Tristan thought you could use some more time away from your place." Lexi shut off the engine and put the keys in her bag. "He should be here any minute."

"When did he tell you that?"

Lexi tapped her temple and she got out of the car.

The feeling of being left out frustrated me and threatened to piss me off. Stepping out of the car, the heat wrapped around me in a stifling embrace. I already missed the cooler Sedona weather.

A car door slammed behind me, and I turned to see Tristan sauntering up to his front door, keys in hand. He looked like he should be moving in slow motion with his sunglasses and tousled hair. His tank top showed off his muscular arms and lean build. I think my mouth actually filled with saliva.

My face flushed and I looked away before he could notice. Lexi on the other hand was looking at me. I dropped my shoulders in defeat and stared at my feet. Why was she always watching me? I almost laughed at the thought when I realized that was her job. I shook my head.

"What's wrong?" Tristan asked, noticing the gesture.

"Huh?" I started, confused, "Oh, nothing, I was just thinking about something." Wow, I was articulate. I hoped the long day I had would justify my stupefied behavior. I scratched at my neck as I followed Tristan and Lexi inside the house. The cool air wafted around me, and I took a deep breath, letting the coldness fill my body.

"Where's your furniture?" Lexi asked, taking in the bare walls and scantily furnished rooms.

"No need for it. This is a place for training and sleep, not a home." Tristan took his sunglasses off and threw them on the counter with his keys.

Tristan's words made me flinch. It suddenly dawned on me how sad it must be for them to be protectors. Never really living their own lives, always following me and watching me. How depressing.

I raked my nails across my arm. I felt a tingling in my calf and scratched at it, then another tingling in my thigh. What was going on? I looked down and saw a brown cockroach crawl up my leg. I shook it off viciously and let out a yelp.

"What's wrong?" Tristan asked concerned, coming to my side.

"There was a cockr--" I stopped midsentence as I saw another one on my right arm. I screamed jerking my arm. When the cockroach didn't come off I swept it off roughly with my left hand. And then I really screamed. Centipedes, cockroaches, crickets, and Oh God help me, scorpions were crawling all over my left arm. I vaguely heard Tristan and Lexi yelling at me to calm down.

My eyes were unfocused, showing me blurred images of my protectors' confused expressions. I didn't want the scorpions to sting me, and I knew I should stay still so I wouldn't provoke them, but I had to move. I had to get rid of them. I rubbed violently at my arm in an attempt to get the nightmarish creatures away from me.

"Get them off!" I screamed.

I couldn't handle bugs, not even a little bit. Then they were everywhere. On my feet, crawling up my legs, violating every inch of skin their twitchy little legs touched. I jerked and flailed, but they wouldn't move. I whimpered.

They were at my waist now, covering my entire lower body, and then my arms. I screamed and screamed and dropped to the floor flinging my arms at my body, but no matter how I moved, they wouldn't come off. Oh God, this wasn't happening! The ground shook beneath me, the shutters clattered, the lights flickered. I shut my eyes tightly and heard Tristan's voice.

"What's happening, Selena?" His voice was so full of fear it scared me even more. I opened my eyes and looked down at my body.

Nothing.

There was nothing there.

Oh please, please don't tell me I'm losing my mind! I scanned my body, my arms, legs, feet, but all the bugs were gone, and the itching had stopped. There were scratch marks from my nails, but no other sign of what I saw. Tristan gently held my arm and inspected the scratches as the house settled.

"Where did they go?" My voice was raspy and shaking from screaming.

"Where did who go?" Lexi asked. Who? Was she kidding me?

"The bugs," I yelled, exasperated. Tristan and Lexi exchanged confused glances.

"There were no bugs," Tristan said softly, keeping eye contact, probably checking my sanity. I wasn't so sure of it myself.

"But," I started, then thought better of it. If they didn't see any bugs, then I must have imagined it. No, there was no way my mind made all that up, it was too real. I felt my eyes fill with tears and looked up in an attempt to keep them unshed.

"Tell me exactly what you saw," Tristan instructed, helping me to my feet. My legs shook under me, but I steadied myself. Tristan led me to the couch against the wall, and I sat. A shiver ran through me as I thought of what happened.

"There were bugs all over me, my arms, my legs, my whole lower body. There were cockroaches and scorpions." Another shiver wracked my body. I looked at Lexi, a look of worry etched into her small pixie face. Tristan was still examining my scratches, his thick, dark lashes hiding his green eyes as he looked down at my arms and legs. "You didn't see them?" I asked shocked. Lexi and Tristan both shook their heads. "Are you saying it wasn't real?" I was scared of what the answer would be and what it would imply if it was yes.

Tristan nodded his head. "Must be Darien again," he said under his breath,

"But, the bats were real. You guys saw them too, right?"

"Yeah, but this is a different kind of magic. He sent the spell directly to your mind, so only you could see it," Lexi explained.

I let out a groan. "Seriously? Twice in one week? Don't evil people have a code or something, a limit to how many times they're allowed to torment a person in one sitting?" I said sarcastically.

Lexi shrugged.

Tristan touched one of the scratches and I jerked my arm back reflexively. A look of... I'm not sure what... flashed across his face.

"Sorry," he mumbled.

"Can't you just do that thing where you undo the damage of a spell? You know, fix my skin?" I asked Lexi. She shook her head.

"I can only undo the effects of the spell, you scratched yourself. It won't work, hon." I slouched back on the couch. This sucked. Images of how I must have looked, thrashing like a crazy person on the floor, ran through my mind and made my face flush with embarrassment.

"Sorry I freaked out so bad. I just really hate bugs." I kept my eyes down and looked at my hands. Some blood crusted around my nails; I must have scratched a lot harder than I realized.

"I want you to lie down," Tristan ordered. "I'll be back."

I laid my back flat against the cushions and felt myself sink in. I wondered if this was where Tristan slept; it was way too soft to just be a couch, especially a supposedly rarely used couch. I closed my eyes and tried to relax my breathing.

This was bad. Darien could get into my head. I opened my eyes and saw Tristan standing above me, studying me. Lexi came to stand beside him.

"What if I was on a mountain or somewhere high and Darien had made me believe something terrible was chasing me? Could he make me jump and kill myself in the process?" The possibility of Darien having so much control over me was petrifying.

"Shh, babe, don't think about stuff like that." Lexi said, gently pushing my hair off my forehead. I knew Lexi avoided directly answering my question because she couldn't lie. Tristan watched Lexi's hand as it ran though my hair, and then he looked away. He closed his eyes and took a deep breath. He placed his hands palm down above my stomach, hovering just inches from my body.

He moved his hands over my waist, hips, legs and feet, never touching me. I wished I could somehow close that gap though. He brought his hands back up to my stomach and then moved them over my arms, chest, neck and head. He left them hovering over my forehead for a moment before finally letting his arms fall to his sides. I had no idea what just happened.

"What did you do?" I looked at my arms, but the scratches were still there, so he hadn't healed me.

"I reinforced a protection spell I had on you," Tristan said. "It's similar to the one Lexi placed on your apartment. I hope it holds this time. I should have known when Darien was able to talk to you telepathically that he must have weakened my spell. I tried to protect you and your mind so he couldn't get anywhere near you." Tristan's jaw clenched and anger flared in his green eyes. I looked again at my body.

"I didn't see that same light this time. Does it mean it didn't work?"

"No, this spell was a little different. It will still protect you, inside and out," Lexi explained.

"So, there is no spell for healing?"

"Not that Tristan or I can do," Lexi said. "Very few witches have that ability."

"I may know one," Tristan said pensively.

"I wouldn't be surprised if you were one of them," Lexi added, dismissing Tristan.

I wondered what I would be able to do once I finally had my full powers... if I ever got them. I was growing impatient with my slow progress and decided it would be a good time to do something about it.

"Can I try teleporting again?" I asked, sitting up.

"You sure you don't want to relax for a minute first?" Lexi asked.

"No, I'm fine. This will make me feel better," I answered. "It'll give me a healthy distraction."

Tristan shrugged, "Okay, go for it."

I stood and focused on teleporting a short distance. I relaxed and believed I could go to the kitchen. Just as quickly, I was there.

"Good," Tristan said. "Now watch me teleport with Lexi, and then you can try." Tristan strode to Lexi, whose face beamed into a bright smile.

I wondered why Lexi looked so happy, and felt my stomach plummet when the thought of Lexi having feelings for Tristan came back to mind. I should have known she would like him, and that he would like her. They were both protectors, strong and brave with so much more in common. I shook my head but felt a small amount of acceptance. It made sense at least. I looked at Lexi, her head cocked at an angle, looking curiously at me.

I smiled to deflect her, and she made a face that said 'what are you thinking?'

I broke eye contact with her to pay attention to Tristan. Holding Lexi's hand, he vanished and then materialized in front of me. The action ruffled his messy hair slightly, giving his face a glow of serenity. Lexi practically giggled. It felt amazing to be able to bend the laws of physics like that. I stared at the area they had just been in disbelief. I still couldn't get used to the thought of being able to teleport.

"Okay, let me try that," I said, taking Lexi's hand. I focused on teleporting us back to the living room, but we didn't move. "What am I doing wrong?"

"Nothing that I can tell," Tristan said stepping beside me. "Here, let me teleport us and maybe you can sense what I'm doing." He placed his hand around my waist, and I held my breath, afraid that if I made any movement he would release me. In a flash we were back in the living room. It felt the same as when I teleported, only it seemed he extended his power to cover me as well.

Lexi walked to us and smiled. I realized then that Tristan still had his arm around me. I reluctantly stepped away from him. I didn't want Lexi to be upset if she did have feelings for him. I know she told me she looked at him as a brother, but I wondered if maybe she just didn't want me to know how she really felt. I would have to talk to her about this later.

"I think I got it," I said, taking Lexi's hand again. I envisioned the kitchen again, but this time focused on spreading my power like a cloak over Lexi as well.

It worked.

I let out a cheer when our feet hit the kitchen floor.

"See?" Lexi said, "I knew we could teach you to control your powers."

I let out a sigh of relief.

"Do you want to try doing something else?" Tristan asked.

"Yeah, but not now. I'm pretty beat. Lexi, can you drive me home?"

"Sure."

We left Tristan's and reached my apartment in minutes. I loved that we didn't have to drive far, especially after our four hour round trip.

"You want me to sleep over in case Darien tries something else?" Lexi asked, walking me to the front door.

I thought about it a moment, then nodded my head.

Lexi's face brightened. "Yay! A sleepover! It'll be like when we were kids."

I laughed and unlocked my door. Lexi walked in first and took a quick look around, making sure there was nothing lurking around the corner.

"Do you remember when we would have sleep overs and write notes to each other while we were sitting in the same room?" Lexi asked.

I smiled at the memory, "Oh, yeah. Why did we do that again?"

Lexi shrugged, "No idea."

I ruffled through my bedroom drawers and gave Lexi some comfortable clothes to sleep in. After changing, we jumped into bed. I was almost in sleeping bliss when Lexi started chatting.

"So, did you have fun today?"

"Yeah, it was nice. Thanks," I said over a yawn, hoping she would get the hint.

She didn't.

"I mean, even teleporting. How awesome is that? You totally got it on lock down now," she babbled.

I smiled, "Yeah, that was pretty cool. I'm just glad I was finally able to do something."

"Just wait. You'll be able to do so many things, your head will spin."

"Thanks, Lex." I rolled over so my back was to her, trying to get into a comfy position.

"When do you think your other powers will pop up?" She asked.

"I don't know, Lex. We'll talk about it tomorrow."

She sighed, "Yeah, okay. 'Night."

I fell asleep before she finished saying the word.

9. MAGIC OR ALCOHOL?

A knock on my door woke me the next morning. I pried one eye open expecting to see Lexi still asleep, but her side of the bed was empty.

The front door opened and I heard murmured voices. I reluctantly got out of bed and washed up before heading to the kitchen.

Tristan sat across from Lexi at the table, both of them drinking coffee. I looked at the creamy liquid longingly and made myself a mug.

"'Morning," Lexi said, when I walked in silently.

I grunted in response.

"So, what do you want to try today?" Tristan asked. There was a note of excitement in his voice, laced with caution.

"I'm not sure," I said.

"How about you try opening the kitchen cupboard?" Lexi offered.

"Are you sure? I mean, I can't even move the Lucy dolls," I pouted.

"I'm sure. You're powers are increasing already, and I have a feeling it will work this time."

I imagined the cupboard door opening, but nothing happened. I shot a 'I told you so' glare at Lexi.

"Just keep trying," she said. "Gosh, you whine a lot. These things don't always happen right away, you know?"

"Fine," I huffed. I took a deep breath and focused, the cupboard door sprang open. I let out a sigh of satisfaction and shock. Finally, what I willed could happen.

Tristan and Lexi exchanged smiles.

"See? You're getting it already!" Lexi cheered.

"What else can I do?"

"According to the prophecy, eventually whatever you want. For now just go slow." Tristan smiled.

"Well," Lexi said, "I was thinking we could try to strengthen your affinity for the elements."

"My what now?" I asked confused.

"You can control the elements. Not only that, you have the ability to manifest them. I want you to become familiar with each of the elements, so you will learn not only to control them, but also respect them. Elements can be your best friend or your worst enemy if you mistreat them, okay?"

I nodded. Lexi stood and walked to her purse on the counter. She pulled out five long candles incased in glass, each one a different color.

"Do you always keep huge candles in your purse?" I asked sarcastically.

"I had a feeling I would need them," Lexi answered, as she pulled out one of the table chairs. "Sit here."

I sat.

Tristan sighed and leaned back in his chair.

"Okay," Lexi started, "we put the green candle here facing north. This is the Earth element. The white candle faces east which represents air," she said, placing the white candle on the floor to my right. "The red candle, as you can guess represents fire, so will be put facing south, and the blue candle, which represents water will be facing west." She placed the final candle to my left, encircling me with their colors.

"What's the purple one for?" I asked. Lexi took my mug of coffee and gave me the purple candle to hold in the center of the circle. I longed for my coffee immediately.

"This one represents spirit. It is who we are, and the source of our magic. This is more New Age type stuff, so we normally don't use candles to call elements, unless it's for a ritual. As witches, we have the ability to connect with the elements without all the visual effects, but you need the introduction course. So, we start with candles until you're comfortable enough where you won't need them." I looked at Lexi who had now busied herself searching for something in my kitchen drawers.

"What are you looking for?" I asked, trying not to move too much in case I ruined something, or accidently put a hex on myself.

"I forgot a lighter. Do you have one? Or matches even?"

"Yeah, top drawer, next to the stove." I answered. I looked at Tristan to see if he was laughing at me sitting on a chair in the middle of candles, but he seemed as serious as Lexi.

"Found them!" Lexi exclaimed as she pulled a little match box from the drawer. "Okay, so now we call the elements to us. This can be fancy if you like, but I prefer a simple, polite request." She stood beside me and faced the white candle first. "Beings of Air, Guardians of the East, welcome." She struck the match, lit the candle and turned toward the red one with a new match. "Beings of Fire, Guardians of the South, welcome." She lit the candle and moved clockwise to the blue candle saying, "Beings of Water, guardians of the West, welcome." Finally she reached the green candle. "Beings of Earth, Guardians of the North, welcome." She lit the candle and a soft breeze swept through her hair as if the elements released a collective sigh.

Lexi smiled in contentment then turned to face me. "You should call on spirit yourself. Just say 'Spirit, source of my powers and all that I am, welcome." I sat up straight and looked at the purple candle in my hands. I placed it between my knees as I took the match box from Lexi. I struck the match, and enjoyed the scent as the stick quickly caught fire. Lighting the candle, I repeated the words. I sat there and looked around.

"What now?" I asked.

"Did you feel anything?" Lexi asked in return. I shook my head. "Huh. That was pretty basic, you should have felt something, happiness, a breeze, something."

"I didn't."

"Did I do something wrong?" Lexi asked. "Tristan, was there anything I missed?" Tristan sat up and looked around.

"Not that I can tell. Seems you did fine. You felt the circle close, I saw the effect it had on you."

Lexi nodded.

"Great, so it's just me then." I looked down feeling defeated. "I don't mean to be in a self-pity mood, but I suck."

Tristan chuckled. "You do not suck. Things like this take time."

"Well according to Lexi, this was pretty basic. I'm defective."

"No, you're not. Just relax and try calling on spirit again. Believe it will work," Lexi said.

"Okay," I sighed. I stared at the flame, mesmerized by its bright heat and called upon spirit. I suddenly felt a peacefulness sweeping over me and through me. I felt like I should be glowing from the inside with the force of this energy. I suddenly smelled the earth, tasted the air, felt the heat of the fire, and the ocean spray of water.

"Wow," Lexi and I said in unison.

"You feel that too?" I asked.

Lexi nodded, "I never felt it so strongly before."

Tristan was now sitting on the edge of his seat, his elbows propped on his knees as he observed us.

"Look," Tristan said staring at the area above my head.

"What?" I asked, worried there was something hovering there I couldn't see.

"Your aura... it's so bright," Lexi said, staring at the same place Tristan was.

"Great. So do I just beam up anytime I use my powers?" I asked.

"Mainly," Lexi answered. "But it also happens when we feel great emotions. Especially happiness or excitement, so we keep it reeled in."

"Remind me to learn that soon." I sighed.

"Wait here a minute. I'll be right back." Tristan stood, and with a few long strides, walked out of my apartment.

"Where else are we going to go?" Lexi asked, after he left.

I watched as she thanked the elements and blew out the candles one by one. As she placed the candles on the counter I decided to take the opportunity to talk to her. Only problem was I had no idea how to broach the subject again. I didn't want her to think I was harassing her, but I just needed to know for sure. I shifted my seat back to the table.

"Lexi?"

"Hmm?" She turned her attention to me then.

"Um, I, uh..." For some reason the words just wouldn't come out. I felt stupid asking her about this and I knew I had no right to.

"Selena, just say whatever it is you need to say." She was patiently waiting, her eyes boring holes into my own.

"Do you like Tristan? Tell me the truth. You can trust me," I blurted, feeling my face flush immediately. I couldn't believe I was actually asking this. I put my head down, unable to keep eye contact, until I heard Lexi laugh. I looked up to see her almost hysterical with laughter.

"Finally! I knew it," she cheered.

"What are you talking about?" My confusion overpowered my embarrassment.

"No, I do not have feelings for Tristan. Like I told you before, I only look at him as a brother, albeit a hot one. I think it's a protector thing, so we don't fall for each other or something. I have no idea, but I really can't think of him that way." She laughed heartily. "I am just happy you finally showed some emotion about him."

She had no idea how much emotion I really had going on inside.

"I was just asking. It doesn't mean anything. I just saw how happy you looked when he approached you before you teleported," I said.

"Whatever! I was excited because I love the feeling of teleporting; it is so cool."

My embarrassment returned; it was such a simple explanation, and I wish I had thought of it before I asked. "I can't believe you can't even be honest with me about your feelings," Lexi continued. "You said I could trust you, and you can trust me. We have been friends for fifteen years, does that count for nothing?" I could see her humor wavering into frustration.

"Of course it does. I just… it's not a big deal, okay?"

Lexi laughed again and shook her head. I felt so stupid. The last thing I wanted was for anyone to know how I felt about Tristan. I was even trying to convince myself that there was nothing there. Obviously that hadn't been working at all. I was surprised at how strong the sense of relief was that Lexi really didn't like Tristan more than a friend.

"What's not to like? He's good looking, strong, protects you, and when he relaxes, he actually has a great sense of humor."

"Doesn't matter, Lex. It's just not the right time." Lexi opened her mouth to say something, but straightened up instead. I knew that was her way of telling me Tristan was coming. I turned to see him walking through the front door with a grin across his face.

"That was fast," I said. "Where did you go?"

"Just went to my house for this." He held a tray in his hands with some random items on it. He placed the tray on the table and I studied it. There was a clay bowl filled with soil, a black candle, a toy windmill, and a clear dish that Tristan lifted off the tray.

"What am I looking at here?" I asked.

"Oh… let's just call it an elemental test kit, for lack of a better name," Tristan said, walking over to the sink and filling the dish with water. He returned and while he set up the items I thought about how I had just given myself away to Lexi, though I knew she had been suspecting it anyway. I looked and saw that Lexi was smiling at me. I hated that she knew me so well. I smiled back and shook my head. She was my best friend; I couldn't be embarrassed around her for long. Tristan finished lining up the items and placed them so they faced me.

"So, in case you didn't figure it out yet, the idea here is to see which of the elements you connect with," he said.

"How?" I leaned closer to the objects as if I could see what made them special.

"Just focus on one element at a time and see what happens," Lexi said, coming to sit beside me.

I looked at the bowl of soil and studied it. I focused only on the moist earth and envisioned flowers and plants growing from its life source. As I felt the nurturing life the earth provided, the soil lifted, grain by grain out of the bowl and swirled for a few moments before falling back down.

"Whoa," I said, as Tristan and Lexi exchanged glances.

I looked at the candle next and realized it hadn't been lit. I studied the wick as images of bright, blazing flames flashed through my mind. I could feel the scalding heat kiss my flesh. I was about to mention the lack of fire, when the wick suddenly burst into flame. Just as suddenly, it was snuffed out, leaving a smoking trail behind.

My breathing grew heavier as I studied the windmill. It was the shiny, toy kind that people put in the ground. I picked up the windmill to get a closer look, holding it upright from its stake. As I studied the colors on the blades, I thought of the air around me, and reflected on its wonder as I breathed it in and out. I appreciated the wind that could gently lift a feather or tear down houses as it willed. Suddenly the blades spun. They twirled so fast, I quickly released the windmill and it was momentarily propelled out of my hand spinning erratically, before falling limply on the tray.

I was scared to look at the bowl of water, afraid of what it might do... or not do. I took a breath and turned my attention to the clear dish. I was mesmerized by the liquid and began to think of the many secrets hidden beneath the depths of the ocean. I saw the waves and heard them as they lapped the shore, felt the rain as it sprinkled my skin and fed the earth. I wondered what would happen if water were lighter than air. I began to believe it was and gasped as the water started sloshing around. It swirled and gathered into a rod shaped tube of water, as if it were being sucked out of the dish through an invisible straw. The water stayed suspended in that position for a heartbeat and then splashed back down.

I took a few shallow breaths before looking up at Tristan and Lexi. Tristan stared at me with his eyebrow raised and his lips puckered in contemplation. Lexi's jaw literally dropped open.

"I didn't think you would have the power to control all the elements," Lexi said, "Or well... at least not yet, I guess." She seemed to be trying to collect her thoughts.

"Ditto," Tristan said.

I felt frustrated and elated at the same time; elated that I was finally gaining my powers, frustrated that without them I felt weak and useless, yet with them, my friends looked at me like I was a pariah, like I was doing something I shouldn't.

"Did I do something wrong?" I asked.

"Nope, not at all." Lexi smiled in awe.

"So, I suppose we will be working on controlling these powers too?" I asked.

Tristan nodded, "Absolutely."

The rest of the day we focused on trying to control the elements, and use them as offensive attacks. We decided that I would try to manifest them…from thin air… tomorrow. The task seemed daunting, and I tried not to feel overwhelmed.

By the end of the day I was feeling exhausted, but confident that I was developing my powers and controlling them – even if it was at a slower pace than I'd like.

"You've made amazing progress," Tristan said, as I calmed the wind I had made blow around us.

"Thanks, coach." I beamed.

Tristan studied me for a moment, making me feel uncomfortable.

"What?" I asked.

He shook his head, and then shook it harder to clear it. "It's getting late; I should go."

"So soon?" Lexi asked, "I was just about to make margaritas in celebration of Selena's big day!"

Tristan hesitated and looked at me.

I smiled and shrugged. "Could be fun."

He nodded and sat at the table. "Alright, just one."

Six margaritas and three tequila shots later we were laughing, and I had fallen on the floor.

"No, Tristan, you should have seen her." Lexi was laughing, and trying to enunciate. "She tried to catch the ball, but it bounced off her hand and hit her in the head – she knocked herself out! How does that happen?" Tristan was laughing along with Lexi, and I was trying not to feel embarrassed.

"So I was clumsy in high school," I said, swaying as I got to my feet. "I outgrew that." I walked to the counter to refill my drink and banged my knee against the chair on my way.

Lexi laughed even harder, tears streaming down her face as she gasped, "Yeah, sure you did."

"Shut up," I said. I stumbled back to the table, and Tristan reached his arm out to steady me. I could feel the heat from his hand spread across my hip.

"You alright?" He asked, clearly much more immune to alcohol than I was.

"Sure, sure, I'm barely buzzed," I said.

"How about you sit down so you don't hurt yourself?" Tristan said, not buying my lie.

"Okay," I dropped onto the chair and tried to balance my heavy head on my weak hand. Ugh, this wasn't going to end well. I tried to focus, but Lexi's laughter at my expense was distracting.

"Selena, you sure you don't want to sleep it off?" Tristan asked.

"No, I'm fine, really," I answered as Lexi snorted.

"The only way Selena will go to bed now," Lexi started, laughing, "is if you," she pointed at Tristan, "go with her."

I felt heat rise to my face and I avoided Tristan's gaze. Damn it, Lexi! I knew I shouldn't have told her how I felt.

Tristan laughed it off as drunk, Lexi talk, but there was a tension I could sense from him. Trying to hide my discomfort, I stood and grabbed the edge of the table to keep my balance.

"Maybe I should go to bed, since I have to try and manifest elements tomorrow," I said. "You guys should stay over."

Tristan stood to make sure I got to my room without tripping and impaling myself on some random object.

The ground beneath me seemed to shake as I tried to maintain my balance. I failed. I fell over and Tristan caught me, cursing.

"Is the ground shaking?" Lexi asked from the kitchen. "Or am I that drunk?"

"The ground is definitely shaking," Tristan yelled, keeping a protective hold on me.

Oh, good. So it wasn't just me.

Cars beeped and blared outside as the rumbling ground disturbed their alarm systems.

"What's happening?" I asked. I held on tightly to Tristan, both for support and enjoyment.

"I don't know."

Lexi rushed toward us, much more sober than I was, and she stood protectively on my other side. "Could it be an earthquake?"

"In Arizona?" Tristan retorted. "No, this has Darien written all over it."

The rumbling ground was flipping my stomach, and it took all my strength to keep my dinner down. This was going to be the worst hangover ever.

"Well, the place is protected," Lexi said, "so he can make the earth shake all he wants, but he's not getting in."

"I don't think he wants to get in," Tristan said, as he looked at the crack that was forming in the ceiling. "There are two floors of apartments above us...he wants us to come out." He released his hold on me and placed his hands palm down, reducing the shaking but not stopping it.

Lexi created a blue, protective bubble that I assumed was her sphere shield. It encased us and protected us from the falling debris.

"That won't protect us if the building collapses, Lexi," Tristan said.

"It should," she said.

"Are you willing to take that chance?" Tristan yelled.

"Can you stop the ground from shaking or not?" Lexi yelled back.

"I can't," Tristan said through clenched teeth, "It's not responding to my magic. I don't know what's causing this."

I held my palms down as Tristan had and tried to still the earth. It seemed to calm only slightly before resuming its aggressive shaking. I wasn't sure if my drunken state hindered me, or my lack of powers, but I felt disappointed all the same. Tristan pulled me into him again, and held me close.

"We need to get out of here," he said.

"Right into Darien's trap?" Lexi retorted.

"We have no choice!"

"Teleport," I said.

Lexi waved her hand, and the protective spell on my apartment evaporated.

"Now!" She yelled as the building shook and crumbled around us. In an instant I was pushed, pulled and twisted, landing in Tristan's house.

"Wait for me," he growled before teleporting again. A moment later he returned with Lexi.

"What... the Hell... happened?" I asked, buckling over and trying really hard not to puke.

"I don't know," Tristan said. "Lexi, seal the house."

Lexi raised her arms, but before she could cast the spell, the house shook, knocking us all off balance and onto the floor.

Tristan regained his footing first and held his hand out for me. I grabbed it tightly and stood on shaky legs as Lexi got to her feet next to me.

"Tristan-" Lexi started, just as the floor boards creaked and rose. Several large, metal blades pushed through the floor, splintering the wood. I jumped out of the way as a blade shot through the floor where I had just been standing.

Lexi and Tristan were dodging the blades as well, but they kept rising until they were at least a foot higher than me.

As I stared at the sharp, shiny metal points, another blade shot up below my feet. I tried to move out of the way, but my left calf and forearm sliced against the cool sharpness.

I gasped as I landed on my side and Lexi ran through the blades like an obstacle course to reach me.

"Are you okay?" She asked, panting.

"Yeah," I gasped, grabbing my arm to staunch the bleeding.

"Come on." Lexi helped me up and we retreated to the corner of the living room. Tristan joined us a few heart-beats later.

The blades ceased their rising, and a blue mist curled its way into the house from the broken floorboards and window frames. The mist swirled and spun and suddenly took on the form of two people laughing as they flew in circles before our eyes.

The holograms (at least that's what they looked like) spun and cackled before coming to a stop before us. The blue, translucent beings smiled wickedly at us, but I had no idea who they were. One was a woman with short, spikey hair and a lip ring, the other a bald man with no memorable features whatsoever, save his cold and calculating eyes.

The woman laughed again and flew straight at me. She stopped a mere inch away and studied my wounds before lowering her head toward my arm. I raised my left arm reflexively to protect myself, and the woman hologram stuck her clear tongue out and licked my cut. I grunted as the action made my wound burn and sting. Tristan charged at the apparition, but ran straight through it. The woman laughed, watching Tristan spin and glare at her.

Lexi's eyes flared with anger and she raised her arms, shooting a white, crackling lightning bolt from her fingers, but it too shot straight through the misty figure. Lexi grabbed Tristan to her side and created her sphere shield to protect us.

The woman threw her head back and laughed, "You think that will keep you safe? We're coming for you, and when we want something, we get it." She spun back to the man. "Come, Yuri."

They flew in a circle, wind blowing my hair back as they spun ever faster before disappearing.

The house stilled, the wind vanished, and we stood trying to catch our breath. I ran to the bathroom and threw up. My head spun, my stomach flopped, and I felt another wave of nausea hit me. When there was nothing else left in my stomach, I washed up and headed back to Tristan and Lexi.

"You okay?" Lexi asked.

I nodded my head.

Tristan strode forward and took my arm to examine the wound. He let out a hiss when he saw that it had begun to fester and puss.

"Ew," I said.

"That bitch poisoned your cut when she licked it," Lexi said.

I looked at the wound on my leg and found that it was a much cleaner laceration. I barely felt it, but the one on my arm stung like a mother--.

"Wait a sec. I know someone who might be able to help," Tristan said. "She just developed the ability to heal, but I wonder…" Tristan took out his cell and started dialing as he walked to the bedroom.

Lexi went to the kitchen and wet a hand towel.

"Here, let me see that," she said.

I gave her my arm, and she pressed the cool cloth on the oozing gash. The water soothed it for a moment before reigniting the pain. I took a breath through clenched teeth and pulled my arm away.

Tristan walked back in then, pocketing his cell.

"Alright, they should be here within the hour."

"Who?" I asked, taking the cloth away from Lexi. I was about to apply it to the wound on my leg but thought better of it. I didn't want to contaminate that one too.

"Just some friends," Tristan answered. "It's okay; we can trust them."

Lexi listened to our conversation and held her hands palm down toward the floor. Slowly the blades retracted, and the floorboards flattened and sealed together in a smooth finish.

"That will never get old," I said to Lexi who beamed. "So, who are these people?" I asked Tristan as I retrieved a clean cloth and ran it under the cold water.

"I met them in school. I've known them most of my life; they're good people."

"Why did you call them? Why not use telepathy?" I asked. If I had that ability, I would consider harassing people with it. I pressed the cold cloth on my leg and it soothed instantly.

"Well it's kind of invasive if you're not expecting it," Tristan explained. "I reserve telepathic conversation only for when it's needed."

The wound on my arm had turned yellow, and my veins became visible, purple paths branching away from the cut and up my arm. My legs buckled beneath me, and there was nothing I could do to regain my balance.

"What-" Lexi began as I fell to the floor.

"Selena," Tristan knelt by my side.

I tried to answer, but my lips wouldn't move. My eyes shifted to Lexi, but I couldn't move a single limb.

10. MUSICAL BEDS

"Look at her arm," Lexi said, panic rising in her voice.

"Son of a bitch," Tristan said through clenched teeth.

"You need to tell your friends to get here now!" Lexi said.

Tristan nodded and closed his eyes. I supposed this qualified as a good reason to reach them telepathically. "Try to heal her," Tristan said after a quiet moment. "If it's magically induced you should be able to reverse it."

Lexi took a deep breath and placed her hands on my arm. She closed her eyes, and I could feel a slight tingling in my arm. The pain eased slightly, but not nearly enough.

"It's not working," Lexi said. "It's either really strong magic, or spelled to not allow healing this way."

My breathing quickened as the panic settled in. Lexi couldn't fix me. I couldn't move, couldn't speak. A tear escaped the side of my eye and into my hair. My vision blurred then doubled, I closed my eyes to stop the dizzying affect.

"It's okay," Tristan whispered. "You'll be fine." His voice was muffled, as if I had cotton in my ears. I opened my eyes, and his image swayed in my vision. I saw him close his eyes, as if trying to contact his friends again, and then he disappeared.

"Man, I really wish I could teleport," Lexi said under her breath. I closed my eyes again, and in my mind I heard laughter. A cackling echo as the poison consumed me. Before my panic could increase even more, I felt the air shift. I dared to open my eyes. Tristan popped back in with a woman. Her green eyes widened as she took in my state. Tristan vanished again as the woman knelt beside me and took my arm in her small hands. A bright light surrounded her. Was she glowing? Maybe she was an angel?

She didn't waste any time. She closed her eyes and I felt warmth spread through my arm and up my shoulder, then increase as it spread throughout my body.

Tristan reappeared with a man at his side and stood behind the woman, watching her work.

As the healing sensation warmed my chest, I took in a deep, jagged breath, and then gasped for more air as if I hadn't been able to breathe the entire time. I almost felt unglued, finally mobile. My hearing cleared but my head spun as I sat up, and I tried to focus by looking at our new guests.

The man was tall and lean, his curly red hair cut short, his brown eyes took everything in. The woman was about my height, with long platinum blonde hair a bit longer than my own. The brilliant glow was no longer there. I must have imagined it.

"Thank you, Genevieve," Tristan said, relief in his voice.

"Of course, anything I can do to help." Genevieve smiled.

"Genevieve, Lachlan, this is Selena and Lexi." Tristan said, calm now that the worst of my injuries was healed.

"It is an honor to meet you," Genevieve said, and looked down at the cut on my leg, "though I wish it were under better circumstances." She healed that wound as well. Lachlan stood nodding beside her. I smiled and nodded back.

"Thank you so much." I flung my arms around Genevieve. She laughed in surprise. I released her and she stood, almost losing her balance. Lachlan grabbed her arm to steady her.

"Are you okay?" Tristan asked.

Genevieve nodded, but held onto Lachlan for support.

"Healing wipes her out," Lachlan explained, and I was surprised to hear a faint Scottish accent.

"I'll be fine," Genevieve said with a small smile. "I just need to lie down. I'm still not used to this, and I haven't healed anything that severe before."

"I'm sorry," I said, feeling guilty. I tried to get up, but I still felt woozy. I sat back on the floor.

"Don't be silly," she said as Lachlan directed her toward the couch.

Tristan offered me his hand, and I gratefully took it, finally getting to my feet. I took a moment for the room to right itself before following Lachlan and Genevieve.

"Who did this?" Lachlan asked as he helped Genevieve lie down.

"I heard the woman say 'Yuri,' so she must be Crystal," Lexi answered glumly.

"Shit," Lachlan said.

"What?" I asked, "Who are Yuri and Crystal?"

"Bad news," Lachlan said.

"They're hired muscle, only… they're not the kind you want to be involved with, even as criminals. They're twisted and sadistic. They have a reputation…" Tristan let the sentence hang.

"For torture," Lexi said, "sometimes for information, but mostly for fun," she finished for him.

"What do they want with you?" Genevieve asked, her voice almost groggy. My guilt returned.

"I can only assume Darien is behind this," Lexi said.

"If Crystal and Yuri want you, they'll get you," Lachlan spoke softly.

"Great, thanks." Lexi rolled her eyes.

"So you guys live around here?" I asked the new couple. They exchanged glances before Lachlan answered.

"We happened to be in the area, but we live… closer to Vegas."

"Oh, well lucky for me you were close by." I dropped on the floor next to the couch Genevieve occupied. My stomach was thankfully settled, but my head was pounding like a hammer. I placed it in my hands.

"Here," Tristan said, holding out a glass of water. "It'll help if you hydrate."

I nodded and took the cool glass, sipping at it cautiously. I didn't want anything to upset my stomach.

"I'm sorry I don't have the strength to heal anything else," Genevieve said quietly.

My heart swelled with appreciation. "Don't be, you've done more than enough. It's just a hangover. It'll pass." I let out a sigh and leaned my head against the back of the couch.

"Tristan, where do you keep your herbs?" Lexi asked as she walked back to the kitchen.

"In the pantry, but I don't have much," he answered.

"I'll make do."

I closed my eyes for a few minutes, trying to forget the pounding that was spreading behind my eyes.

"Swap with me," Lexi said. I opened my eyes to see her holding out a glass with clumpy, green liquid in it.

"What is it?" I asked, giving Lexi my water and hesitantly taking the glass she offered.

"Old family recipe," she answered. "Not everyone has healing powers," she said slightly irritated.

"Your healing did help a bit," I said, trying to build her confidence.

"Yeah, yeah."

I sniffed at the glass, and was surprised that it smelled like melons when the color was such a putrid green.

"Just drink it," Lexi huffed.

I obliged, and actually enjoyed its sweet, creamy taste. It didn't have an instant healing affect, but my headache diminished slightly and I was hopeful I wouldn't suffer from a terrible hangover the next morning.

"Thanks," I whispered closing my eyes.

"I'm sorry it's so late," Tristan said to Genevieve and Lachlan. "I can teleport some beds in if you'd like to sleep here tonight."

"Thank you, but I have to be at the hospital tomorrow," Genevieve answered. "I have a feeling I will be taking some time off soon though, so it may be a good time to let them know." She shot a knowing smile at Lachlan.

"You're going to work tomorrow?" Lexi asked. "Will you be well enough?"

"Yes, a good night's sleep will go a long way," Genevieve said as she sat up.

Lachlan supported Genevieve as they walked toward the front door, and I stood to see them out with Tristan.

"Thank you again," I said, hugging Genevieve goodbye.

"It's my honor," Genevieve responded in kind. "Please call me if you need anything at all."

Lachlan playfully punched Tristan's shoulder, "See ya," he said and walked out with Genevieve.

"Wait," Tristan said following them out. "I'll teleport you back."

I went back inside and sat on the couch. I was so exhausted, all I wanted to do was sleep.

"Do you think my apartment is completely demolished?" I asked Lexi, closing my eyes.

"Probably, but I think I can fix it," Lexi said. "Maybe I should go there now... then again, maybe too many people have seen it destroyed, how would we cover that up?"

I opened my eyes to see Lexi pacing the length of the kitchen.

"Can't you erase their memory like in *Men in Black*?" I asked.

"Oh, no. You can't tamper with people's minds like that," Lexi said seriously. "Maybe I can try to fix the inside only. Hopefully no one would have gone in there yet."

"I have neighbors, remember?"

"Leave the apartment the way it is," Tristan said as he walked into the room. "Insurance will cover it, and it'll get fixed the human way. You can stay here for the time being."

My jaw almost dropped. Stay here? With Tristan? I bit my lip to contain my excitement.

"Lexi, you should stay too. It's safer for us all," he added.

"Sure." She shrugged nonchalantly. "I'll seal the house."

"Come on, Selena, you need some rest." Tristan stood beside the couch waiting for me. I stood and Tristan walked toward the part of the house I hadn't seen before. Past the kitchen, we walked through a small hallway leading to three bedrooms. The first was empty, the second had a bed and nightstand, but nothing else, and the last one had a queen-sized bed, and a single nightstand, with a lamp and book on it. The walls were white and devoid of any art-work, or color.

Tristan swept his hand across the room and before my eyes, the bed and nightstand from the other bedroom app-eared.

"Cool," I whispered. Tristan smiled. A thought came to me then, and I was already angry at myself for asking it. "Are you sure you don't need your space? I mean you have two other rooms, I could stay in one of those."

"Yes, I'm sure. It's easier and safer if we stay close together." Hey, I wasn't about to argue any further. I walked to the nightstand and picked up the book. It was a compilation of the Brothers Grimm fairytales.

"I didn't think you would have time to read," I said, studying the artwork on the cover. It showed a ragged Cinderella reaching for a golden dress hanging from a tree. "I seem to be a full time job these days."

"They're short stories. It's easy to read one or two before bed."

"Why Grimm?" I asked, placing the book back where I found it.

"They're darker versions of the fairytales most people grew up with. I kind of like how they don't always have a happy ending."

"Hmm... I'm the opposite. I'm a sucker for happy endings. You know the ending of a book can make or break the story."

"Like *The Princess Bride?*" Tristan asked. "The edited version has two endings, so I can guess which one you read."

"How did you know I liked *The Princess Bride?*"

"I know a lot more about you than you think." Tristan smiled, and my heart raced.

I slowly walked to the conjured bed, sat on the edge and bounced lightly to feel the firmness of the mattress. Satisfied that it wouldn't disintegrate beneath me, I fell back and stared at the ceiling.

"So what's your favorite book?" I asked.

"The Rock's autobiography," Tristan said.

I sat up, "What?" I laughed.

"It's a fun read," Tristan chuckled, then faltered. "Are you sure you're alright?" He asked, standing above me.

"Yeah, just tired," I answered, and yawned as if on cue. "I just don't understand what's happening. Why am I being attacked relentlessly?"

Tristan sighed and sat next to me on the bed. "Darien is going to come at you from all sides until he kills you."

"I don't know how much more of this I can take," I said, resisting the urge to lean on Tristan. "I'm at the end of my rope... and... this psychic in Sedona said there was pain coming. Could she have meant this? Or is there something else I need to fear?"

"Those psychics aren't always accurate," Tristan said, "but if she is, we'll deal with it. You won't be alone."

"Okay," I sighed. That still didn't mean I wouldn't have to deal with pain in the future.

Tristan nodded and left the room. I crawled under the covers and sank into the mattress. Sleep found me quickly, but didn't last very long.

The red blaze of fire engulfed my vision. I could feel its heat against my flesh as I stared at what used to be my house. I was waiting. My parents would be coming out any minute. I ran outside and across the street like my mom told me. She said she would be right out, that she had to get my dad. They had to come out. The flames were licking the roof and spewing out of the windows. Come on, Mom. Where are you? My heart rate sped up, my hands were clammy, and my nightgown stuck to my little body with sweat. Even from across the street, the heat was fierce.

I heard screaming, an agonizing cry, and I wanted to scream too, but no sound came out. I started to run toward the house, but a strong arm held me back. I looked to see what was holding me and recognized the face of my neighbor. His features were skewed with sadness.

That's when it happened. My house, my sanctuary, the place I ran to when I was scared or needed someone to talk to, the place where I had all my childhood memories, the place where my parents were, exploded.

My neighbor held me back, but I hadn't realized I was trying to escape his grasp. I wanted to go get my parents. Tears streamed silently from my face and dripped on my nightgown. Suddenly I was standing alone, no longer a child.

"Oh Selena, sweet Selena," a whispered voice said "Why do you cry? You will see them soon, so very soon. And so will Lexi and your beloved Tristan. Love complicates things, doesn't it?"

"Who is this?" My voice echoed off the nothingness around me. The voice sounded hauntingly familiar.

I heard a laugh and then saw Tristan and Lexi each tied to a chair. Their hands and feet were bound and they were gagged. A silhouette poured gasoline on them as they tried fruitlessly to escape. A match struck, sparking light in the darkness around me, and then Lexi and Tristan were ablaze. They screamed over their gags in agony, writhing in their seats, trying to break free. The smell of their burning flesh permeated the air. I saw it blister and melt as it fell from their bones.

"NOO!" I screamed and jerked awake.

"Selena?" The lamp turned on, and I saw Tristan and Lexi on either side of me.

"What happened?" Lexi asked, staring at me intently.

"Darien, he was in my dream." My voice cracked around the emotion. I recognized his voice in my waking state.

"How? I reinforced the spell. He shouldn't have been able to break it." Tristan's frustration and worry was etched in his face.

"I don't know but I saw... I saw the night my parents died." I swallowed back a sob and realized I had already been crying. "And then Darien was talking to me, saying I would see them soon and then... and then..." The vivid images of my dream gave it all a sense of realism I didn't like.

"What happened next?" Tristan asked in a soothing voice. He placed his hand over mine and encouraged me to continue with a nod.

"I saw you both tied to chairs and burning. Oh God, it felt so real!" I put my head in my hands and cried. Lexi rubbed my back comfortingly, and Tristan patted my leg gently.

"Shh, it's ok. It was just a dream," he whispered. I wanted to believe him, but I just couldn't shake that feeling of dread.

"You don't understand," I sniffed, wiping my tears with the back of my hand. "You two are all I have. I have *no one* but you. If anything ever happened to either of you, I...I just wouldn't..." I couldn't finish my sentence. I couldn't handle the thought. Lexi, who had been sleeping next to me, got out of bed and headed to the bathroom. Tristan took both my hands in his and rubbed the back of them with his thumbs.

Lexi came back with a glass of water and a box of tissues. I dried my tears and drank the water, pushing the lump in my throat down. I was able to stop crying, but I couldn't shake the feeling.

"I just don't understand why my protective spell didn't work," Tristan brooded.

"Probably because you and Darien-" Lexi started.

"Wait. Let me try something." Tristan interrupted. He placed his hands two inches above my chest and closed his eyes. I suddenly felt warm, and a sense of calmness spread through me. Tristan opened his eyes. "How do you feel?"

"Better, calm."

"See? That worked on you, so my protection spell should too." He shot Lexi a glance and clenched his jaw. She shook her head.

"Why does Darien feel the need to torture me?"

"Because he's an evil prick," Lexi answered, still rubbing circles on my back.

"You already know my theory," Tristan said. "He wants to prove that he knows how to get to you. He's trying to scare you, Selena. Don't let him." Tristan held my hands again. I remembered my dream, and it sent shivers down my spine. I shuddered. Tristan's advice was easier said than done.

"I don't think I will be able to go back to sleep," I whispered, looking down at my hands in Tristan's. It was surprising but nice that he was finally letting me get close to him. At least, I think that's what he was doing.

"Sure you will. You know it might be a good idea for Tristan to do his relaxing thing on you. You should go lay beside him." Lexi said, trying to sound matter-of-fact. Tristan's hands stopped their motion on mine. My heart skipped at the thought of sleeping next to him, but I didn't like that Lexi was volunteering Tristan. I didn't want to bother him.

"I'm sure Tristan enjoys his space, Lex. I'm a big girl. I'll survive on my own."

"Try to relax," Tristan said. "If you're still feeling uneasy, I'm right here, and I can cast another calming spell on you, okay?" He moved back to his own bed. I nodded and put my head back on the pillow. Lexi sighed and crawled under the covers beside me. Tristan turned the light off and got back under his own covers. I tried to calm my breathing, and see peaceful images, but every time I closed my eyes, I saw Tristan and Lexi burning.

I swallowed hard and rolled over on my side. I couldn't shake the image, and the smell of burning flesh haunted me. I flipped over onto my stomach and tried to get comfortable. After a few minutes in that position, I flipped onto my back and stared at the ceiling.

The lump in my throat returned, and tears trickled down the side of my face, into my hair. I wiped at them and searched for the tissues Lexi brought me. I rummaged on the side table and found the familiar box. I wiped away my tears and took a deep breath, but I just couldn't relax.

"Selena," Tristan said from his bed.

I looked over at him, "Sorry, I didn't mean to keep you up."

"Come on." He lifted the covers and shifted himself away from the edge of the bed to make room for me.

"Are you sure? I don't want to bother you."

"Just come on. You'll feel better, I promise."

Oh, I knew I would. I got out of bed and climbed under the comforter with Tristan. His body heat made the sheets warm, and I sank into them. I curled on my side and faced

Tristan, on his side facing me. Tristan moved his hand above my chest again.

"Clear your mind," he whispered.

"I'll try," I scoffed. And I did try, but the image of their demise was burned in my eyelids. I couldn't escape it. I felt a little of the calmness trickle back into me, until my nightmare flashed fresh in my mind again. Tristan sighed.

"Do…" he started, very hesitantly. "The spell would work better if I had direct contact with you." He swallowed, "Do I have your permission to touch you?" He was so nervous. It was odd to see strong, confident Tristan waver.

"Sure, as long as I get to touch you back," I joked. He let out a low chuckle.

"That sounds fair," he said, now more relaxed. He placed his hand on my chest, just below the hollow of my throat. The warmth of his skin was instantly soothing, and I could definitely feel the potency of the magic this way. I was feeling much better already. I placed my hand on his chest, a little lower than where his hand was on mine. I was surprised to find that he wasn't wearing a shirt. How could I have missed that? I didn't mind though, and he hadn't stopped me yet, so I guess he didn't mind either.

His skin was soft for a guy, his chest completely hairless. I didn't know if I would get an opportunity like this again, so I wanted to feel every muscle I could. I ran my hand down his chest and across his abs, and they felt even more amazing than I had imagined. I looked up at him and saw that his green eyes were staring intently at me and his jaw was clenched. I had a theory that when he did that it meant he was holding back.

Or it meant he was really mad.

I moved my hand away.

"Sorry," I whispered looking down at his chest. When I looked back up, Tristan was still staring at me, his hand placed firmly on my chest. Without moving his hand away, he quickly moved so his body was leaning over mine, and he was still looking down at me.

The magic still flowed freely between us, and I had never felt anything like it. He moved his other hand and ran his fingers through my hair, never breaking eye contact. I was borderline hyperventilating, the only thing keeping me in check was his calming magic. He leaned down, his face inches from mine. I could feel his breath on my face, and wondered if this was a dream. My heart rate picked up considerably, and my excitement was off the charts.

"Selena," Tristan whispered, looking above my head.

"Can someone please turn off the lights? I was sleeping," Lexi mumbled from the other bed.

"What is she talking about?" And then I realized that my excitement meant my aura glowed insanely. Crap, this was embarrassing.

"I've never seen your aura so bright. It's amazing," Tristan said. "Don't be ashamed of it."

I guess he could tell my embarrassment through his magical connection.

"It's just…I don't want to be a beacon. I don't want everyone knowing anytime I get excited or happy. It's humiliating."

Tristan smiled, "You will learn to control it."

"How did Lexi see it if she was asleep?"

"Once you get your full powers, you'll have no problem seeing it, and yours is not easy to miss, even with our eyes closed. We can see any person's aura. It's always there, which is why witches learn to control it, so we're not all wearing our emotions on our heads." He laughed quietly. "In this case though, I think it was a good thing she saw it. We could have made a big mistake tonight."

My face fell a little more. "Selena, please don't be upset. It would complicate things if we didn't have boundaries. I need to be able to protect you, and I need a clear head to do that." I nodded, but that familiar ache settled in my chest again. "I'm sorry. I'm not handling this right. How can I ask you to have boundaries when we are in bed together?"

"Do you want me to leave?" I asked over the lump in my throat - that damn thing was persistent tonight.

"No… which is why you should."

I nodded again and slipped out of his bed. I crawled into mine, the cold sheets appropriate for my loneliness. I was confused, part of me was elated that Tristan and I had gotten that close, but a bigger part of me was miserable that it would never happen again. I wasn't sure if Tristan had feelings for me, or if he just got caught up in the moment. My mind reeled and I tried to shut it out.

"Selena, there is something I can do for you though." I looked over, and Tristan got out of bed and stood above me. He gently ran a finger along my jaw, and I saw a longing in his eyes I had never seen before. He placed his hands on my shoulders, and I felt a tingling sensation. Before I knew it, I was in a deep sleep.

11. WHAT THE $#!@

The next few days passed uneventfully, except when my landlord called to make sure I was alright and deliver the news of my destroyed unit. When Lexi and I went over there shortly after to retrieve a few of my belongings, the state of my home upset me a great deal. The walls were cracked, plaster was everywhere, the ceiling was caved in at parts, and my furniture was destroyed. I shook my head sadly, but hoped Lexi would be able to fix it later.

I was grateful that Darien hadn't harassed me in a few days. I came close to snapping after he sent me that nightmare, so having a few days to regain my composure was a blessing. Unfortunately, with the quiet came the paranoia of not knowing when Darien would strike next, or how.

"We need to get back into training," Tristan said one morning.

I groaned.

"I know you don't want to, Selena, but you need to." Tristan rose from his seat on the couch. "We can train outside if that makes it easier."

"Um, no thanks. It's like a bazillion degrees out there," I said in a whiny voice.

Tristan shook his head. "Go, get ready."

"Fine," I huffed.

"Glad it's not me," Lexi whispered as I passed her.

"Yeah, thanks," I mumbled back.

I went to the bedroom and rummaged through my luggage, coming out with yoga shorts and a tank top. I dressed quickly, swept my hair into a high ponytail and slapped on some deodorant.

Ready for my training, I bounded into the living room, and stopped short.

It was empty.

Neither Tristan nor Lexi were anywhere to be seen.

"Hello?" I called, waiting for them to appear. "Where are you guys hiding? You can come out now." I joked, but my nerves were ringing on high alert. It had literally taken me two minutes to change. Where could they have gone in that time? I walked around the kitchen and then the living room, checking behind the couch and corners, but found no one. I went back into the bedrooms, checked the bathrooms, but I was alone.

"Guys? This isn't funny. Please come out," I pleaded, my heart picking up the pace with every silent moment that passed.

I opened the back door and looked out to the yard, then walked around to the front, but it was empty too. This wasn't good. My heart was beating in my throat, my stomach turning. I know Tristan warned me to only teleport to places I knew, but I was scared. I closed my eyes and willed myself to go wherever Tristan was.

My body was squeezed and pulled, and then I was in a room. It was dimly lit, but I could make out two people sitting in two chairs. When my eyes had adjusted, I saw Tristan and Lexi, each tied to a wooden chair at one end of the room. Their hands were tied at the wrists in front of them, rope was wrapped around their stomachs and the backs of the chairs and each ankle was tied to one of the front chair legs. They tried to jerk free of their bindings. Tristan saw me standing there, and I saw panic flash in his eyes. He shook his head as if telling me to leave. My heart sank as I remembered my dream. *No, please no*, I thought.

"Oh, yes," I heard a female voice say. I spun around to see a tall, lean woman that had short, black spiky hair, with chunks of bright blue highlights in between. Her eyes were a cold blue, she had a gap between her two front teeth and she had a ring looped around her lower lip. She stood just outside the doorway. Crystal... she looked different in person than in her blue, smoky image. Had she heard my thoughts? "So nice of you to join us," she sneered, "not to mention predictable."

"What do you want?" I asked, as the panic inside me grew.

"There will be plenty of time for that later. Don't go anywhere." She laughed as she closed and locked the door.

"What the hell is going on?" I asked as I rushed to free Lexi and Tristan. I removed the mouth gags first, wanting them to answer my question. The strip of fabric was pushed in their mouths and tightly tied in a knot behind their heads, and I understood why Tristan and Lexi had failed to remove the gags themselves. Then I went for the knots around their wrists.

"The ropes are infused with magic," Tristan explained when I failed to untie the knot at his hands. I called upon fire, hoping I could burn the ropes off, but only a small flame flickered in front of me before snuffing out.

"We're in an eter room," Tristan growled.

"A What?" I asked.

"The room binds powers," Lexi informed me as she studied the room.

"How?" I asked, fingers fumbling around the bindings.

"There must be incantations and symbols etched into the walls," Tristan answered. I looked at the walls but saw nothing. Maybe they had been painted over.

"What happened?" Frustration was evident in my tone. I ran to the door, but it was locked.

"Crystal and Yuri teleported into the house, cast a paralysis spell and grabbed us," Tristan said. "It all happened so fast we didn't get a chance to react. We were tied up before the spell wore off, and then you appeared. We tried to use magic to free ourselves, or even teleport, but it won't work here." Tristan tried to squirm his way out.

"I thought the house was protected," I said, rushing back to Tristan.

"Well they got past the security somehow," Tristan answered angrily.

"Oh, God. How do we get out of here?" I asked panicked. "Wait, the ropes are infused, but is the chair?"

Tristan's eyes widened. "I don't think so. Try and break it." Before I was able to test the theory, the lock on the door squeaked, and the door swung open. Standing in the doorway were the woman and a tall man with a shaved head. Even his eye brows were shaved, which gave him an eerie look. His eyes were beady and black, and his lips were a thin line.

"Now that we have you all here, we should begin. I'm sure you've heard of us. I'm Crystal, and this is my partner, Yuri." She trailed her finger down his arm, smiled her split-toothed grin and my blood ran cold. Lexi and Tristan were right.

"What do you want?" My voice cracked only slightly.

"We were sent to get you. I'm sure that's no surprise. You," she pointed at me, "Darien wants alive, but your friends here, are for us to play with." She laughed a high pitched cackle that made the hair on the back of my neck stand on end. Darien wanted me alive? Why?

"Please, we can figure this out. I will go with you, no problem, just let them go," I pleaded, one second away from crying. The thought of anything happening to Lexi or Tristan was unbearable. Tristan shook his head in his seat. He didn't like that idea.

"Oh, you stupid girl. They are part of the payment. Not only do we get well compensated for delivering you, we also get to keep your friends. That way they won't be able to interfere with Darien's plans anymore. I'm so excited I can barely contain it." She ground her teeth in anticipation and took a step toward us. I tried to think fast. If our powers didn't work in this room, theirs shouldn't be able to either. Right?

I calculated my chances of being able to take them both down. They were both much taller than I was, but I had the training from Tristan and my karate. I just hoped it would be enough.

Crystal took another step toward me with something silver glinting in her hand, and I took a step back. She laughed, and Yuri just followed her silently. I stood protectively in front of Lexi and Tristan. Whether I could win this fight or not, they were going to have to go through me to get to my friends.

"Yuri, you should probably tie her up." Crystal motioned toward me. "I want to start playing with this one." She walked toward Lexi.

"No!" I yelled, charging Crystal and knocking her on her back. Yuri was on me in a flash, pulling me off his morbid girlfriend.

"Now you get this straight," Crystal started, as she stood and walked right up to my face. Yuri held me back effortlessly. "Darien said he wanted you alive, not that he wanted you in one piece. Make no mistake, I will take great pleasure in dismembering you." She placed the cold metal object at my throat, and I knew then it was a blade; its sharp point pressing against my skin.

"Leave her alone," Tristan snarled, still trying to break free.

"I almost forgot about you," she said, flicking her eyes in Tristan's direction only for a moment before returning them to me. "You will want to make sure I don't remember you right now, boy," she snarled, still looking into my eyes. Crystal pressed the cold metal into my flesh and I felt the sting of it as it broke through my skin. Warm liquid trickled down my neck. I suppressed the urge to whimper. Crystal's lips twitched into an almost smile.

"I thought you wanted to play with me first," Lexi called out.

"I changed my mind," Crystal answered, never once blinking or averting her gaze from mine. I could hear Tristan and Lexi both straining against their bonds, trying to stop her from hurting me, but they couldn't. "This will be much more fun. Yuri, get some rope."

The thought of Yuri leaving gave me hope. I could take her one on one. Just as I had the thought she stood behind me where Yuri had just been. She placed the blade across my throat and held my body tightly against hers so I couldn't move. I tried to think of all the ways to disarm an attacker, but she was holding me too tight. Any way I moved would cause the blade to slit my throat.

Yuri returned too quickly with rope in hand. Crystal tied the rope around my wrists and pulled them up over my head. I looked up at the ceiling and saw the faint outline of a hook. Oh God, this wasn't happening.

My body was lifted a foot off the ground, and I was hung on the hook by my bound wrists. The weight of my body strained my arms.

"Let's see. Where should we start, Yuri my love?" She asked, crooning to her mate as if they were talking about house renovations. Yuri, who had yet to say a single word, just stared at my chest. "Yes, I agree. She's too covered up," Crystal pouted. She swung her blade cutting the thin straps of my tank top. With another slash she had cut my tank straight down the middle causing it to fall to the floor. I hung there in my black bra and shorts.

"What's that, my love? Remove the shorts too?" She said, slashing down the sides of my shorts and cutting my skin in the process. I gritted my teeth, but I couldn't stop the whimper that escaped my lips. "Ah, such sweet music." She placed the blade under my bra strap, about to slice the little clothing I had left.

"Stop hurting her!" Tristan cried out. "Come play with me. I promise you won't be disappointed." He sounded calm enough but I saw the agony in his eyes, and I had to turn away. I couldn't be strong if I saw him like that.

"Shut up. I am playing with you already," she snapped, moving the knife from my bra to swipe the blade along one of my wounds to prove her point. I tensed, not wanting to give her any satisfaction. She handed Yuri the blade while glaring at Tristan, and I saw a flicker in Yuri's eyes. He walked to me slowly, tilting his head right and left trying to decide what he wanted to do. My heart raced, my arms shook, and they ached with the weight of my body. I had to get out of there. I couldn't let them keep going.

Yuri pressed the blade against my rib cage and sliced my skin diagonally downward, mirroring my ribs. I tried to be strong, but I couldn't. I cried out in pain. I vaguely heard Tristan and Lexi yelling, but Yuri kept cutting, at least five slices on each of my sides.

I felt my blood stream down my legs to pool on the floor. My tears ran hot down my face, and I tried not to look at Lexi or Tristan. Yuri gave the blade back to Crystal and her face lit up with anticipation. She kissed him roughly. She was not artistic like her mate. She was savage. She stabbed the front of my left thigh, hard and deep and dragged the blade down to just above my knee. I screamed out in pain, and black spots played across my vision. Crystal laughed as she watched me writhe in agony. "Selena! Selena, oh my God," Tristan called. I couldn't answer. A sob escaped my throat instead.

"I have an idea," Crystal said. "Come Yuri."

They left, locking the door behind them, leaving me hanging and bleeding.

"I'm so sorry. So sorry," Lexi repeated shaking her head. She still wriggled her wrists hoping to loosen her ties.

"Those sick sadistic fucks. I will kill them!" Tristan snarled, viciously thrashing in his chair, trying to break free. Then I saw a spark in his eye. He squirmed, lifting his body as far from the chair as he could, and reached into his pocket. He fussed for a few moments, reaching his fingers in as far as he could, until his hand came out with a pen between the tips of his index and middle finger. He shifted the chair closer to the wall and started searching with his eyes.

"What are you doing?" Lexi asked.

"Trying to find the incantations." Tristan seemed to have spotted whatever he was looking for and hacked at a small spot in the wall with the pen.

I don't know how long I was hanging like that before the door unlocked once again. Tristan stopped his vandalism quickly. I was on the brink of fainting from blood loss, but fear still rushed through me. My heart raced, beating so hard it knocked against my rib cage. Crystal and Yuri entered carrying something large and metallic. It looked like the head of two pitch-forks attached together at the neck, with two handles at the end. My stomach flipped. Bile rose to my throat and I tried to swallow it down.

Yuri walked toward me with Crystal at his heels, nipping his ears playfully. The bile started to rise again at the sight. He pulled open the handles of the object, and the two heads opened apart like giant salad tongs. My eyes widened, my heart beat in my throat, and my body shook with fear. What was he going to do to me?

"Oh God, no!" Lexi cried at the same time Tristan yelled,

"You get away from her!"

Crystal just laughed. Yuri was so focused, he didn't even flinch. He wrapped the disturbing tongs around my bare waist. The cold metal sent shivers through me and I wished I could be somewhere else. Anywhere else. Then he squeezed.

My ribs cracked.

I screamed. I screamed until my throat was raw.

Then he squeezed tighter and I felt more of my ribs break. I tried to scream out again, but I could barely take a breath without reigniting the pain.

It was excruciating. I blacked out, but only for a second. When I came to, Yuri and Crystal still hovered over me, delighted with their new toy. My eyes blurred, and my hearing became muffled. I looked over at my friends, a snarl plastered on Tristan's face, but knowing Crystal and Yuri were preoccupied with me, he was working on the wall. I faintly heard Tristan speak, but I couldn't make out what he was saying at first. My senses dulled and then came back into focus with another rush of pain. Then Tristan's words rang clear.

"I will kill you. I will gut you. I will slice you open from navel to nose, and I will make your torture devices look like toys. You will beg for death. I damn you to Hell! And I will make sure I send you there myself." His voice was cold, quiet, and he was ready to snap. It was more frightening than if he had been yelling. Then he smiled.

That's when I heard it.

The loud crack of wood buckling. The war cry of Tristan as he charged for Crystal using his bound hands like a hammer and hitting her hard in the face. She went down quickly, but Yuri stood fast. Yuri ran toward Tristan, but Tristan was faster, dodging out of the way at the last minute and pushing Yuri in the back with such force, he slammed head first into the wall, falling motionless. He grabbed Yuri's head and smashed it once against the floor. A clatter sounded from somewhere outside the room.

Tristan was about to smash Yuri's head again, when Lexi called, "Tristan. We don't have time. We need to get out of here," as she cast a shatter spell to break her own chair. That seemed to snap Tristan out of his rage temporarily. He looked at Lexi and then moved quickly to me. I looked where he had been sitting and saw that all that was left of his chair were wood splinters. The rope that had been around his waist and ankles was in the debris.

"Oh God, Selena, I'm so sorry." Tristan awkwardly removed the clamp and lifted me up and off the hook, and I fell limp into his arms. He carried me with some difficulty; his hands still bound, and he ran out of the room. Each step he took made me cry out in pain. I heard another noise coming from behind us this time.

"Teleport!" Lexi yelled, and in a pulling, twisting flash we landed outside an unfamiliar house.

Tristan knocked on the door, placed me on the ground and then teleported, returning with Lexi just as the door opened. Genevieve stood inside, her eyes widened in shock.

That was the last thing I remembered as blackness swallowed me into its painless embrace.

12. FAILED
-TRISTAN-

"What happened?" Genevieve cried. Lachlan came running behind her and with one swift movement, picked Selena up and took her inside. She was thankfully unconscious.

"Crystal and Yuri," Lexi said, gasping for air.

"Shit," Lachlan mumbled.

"Exactly," I growled. "I should go back there and finish them off! If Darien hired them, they won't stop until they get us." My rage was boiling over.

"You can't do anything with your hands tied like that," Lexi said. "We need to get these off, and then we can go back there. I will come with you."

"I can smash their heads in the ground," I snarled, recalling the satisfaction that had brought me. Lexi gave me a reproachful look.

Geni quickly cleared the kitchen table and Lachlan gently placed Selena on it. Her body was shaking from the pain and blood loss. She kept dozing in and out of consciousness.

"Holy Hell, what did they do to the poor girl?" Geni asked astonished.

"Can you heal her?" I asked, my voice a rough whisper. Seeing the blood caked on Selena's body made my rage flare all the more. She didn't deserve this; no one did.

"I should be able to heal most of her injuries, at least to stabilize her. Beyond that I'm not sure." Genevieve tried to be gentle, but it was no use, Selena let out a whimper every time Geni touched her. I stood beside Selena and took her hand. I couldn't stand to see her in pain, and I felt useless watching her go through this.

"It will be over soon. I promise," I soothed. Selena looked at me before shutting her eyes. A tear trickled down her face and I gently wiped it away.

Genevieve placed her hands on one wound at a time starting with Selena's neck. It seemed to be painless, as Selena gratefully took the relief it provided. Her skin began to mend itself back together. Then Genevieve moved to the ribs and began sealing the wounds one by one. Slowly, Genevieve went through each cut down Selena's sides, first one side, and then the other. She felt around her ribs and gasped.

"All of her lower ribs are broken," She whispered, her eyes glistening with tears. I clenched my jaw, imagining the pain I would inflict on Yuri and Crystal in return. She set to work on those next. Unfortunately healing broken bones wasn't as painless; she had to re-break Selena's bones back in place. As each rib snapped back together, Selena screamed. She blacked out at one point, but came to a moment later. She seemed able to breathe easier at least.

Genevieve knelt down, taking a moment to regain her composure and her strength. She teetered slightly, and Lachlan knelt beside her.

"Can you finish?" He asked.

Genevieve swallowed, closed her eyes and nodded. A moment later she took a deep breath, and with a reassuring pat from Lachlan she stood and worked on the slashes down the sides of Selena's thighs where Crystal had cut her shorts off.

Finally Genevieve reached her leg. Selena gritted her teeth when she touched the area around the laceration.

"This one is very deep. I don't think I have much strength left to heal it all at once." Geni looked Selena in the eye to make sure she understood. Selena nodded to reassure her. Genevieve focused her energy onto the large gash in Selena's thigh, and I could see the first layers of tissue mend, but the wound stayed open. She tried again, but it wouldn't completely heal. "Some of the deeper tissue has mended itself, but..." She fell back against Lachlan, who directed her toward the couch. "No," Genevieve stopped him. "I have to wrap up her leg. We won't be able to heal it anymore until tomorrow."

"Then sit down and do it," Lachlan said, bringing a chair to Genevieve. She dropped onto it, physically drained.

"Thank you." Selena's voice cracked and was coarse from screaming. Genevieve smiled warmly at her.

"Lachlan, get the girl some clothes. And find a way to remove those ropes off Lexi and Tristan, will you?" Yes, please. I needed to go and finish what I started. Each passing moment I stayed here gave Yuri and Crystal a chance to escape, and that I could not accept.

"Aye. One thing at a time, woman," he responded as he left to get some clothes. Genevieve tried to stand, but faltered.

"What do you need?" Lexi asked.

"In the linen closet, beside the bathroom, I have a first-aid kit. I'll need that and a wet towel," Genevieve answered. "I wasn't always able to heal," she threw in for Lexi's benefit.

"I'll be right back," Lexi said as she left the room. She came back with the items in her bound hands. Genevieve opened the kit, took out wound dressings and a wrap. She cleaned the blood off Selena's leg, placed the dressings on the cut and then used the wrap to keep it all in place. She had to wrap the entire top half of Selena's leg. Then she wiped the dried blood off her sides and stomach, along with anywhere else it trickled down to.

"I can do that," Selena offered, her voice a whisper. Genevieve waved her off.

Finally Lachlan returned with a sweater and loose fitting pajama pants.

"These should do the trick," Lachlan said handing the garments to her.

"Thank you." Selena eagerly put them on, shivering. She went and sat down on the couch once she was dressed, and I sat next to her, awkwardly wrapping my infuriatingly bound arms around her shoulders to comfort and warm her. She looked surprised, but I didn't shift my hold.

I managed to relax only slightly now that she was healed. I held Selena close, wanting to feel like I could protect her this time. My failure at keeping her from harm engulfed me, almost suffocating me. The only way I could forgive or redeem myself was to make sure Crystal and Yuri could never hurt her or anyone else ever again.

Lachlan helped Genevieve to the living room. She sat in the arm chair heavily, as if her limbs were weighed down.

Genevieve tried to stand, "Lachlan, can you get Selena some juice?" She asked. Lachlan gently pushed her back down onto the chair before going to the kitchen. He came back with a glass of orange liquid.

"You lost too much blood. Drink some orange juice to rehydrate and get your blood sugar back up," Genevieve said, as Lachlan placed the glass in Selena's hands. She did as she was told.

"So how do we get these things off?" Lexi asked, pointing to the rope with her eyes. Lachlan ran a hand over his face in contemplation.

"Go get my spell book, will you?" Genevieve asked Lachlan. He let out a huff as he left, and came back a moment later with a thick, black, leather bound book. Genevieve took it from him and started flipping through the pages.

"We need to hurry," I said. "I'm sure Crystal and Yuri have come to by now and I want to kill them before they contact Darien." The fury in my voice was unfamiliar to me.

"Please stay," Selena whispered, placing her hand on mine. "you don't have to do this." Her eyes pleaded.

"Yes I do. For you."

Selena averted her gaze.

"Here it is. I knew I saw it in here before. They should really teach us this stuff in school," Genevieve said, reading the page in front of her. "Okay, it says we have to remove the charm placed on the object by cleansing it. Huh, it's kind of like crystals, you charge them and cleanse them the same way. Okay, you two come with me. We're going to wash the rope and infuse them with our new intention, which is to remove the charm."

"You're not goin' anywhere," Lachlan said, taking the book from her. Genevieve didn't protest, she seemed very close to passing out.

"Is there anything I can do?" I asked her.

"No, I'll be fine, really."

"Come on then," Lachlan said.

I hesitated for a moment before leaving Selena. Seeing her huddled on the couch in oversized clothes, made her look so young and breakable. It was hard to think of her that way when I knew how strong she was. The three of us walked to the bathroom, leaving Selena alone with Genevieve.

I was eager to get my ropes off first as Lachlan turned the faucet on. I placed my bound wrists under the water. The coolness soothed the rope burn from trying to wrest free. I imagined the ropes unbinding themselves, charging them with a new purpose as the water cleansed away the old one. Finally the rope fell loose, and I breathed a sigh of relief.

"I need to leave you here for a little while. Will you be alright?" I asked Selena as I came back into the living room. Selena nodded even though she didn't want me to leave. She was petrified, but I couldn't afford to let my emotions guilt me into staying. Before I could reconsider leaving, I teleported out of the house and found myself back in the building we had just escaped. I ran through the hall and back to the room we were held captive in. I expected to see Yuri still lying lifeless on the floor, but he was gone. And so was Crystal. I ran through the hallway to the other rooms, but they were all empty. With an angry growl that sounded suspiciously like a wild animal, I teleported back to Selena.

13. HAUNTED
-SELENA-

"He left already, didn't he?" Lexi asked as she came into the room a moment later, rubbing her newly freed wrists. I nodded. "What an idiot. He's going to need my help," she whined as she sat down on the couch next to me. She wrapped her arms around me in a light hug, afraid she'd hurt me even though I was mostly healed. I shrugged my shoulders, but my gut twisted with fear. What if he teleported and Crystal and Yuri were ready and waiting for him? What if they got backup? What if he got hurt? The possibilities ran through my mind.

"Let me teleport us to him," I whispered to Lexi, glad my voice didn't betray my emotions.

"Selena, you're too weak. You need to rest."

"I don't care. He could be in trouble," I cried. I stood, unsteady at first - I had lost too much blood, but I was determined to get to him. Before I could think of where I wanted to be, Tristan materialized in front of me. I let out a sigh of relief and felt my body relax.

"They weren't there," he huffed impatiently. "They must have booked it as soon as they came to. I knew we took too long."

Lexi spoke up, "What if we went--"

"No," I interrupted. "No one is going anywhere. Please, please just stay here where we're all together and safe. Please?" My voice cracked at the end, and I held back a sob.

"Shh, it's okay," Tristan soothed. "No one is going anywhere, okay?" He lifted his arm as if to wrap it around my shoulder again, but hesitated. "Come on, you need to rest."

"I am going to put a protective spell on the house. Make sure no one will be able to teleport in here." Lexi went to the kitchen where I saw a blue light shine, spreading its seal across the walls. I felt better knowing the spell was in place, even though it didn't work last time.

"Do you have any guns around here?" I asked Genevieve.

She shook her head, "No, we've never had any use for them... they don't work where we're from."

Damn.

"Where are you from? Is this not your house?" I asked.

"It is more of a...second home," Genevieve said. "You and Lexi can sleep in the spare room, top of the stairs and to your right. Tristan, you can sleep across the hall from them in the den."

"Cool," Lexi called from the kitchen. I walked a few steps, trying to put weight on my injured leg, and cringed every time I did. Tristan picked me up effortlessly and carried me up the stairs and into the room, laying me on the bed and tucking me in. He took a step away from the bed, and I grabbed his hand.

"Please don't leave me," I pleaded. I knew there were boundaries, but I couldn't justify following them just then.

Tristan hesitated, a million expressions crossing his face before it settled on defeat.

"I'm not going anywhere," he said softly. "I was just going to come around to the other side of the bed." I'm sure he noticed the shock on my face, but he didn't say anything about it. I wrapped my arms around my body. I couldn't stop shaking.

"Maybe I should get you some water, or something to eat first."

"No. I'm fine. Just lie with me." I didn't like being so clingy, but I was scared to death. Every time I closed my eyes, I saw Crystal and Yuri. I was scared that I would always be hunted or that I would be hurt again. Although most of my wounds were healed, I could still feel vestiges of the pain, searing through my flesh and into my tissues. Seared into my memory.

Tristan crawled into bed beside me, and I curled into him. He gathered me in his arms and held me tight.

"Can we buy a gun?" I asked, feeling an extreme need for the safety it would provide.

"Guns don't work for witches. Our magic interferes with human weapons for some reason."

My stomach sank at the news, I wanted to feel safe.

"Nobody knows why?" I asked.

"We have magic, so there's really never been a reason to study why they don't work."

"I'd say we just stumbled on a pretty good one," I mumbled.

"Think of it this way," Tristan started. "One of our most severe punishments is to bind a witch's powers. Say we figured out a way for witches to use guns, and all of a sudden every violent witch whose powers have been bound now has a secondary means of killing. To be honest, most of the time, being unable to use guns is a blessing that no witch would want 'fixed'."

Tristan held me tighter as if to compensate for the lack of weaponry.

"You still have knives, and probably explosives," I mumbled.

Tristan chuckled. "That's true, but guns are just one less thing for us to worry about."

No matter how warm I got, my body wouldn't stop shaking. Tristan ran his hand up and down my back, speaking soothing and reassuring words.

"I'm so sorry," he whispered.

"What for? You saved me again," I answered.

"I should have stopped them before they laid a single finger on you. I should have been better prepared, so that when they came into my house, I would have been ready."

"How could you have known that was going to happen? You can't be so hard on yourself."

"Selena," Tristan paused for a moment, deep in thought. Finally he continued, "You are everything to me. Seeing you hurt..." he clenched his jaw and looked away. My heart picked up a beat. "I never want you to be hurt ever again for as long as you live. And I will get those bastards for what they did to you." His eyes blazed with rage, his jaw clenched and un-clenched as he no doubt plotted his revenge.

"I'm sorry I didn't take your training seriously enough. All that time and effort for nothing. What a waste."

"It wasn't for nothing. There was nothing you could have done differently. Not with the way they restrained you. But I will train you better and work you harder and make sure you can kill anyone who comes after you," he promised.

"I'm too weak. It doesn't matter what you teach me. Obviously even with all that training I had, I blanked anyway. I won't be able to overpower anyone."

Tristan scoffed, "Are you kidding? You are the strongest woman I know. You just need to learn more technique, and now that you know what you're up against, you will know how to apply it."

As the adrenaline left my body, I felt my eyelids droop, and my muscles felt like they were turning to mush. Even though I was still traumatized, my exhaustion won out.

My dreams were riddled with Crystal and Yuri, her cold blue eyes, and creepy split-toothed grin, and his black eyes, and expressionless face. I saw the knife and the vice grip, felt the pain, and I woke up to a blood curdling scream. It was moments before I realized I was the one screaming.

Tristan was there, holding me, shushing me, calming me. My body wracked in shivers and Tristan held me tighter, trying to hold me together. He swept my damp hair off my face, and again I saw the anguish in his eyes. He held me against his chest. The safety from his muscular arms was comforting, and soon my shivers became small tremors.

I couldn't fall back to sleep after that, and when Genevieve made dinner, I ate only bits and pieces, just enough to appease Tristan. I stayed awake the rest of the night, long after Tristan fell asleep with his arm wrapped protectively around me.

The night passed while I watched the moonlight transform into sunlight, shifting the shadows from the blinds to creep across the ceiling. My body ached, and I was exhausted, but I couldn't sleep. I was too scared. Sometime during the night Lexi came in and took Tristan's place. I was glad for her support, but it was Tristan I wanted beside me.

There was a soft knock on the door and Tristan poked his head through. He didn't look like he had slept much either.

Lexi shifted next to me, rubbing a hand over her face as she woke.

"Did you sleep?" Tristan asked, voice still groggy.

"A little," I lied, not wanting to worry him.

He nodded unsurely, as he came up to the bed. "How are you feeling?" He gazed into my eyes, trying to read my thoughts. His green eyes blazed with concern. I clenched my jaw, scared that if I spoke I would cry. I shrugged my shoulders instead. Tristan let out a sigh and ran a hand through his mussed hair. He leaned over and moved my hair away from my face.

"I'm going to wash up and see what's for breakfast," he said, stepping away from me.

"We should probably leave afterwards," Lexi said. "No need to impose on Genevieve any more than necessary."

I nodded and stayed in bed for a while after Tristan left. Lexi went to wash up after a bit, and then I followed suit. I really needed to wash the previous day off me. A quiet yelp escaped when I put pressure on my leg. Then I thought of ways I'd have to wash myself around it. I stared at the wrap with frustration, hating it for preventing me from already being in the shower. Blood had soaked through the dressings, and I decided to find Genevieve to see if she could heal it some more.

Then I stopped. I unwrapped my leg, and placed my fingers on either side of the wound. It was a long and gaping monstrosity, even with Genevieve's previous handy work. Closing my eyes, I imagined the cut healing and my skin sealing itself closed. I felt the warm tingle in each layer of tissue as it mended together. It was as if I could sense what needed to be done, how my body needed to be healed, and my body responded. I wondered if this was what Genevieve sensed and felt when she healed others. I suddenly felt light-headed, and my lack of sleep all at once, but the sensation left as quickly as it came. My admiration toward Genevieve grew as I realized the exhaustion she must have felt the night before.

When I opened my eyes again, my leg was completely healed, but like my other wounds, the ghost of its pain lingered. I gasped in astonishment.

Grateful that I could shower freely, I skipped quickly to the bathroom and started the water. Before I could get undressed there was a knock on the door. I opened it to find Lexi standing there with some towels and clothes.

"I thought you could use these, they're Genevieve's," she said quietly. I smiled, wondering how I could have forgotten to make sure I had a change of clothes myself. "Listen, I didn't get a chance last night, but I wanted to thank you."

"Thank me? For what?" My eyebrows knitted together in confusion.

"If it wasn't for you, Crystal would have tortured me first. I'm just so sorry I couldn't return the favor before..." She lowered her gaze to the floor. My body twitched at the mention of Crystal's name. I took the towels and clothes from her, placing them on the counter, and then gave her a hug.

"I would do anything for you. You are my best friend, and I love you. Don't feel bad, there was nothing you could have done, okay?" I asked, knowing it was just hours before that Tristan had told me something similar. I felt her nod, still holding me in a hug.

"Yeah, but I'm supposed to protect you, not the other way around." She sniffled into my shirt.

"You've been protecting me my whole life. It was my turn."

She let me go and wiped at her eyes. "Okay, well, um, breakfast will be ready soon, so come down when you're done."

"Hey, Lex?" I called as she reached the door. She turned to face me and I showed her my leg.

"Wow, I thought she hadn't been able to heal it." She examined my leg closely.

"She hadn't. Well not entirely anyway."

Lexi shot up. "No way!"

I smiled sheepishly. "This is good, right? My powers are finally increasing, right?" I searched for reassurance, half excited and half terrified with my daily discoveries.

"Yes, this is good." She gave me a quick hug.

I nodded and closed the door after her, anxious to get to the hot running water. I undressed quickly and stepped over the tub ledge into the shower, feeling the steam loosen my muscles and wash away the blood and misery from the night before. I tried to relax and really enjoy my shower but I felt broken. I cried instead, sobbing quietly as the water ran down my hair. Each memory ran through my mind like a flash of pain. My sobs diminished to whimpers as the water started to cool down. I took a deep breath and tried to focus on the positive. I was able to heal myself, my powers were growing, and Genevieve was able to undo the majority of physical damage I endured. I could at least take some comfort in that.

I dried off and dressed quickly in the jeans and t-shirt Lexi gave me; they were a little tight, but fit for the most part. I ran a brush through my hair and let it fall in wet strands down my back. My eyes were ringed with black circles from lack of sleep and they were slightly puffy and red from my recent cry. Unfortunately there was nothing I could do to hide that.

I shook my head at my sad-looking reflection before heading downstairs.

"There's got to be something we can do to be proactive." I heard Lexi say in hushed tones, and I stopped outside the kitchen to listen.

"What do you want me to do? I have no idea where they are, or who they're with. It could be a suicide mission if we do this wrong," Tristan whispered.

"What if you got Selena to teleport you *to* them?" Lexi offered.

"What do you mean?" Genevieve asked.

"Selena doesn't have to know where she's going to teleport," Lexi said excitedly. "She can simply go to whomever she wants."

"How?" Genevieve whispered.

"I don't know, but that was the only way she could have gotten to Tristan and I, right Tristan?"

Tristan was quiet a moment. "There was no other way she could have found us, true, but she needs to be kept out of it. At least until she's had time to heal physically and emotionally. Last night took a devastating toll on her. She barely slept." Tristan argued.

"But-" Lexi started, but stopped short as I walked into the kitchen. Lachlan and Genevieve sat on one side of the table while Lexi and Tristan sat across from them. All four of them looked me over as I sat at the table. There were plates of scrambled eggs, pancakes, bacon, and sweet bread laid out before me. Smelling the food made my stomach growl, and I was glad I had some semblance of an appetite.

I filled my plate in the awkward silence and started eating while everyone stared at me.

"What?" I asked over a mouthful of pancake.

"Nothing," Lexi said while the others shifted in their seats.

"Look, I am shaken up, absolutely. Anyone would be if they experienced what I did. But I will be fine in time. Please don't treat me like a child." I took a bite of bacon and chewed the tough meat for a moment.

"How's your leg?" Genevieve asked, breaking her silence.

"Good, I healed it. Thanks for healing the rest of me." I smiled, and then took another bite of bacon.

"You healed yourself?" She asked, eyes slightly widening.

"Yeah, I know, I was surprised too," I admitted.

"You healed it in one shot?" She pressed.

"Yeah, why?" I asked nervously. "Did I do something wrong?"

"No, it's just that it was very deep, and healing that takes up a lot of energy. Usually lacerations like that can be healed in two or three separate sessions, if not more." Genevieve explained.

I smiled sheepishly. "It worked okay today. Maybe it wasn't as deep as we thought." I changed the subject. "I'm not sure what the plan is, though by your whispers I'm sure you're trying to think of something. I personally think we need to call the Charge." I forked a chunk of scrambled eggs, and took another bite of my pancake.

"How do you know about the Charge?" Tristan asked.

"Lexi told me. Anyways, I think they should know about Crystal and Yuri and we should find out if they can help us."

"Alright," Lachlan said. "I'll give 'em a call." He pushed his chair back and left the room.

"Can you just call them? Like 911?" I asked. Tristan poured me a glass of orange juice, and I drank it greedily.

"Yes, we have an emergency number to reach them, and a distress code for the times we call them telepathically."

"Cool," I said and finished off my plate.

"Alright," Lachlan said, taking his seat at the table. "They'll send the investigators over as soon as they can."

We sat in silence a moment. "Aren't you guys going to eat?" I asked, feeling self-conscious.

Slowly they all filled their plates, but I knew they were only eating to make me feel better.

"I've been thinking," I said as the others slowly ate. "I'm developing my powers, and I intend to use them whenever possible, but after yesterday it's pretty clear I need to make sure I can defend myself without them. Maybe we could train just until the Charge arrive?" I asked Tristan.

"You sure you're up to it?" Tristan asked studying my appearance.

"Yes. I need to know I'm doing something productive and I don't want to take any chances of being caught like that again."

"Okay," Tristan said. I nodded.

Genevieve stood to clear the table, her plate barely touched. Tristan and I helped, removing the plates and glasses. Lachlan was the only one who ate more than a few bites of food. He actually ate more than I did.

Genevieve looked at him curiously.

"No point in wastin' the food, now is there?" He asked over a mouthful of eggs. I smiled appreciatively. Genevieve and I finished cleaning the kitchen as Lachlan finished his meal and headed to the living room with Tristan.

I caught Genevieve eyeing my leg now and then, and it made me feel uncomfortable.

"How did you do it?" She finally asked.

"I just pictured it healing all the way through and it did." I put the last dish away. "I did want to ask you what it feels like for you to heal. I had a sense of my body responding to my magic and knowing how to heal itself."

Genevieve shook her head in astonishment. "My experience is a little different. I can sense the area that needs to be healed, but I sense the cells that need to be repaired, or the bacteria that needs to be destroyed. I need to understand what is happening within the body, I can't just think it will heal, I need to know how to heal it."

I nodded, "Did you work at the hospital to understand your healing powers?"

"No, I was already working there as a nurse when I developed my powers, so I already had an in-depth knowledge of anatomy. Witches who develop the power to heal, do have to study medicine to practice it. Another reason why I am surprised you were able to heal yourself so easily. Your abilities truly are a wonder," she said in awe.

I bit my lip, feeling like a pariah again. I mumbled a "thanks" and then headed to the living room to join the men.

"So the plan so far is that you two are going to train, but what should we do?" Lexi asked.

"Just wait for the Charge and let us know the moment they arrive." Tristan answered.

Lexi nodded and talked to Genevieve and Lachlan. Tristan took my hand and led me to the back of the house. He opened a glass door and escorted me to the back yard. Plush grass filled the area within the white picket fence. Rose bushes edged the front of the fence, full and colorful, with a scent so strong I could smell it from across the yard. I couldn't believe we were actually still in Arizona. Wait…

"Where are we?" I asked, looking around us.

Tristan chuckled. "It's a half-way house, though not the way you know it."

"What does that mean?"

"Genevieve has an identical house or, well, cottage, I guess, somewhere else. She knew she would be needed, so she created this house closer to you, but it keeps all the characteristics of her actual home."

"Where are we exactly though?"

"Let's just say somewhere between her real home and yours."

"Cool! Where does she live?"

"The Hidden City."

"The what now?" I asked.

"I'll tell you all about it later. I may even take you there." He smiled, and my heart fluttered at the idea of a trip with Tristan, even if it was to some weird, unknown place.

A small metal table with two chairs surrounding it stood to the side of the patio door. Tristan led me there and I sat down, taking in the beautiful, clear blue skies and warm breeze.

Tristan crouched in front of me. "Are you sure you want to start training right now? I'm worried it will be too much too soon. You have just barely healed, and last night was…" He let the sentence hang. I shivered at the memory.

"I have to try. If it becomes too much, I'll stop." I ran my hands up and down my arms in an attempt to flatten the goose bumps. Tristan took a deep breath and nodded, standing up.

"Alright, come on." We walked to the middle of the yard and he turned to face me. He charged at me and I flinched, curling into myself, and stepped out of his way. My heart beat picked up. Maybe I wasn't ready for this yet. Tristan stopped and turned to face me, his expression blank, but I knew he was waiting for an explanation.

"Sorry. I was kind of caught off guard." I swallowed hard. "Let me try it again."

"You sure?" Tristan raised his eyebrows, his face filling with concern. I nodded and held my head high. He stood across from me, and again he charged. I quickly lowered my stance, hitting him in the stomach with my shoulder and taking him down. He let out a quiet *oomph* as he fell. Quickly getting to his feet, he dusted himself off and gave me a smile.

Without warning he threw a punch at me. Again I flinched and curled in on myself. I closed my eyes tight, waiting for his fist to make contact, but it never came. I opened my eyes and saw Tristan standing before me with so much worry etched into his face that I had to look away.

"Selena, you're not ready."

"Yes, I am," I said defiantly. But I couldn't make myself stand tall this time. I was scared. I knew Tristan wouldn't hurt me; I wasn't scared of him. It was his movements, his actions, knowing there would be pain if I didn't move fast enough.

Tristan studied my face, and let out a sigh. "You're a terrible liar."

"I am not," I answered, but I averted his gaze

With one long stride Tristan was in front of me, and pulling me into his arms. I hesitated, caught off guard, and then decided to go with it. I rested my head against his chest and heard his heart beat through his thin shirt. I had the sudden urge to cry, but I refused to let him see me weak again. I took a deep breath, inhaling the crisp scent of the soap he used and felt myself relax. After a moment, I pulled away and looked into Tristan's eyes.

"I can do this." I could see Tristan's jaw setting stubbornly, doubting the truth of my statement. I could read it in his face. I pulled back and got into a fighting stance. Tristan shook his head, but he stood across from me, ready to attack.

He came at me with a punch. I grabbed his wrist and pulled it behind his back. He twisted and righted himself again, throwing a punch at my jaw with his free hand. Again I grabbed his wrist, but this time I kicked him in the stomach. He hunched over slightly, then righted himself quickly, accidentally head butting me in the process. It was a hard hit, and it dazed me. I let go of Tristan's arms and tried to regain my balance.

"Oh my God, Selena, are you okay? I swear I didn't mean to actually hit you." I could tell he wanted to laugh at the situation, but he was scared; scared that he really hurt me, and scared that it was too much for me to handle. He walked to me quickly and lifted my head. He gently pressed his fingers under my right eye, and I flinched from the pain. "I cut it. I'm so sorry," he whispered.

"It's okay. It's what we train for." I pressed my fingers under the cut and healed it.

"Whoa," Tristan mumbled under his breath. It was nothing, but my skin trembled, as if it were afraid, tormented by the memory of being cut and hurt. I shook it off and stood ready again.

Tristan shook his head, "No. No more right now. I can't do it." A part of me was annoyed, because I really needed to practice, but another part of me was relieved. Despite my big talk, I really wasn't ready.

"Do you think I can defend myself with the amount of training I have at this very moment?" I asked, half-heartedly wanting to push myself.

"Yes. You are incredibly strong. You deflected my attacks pretty well. You just need to perfect your technique, but it won't be today. I'm sorry," he said with a finality I couldn't, and didn't want to argue with. I took the escape he provided, and felt ashamed.

"What's wrong?" Tristan asked, trying to read my expression.

"I want to be stronger than this."

"You are strong. I already told you this. You just have to be realistic. You can't expect to go through what you went through and wake up training. You need time to heal. Not just physically, but mentally and emotionally. I promise I will keep you safe. I promise you will not have to fight *anyone* without your powers. We can wait." He brushed his fingertips across my jaw, making my heart hammer inside my chest, and then dropped his hand.

"Come on, Firefly," he said, leading me back into the house.

"Firefly?" I asked, still slightly unfocused from his touch.

"Yeah, you're glowing again." Tristan laughed.

Damn my stupid glowing emotion crap!

We walked inside the house and saw Lexi sitting on the couch next to Genevieve, and Lachlan sitting in the armchair.

"Training over already?" Lexi asked, looking up as we entered the room. "What happened, Selena? Did you get your ass handed to you?" She teased. My face flushed with embarrassment. Tristan shot Lexi a glare.

"We decided to take it slow. We did a bit today, and that's enough for now. Okay?" Tristan stared at Lexi.

"Okay. Calm down." She made an exaggerated what's-his-problem face to Genevieve.

"You really need a filter," Genevieve whispered.

"Wha-" Lexi started, leaving her mouth hanging open as Genevieve shook her head for Lexi to stop talking.

I sat down on the love seat and Tristan sat next to me.

"What's taking the Charge so long?" Lexi asked, rolling her eyes out of frustration. She didn't like just sitting around doing nothing.

As if on cue, there was a knock on the door. I jumped, startled at the noise.

Genevieve hopped up and answered the door. She returned a moment later with two men. They looked an awful lot alike. Their hair was dark, but shaved very short, their eyes were dark and probing, as if they could see our thoughts, and they stood still and tall in an intimidating way. They wore dark navy pants and a matching shirt, and on each of their forearms was a tattoo of a shield with a calligraphic C in the center.

"We're from the investigative unit of the Charge," one of the men said. "I'm Bronson and this is my partner Diggs." Bronson waved his hand toward the man next to him.

"We received a call that you had a disturbance last night," Diggs said.

"We'll start by reviewing a visual account of your experience, and from there hopefully we'll be able to track down the attackers," Bronson added. "Who witnessed the incident?"

"These three 'ere," Lachlan said, pointing Tristan, Lexi and I out.

"Visual account?" I asked, getting to my feet.

"Yes, ma'am," Diggs said. "This will only take a moment."

Diggs reached and clasped my hand between his two large ones, as Bronson took hold of Lexi's. They closed their eyes and the room became perfectly still. A few heartbeats later, Diggs and Bronson opened their eyes in unison, looked at each other and after a silent moment that looked like one of Lexi and Tristan's telepathic conversations, they nodded. Bronson stepped in front of Tristan and repeated the process. Tristan stood with his hand in Bronson's almost looking bored.

"This situation is more hostile than we anticipated," Diggs said, eyeing me openly. He then turned to Bronson and nodded, "She's the one Captain was talking about. The prophecy is real. It is an honor to meet you ma'am," he said, turning his attention back to me.

My face flushed and I shifted uncomfortably. "What did you just do?" I asked.

"We have the ability of sight, so we're able to see everything you experienced from your point of view," Bronson answered. "All investigators must have this gift. It helps us weed out the truth."

"We know who the assailants are," Diggs said. "We have been monitoring Crystal and Yuri, but we haven't been able to apprehend them. They seem to know when we find their location, and leave just before we arrive."

"We suspect there may be a mole in our unit," added Bronson. "Someone feeding Crystal and Yuri any leads we obtain, which is disturbing. Our code of conduct is sacred."

"Please, have a seat," Genevieve offered. "Can I get you something to drink?"

"No, thank you, ma'am," Diggs said. "We won't be here long."

"Is there anything you can tell us that will help us protect ourselves?" Tristan asked.

"Perhaps taking a proactive approach may help," Bronson said.

"However, as investigators we're not supposed to release the information of the assailant's last known where-abouts to civilians," Diggs said. "We shouldn't encourage you to take matters into your own hands; we wouldn't want you to get hurt."

"We're really not supposed to tell you if there were rumors that Crystal and Yuri were hiding in a small shack an hour west of here," Bronson winked.

"We're also not able to tell you if we followed this tip and found the shack abandoned." Diggs pulled a pen and a pad of paper from his pocket, and scribbled some words across the blank sheet.

"Please look after yourselves," Bronson said. "We'll continue to look for them, and if we find any information, we'll find you." He nodded to us, and they turned toward the door. A sheet of paper fell from Diggs's hand to the floor, and I grabbed it.

"Uh... off- investigator?" I called. He turned around. "You dropped this."

"Pardon me, ma'am," he said. "Perhaps you could throw that out for me?"

I looked down at the paper and found it was an address.

"Sure," I whispered. He smiled and stepped out into the night.

"We should check the address Diggs gave us," Lexi said a few minutes later.

"It was abandoned," Tristan said. "The investigators don't even know where to find them."

"So best way is for me to teleport you guys then, right?" I said after some more thought.

"Wrong," Tristan answered. My body had started to ache again and I felt myself sink in the soft cushions.

"Why not?" I pushed.

"Because we have no idea where we would end up, or who else could be there," Tristan said. "And for the last time, you need to rest." He almost yelled the last part. I cringed.

"Fine," I said through clenched teeth.

"It doesn't hurt to check out the shack," Lachlan said.

As the others discussed strategy, my mind kept wandering to Yuri and Crystal, and I spent most of my efforts trying to block them out. The more I thought about it, the more I feared that I wasn't the one in the prophecy. I mean, yes, I had powers some of the others did not, but what kind of pre-destined savior can't fight off two witches?

I barely spoke a word, and Tristan started to eye me, concern evident on his face. Occasionally I smiled to reassure him I was fine, even though I wasn't. My brain was a jumble of thoughts and worries, and I just couldn't focus on what was going on around me.

As my mind wandered, the couch started to feel really good, and my eyes shut of their own accord.

I was in my black bra and underwear, hanging from a hook in the ceiling. Suddenly Crystal and Yuri were standing in front of me, appearing out of thin air. Crystal cackled as she admired a chain saw. Its teeth cut the air around it in an ear-piercing noise. Yuri opened and closed the vice grip around my waist, holding me in place so Crystal could cut me to pieces. Behind them, Darien stood watching, arms crossed over his chest, his posture tense. I heard the blade of the chainsaw, felt the pressure of my ribs breaking.

"No!" I screamed, flailing my arms in front of me as I jerked off the couch.

"Selena? What's wrong?" Tristan asked as he ran into the room. "Another bad dream?" He asked quietly, when he saw my appearance. I nodded and swallowed hard. He knelt in front of me and took my shaking hands into his warm, steady ones. "You are alright. You are safe, and I won't let anyone hurt you. Okay?" He said it soothingly, almost hypnotically, and I found myself nodding. He moved and sat next to me on the couch.

"I need a minute," I said, standing up. Tristan looked slightly startled at my abrupt movement. I smiled reassuringly and headed for the bathroom. I washed my face and stared at my reflection. My hair had dried in waves down my back, the black circles were still around my eyes and they were tinted red from lack of sleep. The puffiness was gone, but the rest of me looked like death. I really wanted to sleep. My body wanted the rest, and my mind wanted the escape of dreams, not the torment of nightmares.

I sighed and headed back to Tristan, still sitting on the couch.

"You okay?" he asked.

"Yeah, I feel a bit better. How long was I asleep for?"

"A little over an hour."

"Should we go back to your place then?" I asked, trying to get a sense of comfort, "Or mine even?"

"Soon. I think it would be better to deal with Crystal and Yuri first, strength in numbers. I actually picked up your bag from my place."

Great, that meant we were here to stay. I groaned.

"Okay," Lachlan said as he entered the room, "so I made a few calls to see if anyone knew about the shack, or Crystal and Yuri's whereabouts." Lachlan shot a glance at Genevieve who stiffened, then looked away before continuing. "Most of my contacts didn't know anything, or didn't want to say anything, but one gave me Gianni Martone's number."

Tristan tensed at the name.

"Who's Gianni?" I asked.

"He's another witch with a bad reputation. He knows Darien well," Tristan answered. "What did you find out?"

"Well, he didn't want to tell me anything at first," Lachlan continued, "but when I told him who I was trying to help, he loosened up a little." He turned to me. "You're the reason he stopped running with that crowd, you know. He's a real believer now. Anyway, he said that he ran into one of his old friends Thursday night, and here's where it gets interesting. This guy was telling Gianni how he's been camping out in the woods. Whoever he's working for now is real touchy about not getting found, apparently they're high on the Elders' priority list, so they've been avoiding the cities."

"So, wait," I started, processing the information. "You're saying that Gianni's friend is working for Yuri and Crystal and they're hiding in the woods?"

Lachlan nodded.

"How do we know it's them?" Lexi narrowed her eyebrows at him.

"Two," Lachlan replied. "Two leaders. That's what he said. Gianni said the guy hinted more than once that it was them. It sounds like Yuri and Crystal to me, and it sounds like they won't be expecting us."

My stomach turned with fear and anticipation.

"Do I want to know how you have these kinds of contacts?" I asked Lachlan. He smiled and winked at me.

"I suggest we teleport to their camp," he said. "We scope out the area, number of people, so on and so forth. Once they're out of the way and not hunting you, we can proceed to go after Darien."

"If we don't get killed first," I whispered under my breath. Thankfully no one heard.

"This is still very risky. We could easily be outnumbered. If I teleport with one of you and we get caught, then what?"

"I can teleport too," I added. "Can't I teleport more than one person at a time?"

"It's never been done before," Genevieve said.

"Why not?" I pressed. "Wouldn't the same magic apply, just to more than one passenger?"

"The veil is only strong enough to carry one extra person," Tristan answered.

"Let's just try!" Lexi jumped to her feet. "Come outside, we'll teleport from the back of the house to the front."

I shrugged and stood. Tristan placed his hand on my

arm to stop me.

"You don't have to do this right now."

"I'm okay. Really. It's not that far, it's just a test." I smiled reassuringly at him until he released my arm.

We all gathered outside in the backyard. Lexi stood next to me, and I motioned for Tristan to come over as well. When they were shoulder to shoulder with me, I took their hands.

"Remember, just to the front, okay?" Lexi reminded. I nodded, and envisioned my teleporting power to expand and cloak Lexi and Tristan. In a flash we were pushed, pulled and twisted, landing on our feet in the front yard. Before I could overthink my success we teleported back to the others.

"Wow!" Lexi said.

Tristan nodded silently, but there was a shimmer in his eye that told me he was proud.

"Let's try more," Lexi chirped.

"I'm not sure that's a good idea," Genevieve said. "It might wipe Selena out, or leave someone stuck in transition."

"Actually, you don't get stuck," Tristan countered. "Either you teleport or you don't. Worst case scenario, one person gets left behind."

"Alright then, Lachlan, come here, Tristan you stay on the other side of Selena," Lexi instructed.

"Do we all have to touch Selena, or is holding hands with each other enough?" Lachlan asked Tristan.

"I'm not sure, let's try holding hands and see what

happens," Tristan answered. I took a deep breath as Tristan took my hand. A warm sensation spread throughout my body and I smiled. Lexi took my other hand and Lachlan took Lexi's free hand. Again I teleported the group to the front yard. When I opened my eyes, all four of us were there. I let out a laugh of excitement.

"Wait, get us back," Lexi ordered. I did.

"Does it make you feel tired? Is it harder to take more than one person?" Genevieve asked.

"Not really, no. It all feels the same," I answered honestly.

Genevieve came and held Tristan's hand. "Are you sure this won't be too much?"

"We'll find out." I smiled and checked to make sure we were all linked, and then teleported us into the front yard.

I heard chuckling, and then laughter and cheers. Only then did I open my eyes. I had brought every single one of my friends with me. I stood rooted to the ground, staring out at the forest in front of me, suddenly grateful there were no other houses around. What would people think if they saw this? The sky was a crisp blue, and it seemed the ground and trees were applauding me. But what did this mean? Was I really the one the prophecy spoke of? Or just lucky?

"Take us back," Tristan ordered, and we all linked hands, and landed softly in the backyard.

Lexi cheered jumping up and down.

"Hell, I never heard of anything like this happening

before." Lachlan laughed a throaty laugh, while Genevieve stood wide-eyed taking it all in. Tristan hugged me and lifted me off the ground.

"You're amazing," he whispered to me before setting me down again, taking a quick step back as if he realized he wasn't supposed to do that. He was giving me mixed signals and I wasn't sure what to do.

"Good. Now that we established that, let's go back inside and finish this plan," Lexi said. We all followed merrily inside.

"Okay, so since Selena can teleport all of us, it should reduce some of the risk, right?" Lexi asked, sitting on the couch.

"Well, some of it, but we may still be outnumbered," Tristan started. "Or if Gianni's information is wrong, or if it's a trap. We could end up in an eter room for all we know. We should have two teams. I don't like splitting up with Selena but since we are the only two who can teleport we have to."

"So let's take weapons in case we find ourselves power-blocked," Genevieve offered.

"That's a good idea." Tristan nodded, "I will take Genevieve and reinforcements. Once we know the area's safe, I'll call Selena to teleport Lexi and Lachlan to us. That way we won't all be sitting ducks. You three will be able to get to us if we're not in a secured location. Sound good?" Tristan finished.

"So we're going after Crystal and Yuri first, right?" Lachlan asked. My heart rate picked up.

Tristan nodded. "We need to get them out of the way first. Then we need to find out what Darien is up to."

"So should we go there tonight?" Lexi asked.

"Actually, I still need to get myself ready," I said. "Last night was a lot to handle, and I could use another day to recoup. Is that okay?"

"Of course," Genevieve said gently.

"We'll leave it for tomorrow night," Lexi said.

Everyone nodded in agreement.

"Are you okay?" Tristan whispered to me.

"Yeah, I just need to gather my wits," I smiled.

So I had two days before my friends risked their lives to ensure my safety. I would have to follow through with my own plan before that.

I played along throughout the rest of the afternoon. The truth was, I was the only one going. I was the only one who would risk my life. The others needed to be safe. I still wasn't convinced that I was the one in the prophecy, so why should these wonderful people get hurt for a phony? No, I would handle this myself.

Tonight.

I was terrified but determined, and now that I had my own plan, I was feeling better. I just needed to figure out the right time. I took a deep breath and exhaled, feeling the odd relief wash over me. Just then I turned to see Tristan studying me.

Damn.

"What are you thinking?" He whispered to me. "I can

tell you're up to something." He clenched his teeth. I shook my head and went out through the back door. The fresh air hit me immediately, and I savored it. The mid-day sun shone brightly, and I absorbed its rays like a dying flower.

"Don't think I didn't notice that you avoided my question." I spun to see Tristan standing behind me. I didn't even hear him come out.

"It's no big deal. My thoughts have been a mess today, and I just didn't want you to worry about me," I half lied.

"I do worry. Whether I know what you're thinking or not, I can tell you're not well. I don't expect you to be either. It's only been a day, and I think you keep forgetting that."

"I'm not. I told you I need another day before we do this," I said.

"You'll need more than a day. What you went through was traumatic, and you'll need a lot more time to get over it. I feel like you're trying to be tough so you're not letting yourself get better in your own time. You have no one to impress, Selena."

"How can you say that?" I clenched my hands into fists at my side. "I have a room full of people who would risk their lives for me. I can't let any of them down. How can I be a hero or whatever when I'm too weak to get over yesterday? Too weak to have defended myself in the first place!" My voice rose as my anger peaked. The wind blew around us, whipping my hair around. "You have no idea what I'm feeling, how guilty and horrible I feel. I am not good enough to help anyone. The least I can do is put on a brave face, so they don't know how weak I really am." I stormed past Tristan and went back inside.

I ran up the stairs to my room, taking them two at a time and slammed the door behind me. I sat on the bed and fumed. The prophecy was wrong. I was not the one. There was no way I could be. How sad it would be for all the witches to rest their faith on weak, stupid me.

There was a knock on the door, and my mind snapped to attention.

"Selena, can I come in?" Tristan's voice sounded muffled through the door.

"I need time alone. Please just leave me for now," I answered. I heard Tristan sigh through the door and then his footsteps receding as he walked away. I took a deep breath to clear my thoughts and went back to breaking down my plan. I needed to think of all the possible scenarios and make sure I was prepared. Another knock on the door interrupted my thoughts. I clenched my teeth out of frustration.

"Tristan, I told you to leave me alone," I yelled.

"Um, actually it's me," Lexi answered.

"Oh, sorry." I opened the door.

"How are you holding up?"

"Fine, I guess. Just frustrated."

"About Crystal?"

"Yes, I'm just so scared. I don't know what to expect and I just want it to be over."

"I know you do." She wrapped her arm around my shoulder. "What else is bothering you?"

"I'm just confused about…" I let the sentence hang.

"About Tristan?" She asked softly.

I nodded. "It's stupid, I know. Especially with everything else that's going on but he keeps giving me mixed signals. Like one minute he lays beside me in bed, the next he runs away when he hugs me. Then he lectures me like he has some say in what I think and do." I sighed.

"I don't know what you and Tristan are fighting about, but he cares about you. Let him in. I'm sure if you explain yourself, he'll be more than willing to listen."

"I explained myself already." Were we fighting?

"Tristan tries to be strong and hide his feelings, but I can tell when he's upset. Just give him a break, okay?"

I rolled my eyes. "I'll do my best."

Lexi opened the door and strolled out, closing it quietly behind her. I threw myself on the bed, and let out a sigh. She was right, of course. I would give him a break when I gathered my thoughts and calmed my nerves.

I thought through my plan again, and then I allowed myself to think about Tristan. I was being snappy; Tristan was just looking out for me, and I was being defensive. I just wish I knew where I stood with him.

Someone cleared their throat outside the room, making me jump. I got off the bed and opened the door. Tristan stood outside my door smiling crookedly. He ran a hand through his shaggy hair, and my heart skipped a beat. I mentally cursed myself.

"Can I come in?" He asked.

I sighed, but opened the door wider for him.

"I know this isn't easy for you, but you need to remember that we know that," he started. "No one expects you to be a machine. We will get through this together, with combined strength. It's not all on you." He took a step toward me and gazed down into my eyes. I almost stopped breathing.

"I don't mean to be dramatic. I'm just frustrated," I said, maintaining eye contact.

"I get that, but you're not alone," Tristan whispered, stepping even closer to me.

"I'm not?" I asked dazedly.

"No." Tristan slowly lowered his face and softly brushed his lips against mine. Was this really happening? I hesitantly kissed him back. Tristan pulled me up against his body and the passion exploded between us. I ran my hands through his hair, down his back, holding him, needing him. He had one hand in my hair, the other on my hip as he deepened the kiss.

Head reeling, I broke the kiss first.

"What happened to boundaries?" I asked breathlessly. I didn't want to stop kissing him, but I needed to know he wasn't going to act cold toward me again in five minutes.

"You're right, I just… I couldn't… it won't happen again." He turned on his heel and out the door before I had a chance to process his words. What just happened? My heart ached and my mind reeled. I closed the door and threw myself on the bed, burying my face in the sheets. I allowed myself two minutes of anger, confusion and heart ache, and then I composed myself before heading back downstairs.

Everyone seemed to be in brighter spirits, now that they knew there was a plan. Now that they weren't sitting down and being useless, they were happy.

I was terrified.

I went through the best way to follow through with my plan. I would have to wait until everyone was asleep tonight. That much I knew for sure. Other than that, I was kind of winging it.

Tristan had avoided me like I suspected he would. Back to being cold and professional. I pushed my disappointment aside; I needed to focus.

Finally night came, and I managed to keep my plan to myself. One by one everyone went to bed, first Genevieve, followed by Lachlan, then Tristan and finally Lexi.

"You coming up?" She asked as she stood on the stairs.

"Yeah, in a minute. I just need some alone time," I answered, tucking my legs beneath me on the couch. I tried to look cozy and comfortable, so there would be no indication I was up to anything.

"'Kay," Lexi said and went upstairs.

I waited half an hour and listened for any movement upstairs. It was completely still and quiet. All the lights were off in the house, all bedroom doors were closed. Perfect.

I went into the kitchen and opened the drawers until I found what I was looking for; a flashlight and a knife. I crept to the door; I wanted to make sure I was out of the house and far off the property before I teleported, just in case.

Before I could open the door, the stair light flickered on, and the weight of someone coming down the stairs made each step creak. I didn't have time to open the door or they would hear me. I closed my eyes and pictured Yuri and Crystal. I started feeling the familiar pull of teleporting when *whack!*

14. ALARMS HURT

It felt like I slammed into a brick wall, throwing me off my feet. When I opened my eyes, I was on my back, my head throbbed, and there was an annoying chirping sound. Was that in my head? Or around me? Within seconds Lexi was standing above me, Lachlan was standing at the base of the stairs, and I heard voices talking anxiously from the top floor.

"What the hell? Selena?" Lexi asked, studying me.

"What?" I asked, trying to sit up, but my head felt like it weighed a ton. The others had joined us, expressions of confusion on each of their faces.

"Selena, are you alright?" Tristan rushed toward me and knelt beside me. "What happened?" He was alert and looking around, trying to find out who hurt me.

"Don't feel bad for her just yet, Tristan," Lexi said hotly.

"What? Why?" He asked Lexi, and then turned back to me, studying my face.

"What were you doing down here, Selena?" Lexi

asked, walking around me like I was a suspect in a bad cop movie. The others quietly awaited my response.

"Nothing, I thought I heard a noise so I decided to check it out," I said. Tristan looked around and saw the flashlight and knife in my hand.

"So you decided to check it out alone? And why didn't you just turn on the light? Why would you need a flashlight?" He asked.

"I was trying to be all stealthy. I was sitting in the dark and didn't want to alert…whoever."

"I was coming down for some water. Was it me you heard?" Lachlan asked.

Finally, an out! I was about to agree, but before I could answer, Lexi was talking again.

"Oh please, Selena, enough! You were trying to teleport. Where were you going?" Lexi yelled.

"Teleport? Why?" Tristan added, disappointment written on his beautiful features.

"I—I-"

"Save it. When I sealed the house, I made sure no one could teleport in, and just in case that failed, they wouldn't be able to teleport out. If anyone tried, they'd be blocked and an alarm would sound," Lexi explained, and the chirping sound stopped as if on cue. Lexi crossed her arms over her chest in judgment. "So again I ask: where were you going?"

"So that's why you were so adamant about teleporting from the back yard to the front only?" I asked. I wished I had figured that out sooner.

"Don't try and change the subject, Selena. Where were you going?"

Before I could muster the courage to answer, Lexi huffed, strode forward and grabbed my hand.

"Hey!" I tried to pull my hand back.

"Let me guess," she spat, gripping my arm tightly. I had never seen her look so angry. "You were going to find Crystal and Yuri on your own because you don't think you're worth risking our lives for. Did I get that right?" She released my arm.

Tristan's eyebrows knitted together in confusion, and his green eyes dimmed a little.

"How did you-" I started.

"How could you think that?" Tristan asked softly. I tried to sit up, but I still couldn't lift my head.

"Hurts, don't it?" Lexi chirped. I sighed.

"I just don't think that I am the one the prophecy was about. I mean, I got bested by two witches. How can I be expected to save people or lead them or whatever it is I'm meant to do, when I can't even take care of myself?" I rambled. Tristan sat back on his heels and ran a hand through his hair.

Surprisingly, Lachlan stepped forward. "I have never seen anyone teleport more than one person at a time. That's pretty amazing."

"You also healed your leg in one shot," Genevieve added. "No healer I know can do that."

"Look, I appreciate your reassurances, but I just don't think that's enough. I think whoever the prophecy is about has a strong personality and character, not just magic."

"This is hopeless," Lachlan said, getting himself a glass of water, and then he started up the stairs. "Since nothing urgent is happening just now, I'm hittin' the sack."

"How long will this last?" I asked Lexi after I tried and failed to lift my head another time.

"As long as I want it to." She paced around my still form. "You are unbelievable, you know that? I am so mad at you! How could you even think to leave and do this on your own?"

"So you agree that I am too incompetent to beat them alone?" I added snidely.

"Ugh!" Lexi grunted and threw her arms up in frustration. "I am so sick of your pity party, Selena. You already have more power than any witch I know. What will it take for you to believe in yourself?"

"We've talked about this before and I thought you had accepted it. Why are you doubting yourself again?" Tristan asked.

"I don't know," I blurted. "I just feel like whoever the prophecy is about needs to be spectacular, and after Crystal…" I held back a sob. "They broke me." I whispered.

"I get it," Genevieve spoke up. "You wanted to go after them alone to redeem yourself. If you could beat them without anyone's help, you could prove to yourself that you are strong enough to be the prophesied."

I hadn't thought about it that way.

"Can you please let me up now?" I asked Lexi. She

sighed and waved her hand over me. Immediately I felt lighter, and I sat up easily. "Thank you." Standing up I saw Genevieve turn to the stairs. Feeling defeated I headed that way too, hoping I could bury myself in the sheets and hide from embarrassment. I couldn't even pull off an escape.

"Wait," Tristan called after me, and I stopped short of the stairs. "What were you thinking?" He was trying to keep his voice down, but I knew he was mad.

Lexi cringed, "I guess that's my cue. See ya!" She ran upstairs behind Genevieve and away from the verbal lashing I was about to receive. She just left me. That ass.

I turned to face Tristan and my heart ached when I saw how hurt he was. "You could've gotten yourself killed! How could you be so selfish?"

"I was trying to be the opposite of selfish actually. I didn't want anyone to get hurt over me. That's all. I wanted to handle it myself."

"I understand that, but by leaving and potentially getting hurt or killed, you were being selfish. You weren't thinking about how your absence could affect others. How it could affect me."

I looked down at my feet. I hadn't thought about that either.

"I'm sorry. I just...I don't know, I didn't think. I'm sorry."

Tristan took a step toward me and lifted my face to look into my eyes. "Don't ever do that again. If anything happened to you..." He ran a hand through his hair, "Don't do that again." He spun on his heel and went up the stairs.

I paced the living room for a minute then headed outside for some fresh air. I stared at the stars above and asked for guidance. A moment later, I teleported to Crystal and Yuri's hideout in the woods.

I understood what my friends were telling me, but the thing was, this was something I had to do for myself. They could reassure me all they liked, but honestly, it didn't mean a thing until I could believe it. I landed a few yards away from the spot Lachlan's source had told us about. In the cover of darkness, I crept between the trees, hearing the crickets chirp and an owl hooting in the distance. It felt like I was walking for hours as my fear and anticipation grew, but really it was only minutes until I saw the light of a campfire flickering against the black backdrop of the night. I heard quiet conversations, whispering and grunting as I reached the area where the trees began to thin out.

At least twenty witches occupied the clearing, some sitting alone, others standing and talking in groups. The fire crackled, heating the area and cooked some unknown meat on a spit. The smell filled the air, reminding me of the time my parents took me camping one summer. This was much different than that happy, peaceful time.

I looked around at the group, a mixture of men and women, ages ranging from mid-teens to mid-forties. Two women were getting into a heated argument, their voices rising, but I couldn't make out the words. Suddenly sparks shot out of one of the witch's fingers at the other, who blocked it and cast her own electric spell at her foe. A fight broke out and some of the others stopped their conversations to watch.

I was completely outnumbered. What was I thinking coming here alone? Suddenly Lexi's and Tristan's chiding echoed uselessly in my mind.

Damn.

Okay, no problem, I would just teleport back, sneak into the house, and no one would know I ever left.

I backed away, slowly creeping back into the cover of the trees to teleport. I closed my eyes and pictured the cottage, envisioned being there, but before I could begin to teleport a strong hand grabbed the back of my neck, and I gasped just as another closed over my mouth. The smell of sweat and earth invaded my nose as I tried to squirm free. The hand lifted from my mouth as I was turned to face a large man, well over six feet tall and definitely on whatever the witch equivalent to steroids was. A jagged scar marred the right side of his face in a zigzagged trail that started at his forehead, traveled over his eye and onto his cheek.

"Look what we have here," he said in a fittingly deep voice. His face split into a grin that revealed several missing teeth. "Yuri," he yelled over my head. A chill coursed through my body. I didn't want to wait for Yuri to show up. I thought I was ready, but I was wrong. I couldn't face him or his nasty girlfriend. I tried again to teleport back to the cottage but nothing happened. This wasn't one of the scenarios I had planned for.

"I have a few gifts of my own," the huge man said, raising his scarred eyebrow. I tried willing his hand to burn and release me, but again nothing happened. He stood, still smiling at his accomplishment. So he could stop me from using magic. Great. But could he stop... I threw a punch at his face. He grunted in surprise, loosened his grip minimally but didn't let go. I heard footsteps approach and the witch turned me to face Yuri.

My stomach dropped and my mouth went dry. No, I wasn't ready for this. Stupid, stupid, stupid. Yuri tilted his head, his black, lifeless eyes assessing me. I refrained from whimpering.

Yuri raised his eyes to meet those of my capturer and nodded his head. I felt pressure on the back of my neck and everything went black.

15. HIDEOUT
-TRISTAN-

"Damn it, Tristan, wake up!" Lexi yelled in my ear and I jerked awake. "Selena's gone." She stood, wide-eyed and panicked.

"What do you mean?" I asked, throwing the covers off and reaching for my clothes.

"I mean she left. After all that talk, she up and left anyways. I think she went to Crystal and Yuri."

I let out an oath as I threw my clothes on.

"Wake the others and meet me in the living room." Lexi nodded and left. I grabbed my knives and ran down-stairs. A few moments later Lexi ran down with Lachlan and Genevieve.

"You've got to be kidding me," Genevieve said, tying her long hair back in a ponytail.

"Are we considering this the ambush?" Lexi asked as we ran through the front door.

"No, just a rescue mission," I answered angrily. How could she do this?

"What if she doesn't need to be rescued?" Lachlan asked. "What if she just went for a walk or somethin'?"

"You know she didn't," I said. "We will teleport outside the site and work our way in. If Selena's there, we'll find out. If we can take on however many witches there are, then fine, if not, we get Selena out and regroup. Clear?"

"Clear," Lexi answered.

"Okay," Genevieve said as Lachlan nodded his head.

"Good." I took Lachlan's hand and teleported him to the woods. The area seemed clear, no witches in sight. I teleported back with Genevieve and then Lexi. We spread out and crept through the trees as quietly as we could. We walked about a hundred feet before we spotted the campfire and the two dozen witches surrounding it.

"Damn," I whispered. There was excitement in the air as the witches gathered and talked to one another. I crept along the trees, the others on my heels as we tried to find a lone witch, anyone we could get some information from. It took everything I had to not rush in there, but after ten minutes that felt like an hour, I finally saw an opportunity. One of the witches finally stepped into the trees and began unbuckling his belt only a few feet from me. I shot a grateful glance at the heavens and I pulled my knife out. I motioned for the others to follow as I crept quietly behind the man who began to whistle. I quickly covered his mouth, and pulled him into the shadows, thankfully unseen. I dragged him deeper into the woods to where I hoped I wouldn't be heard.

"Where is she?" I snarled at the sniveling witch,

pressing the blade below his jaw.

"I-I don't know who-" he started.

"Don't play games with me." I grabbed the man's throat and squeezed. "Where is she?"

The man shook his head. I pocketed my knife, pulled back my fist and punched him in the jaw. The witch fell to the ground gasping.

"I don't know anything," he whimpered.

"The hell you don't." I grabbed him by the throat and lifted him a foot off the ground. The man choked and wheezed as his feet tried to find purchase.

"Okay," he coughed out and I loosened my grip marginally. "She's in the lodge."

"Take us." I dropped the man and cast a spell that would keep him attached to me, and silent so he couldn't scream for help – mentally or vocally. As he moved forward, I did as well. The others followed behind.

The witch led us deeper through the woods, farther into the darkness of the forest as the large trees blocked out the moon and stars.

Finally we saw the lodge; a wooden beamed one-story cabin with barred windows, and smoke streaming from a crumbling chimney. As we approached the lodge I released the man of the spell, not wanting him to get in my way. I knocked him unconscious and stepped over his body, ready to get Selena.

16. YAY OR NAY
-SELENA-

When I came to, I was tied to a chair in a dark room with the moon shining through one barred window as the only source of light. Yuri and Crystal stood in front of me, and I turned my head to see the humongo-witch standing behind me, hand still wrapped on my neck to make sure I didn't use any magic. If only I could get away from him, I could defend myself and maybe even end this now, but my binds were too tight as was the witch's grip.

"You're awake I see," Crystal said, walking toward me. "That's good; it's more fun that way." Her split-toothed grin spread across her face.

"Let me go," I said through clenched teeth.

"Really? You're going with that?" Crystal laughed. "Oh no, thanks to Matthew here," she gestured to the witch behind me - so he had a name, "I will get to enjoy myself so much more than I had planned. Darien will be here soon enough, but until he comes, I see no reason why I can't play."

It felt like my lungs collapsed. I could only take shaky,

shallow breaths through my nose as my fear grew tangible around me. Not again. No, I was supposed to come out on top and regain my confidence, not have it re-shattered.

"Too bad you're such a coward you need Brutus here to restrain me," I said, as I heard Matthew grumble at his nick-name. "Otherwise we could really have some fun. Untie me. I dare you." I forced myself to glare at Crystal without blinking. Her lip ring twitched as she strode closer to me.

"Here's my idea of fun." Crystal back-handed me across the face. "I'm sure you couldn't have forgotten in such a short period of time." She grinned like the Cheshire cat. I spun my head to face her again and spat in her direction.

"That all you got?" I said, surprised that I could pretend bravery so easily. Crystal's smile transformed into a snarl as she formed a fist and punched me in the jaw.

"You're lucky Darien is on his way or I would tear you apart again." Crystal scraped her nails under my chin and I jerked away. "Come to think of it, I don't see a scratch on you. How disappointing." She pouted. Yuri stood behind Crystal, silently observing. How was I going to get out of this one?

"I'm stronger than you think," I said evenly.

"That so?" Crystal pursed her lips. "Yuri, get Joe." She paced in front of my chair as Yuri obeyed. I tried not to think of who Joe was or why Crystal would want him. Instead I tried to think of ways to get out of the chair and Matthew's grip.

Squirming was useless and so was my magic. This couldn't be happening again. Yuri walked into the room with a young man trailing behind him. Joe, I presumed, was thin as a rail and mousy, walking in with his head down and his shoulders slouched.

"Drink," Crystal ordered him.

What?

Joe nodded and took one long stride to stand in front of me. He placed his hands on either side of my head to keep me still and pressed his wet lips to my forehead. Suddenly I felt all my energy drain out of me in a hot torrent from my feet and up though my head into Joe's lips. I gasped as he finally released me and slouched in my chair. Shivering and weak, I looked at Joe and saw him buckle over as light shone throughout his body. His back snapped straight, his arms shot out and then his body began to thicken and grow to challenge that of Matthew. He grew tall and strong and stood straight, hovering over my weakened form.

"Now that's better," Crystal said. "Darien will be so happy you dropped by," she said to me, "and all alone."

"Who said she was alone?" I slowly angled my head toward the door to see Tristan standing just outside of it, flanked by Genevieve, Lachlan and Lexi. My relief quickly turned to shame and then dread. They were going to be so pissed at me if we got out of this. I wasn't sure who I was more scared of just then.

"Great, here comes the rescue squad," Crystal snarled. "Bored now." She took Yuri's hand and ran through a hidden door I hadn't noticed before. Tristan started to pursue them, but ran right into Joe's large form. Tristan swung a punch into Joe's gut, but he barely flinched. Lachlan stepped next to Tristan, fireballs sparking from his fingers, as Genevieve and Lexi ran toward me. Matthew stood in front of me, barring their way. Genevieve hurled an icicle at Matthew, distracting him enough for Lexi to pass him.

"Are you alright?" She hissed as she untied the ropes. Thankfully they hadn't been infused with magic this time.

"Just... weak," I whispered. "Super Joe sucked the life out of me." I gestured to his large form with a nod of my head.

"Well, we'll just have to get it back." Lexi helped me to my feet and dragged me out of the room. I couldn't even muster the strength to try and cast a spell. I had nothing left. "Tristan, I got her. Come on!" Lexi yelled from outside the door.

"Coming," Tristan grunted as he took a hit from Joe. Lachlan's fireballs sizzled into nothing as Joe deflected each one while Genevieve was working to freeze Matthew in place. She pressed her palms together and ice shot forth, wrapping Matthew in a frozen cocoon. Lexi cast her sphere shield over Lachlan and Tristan, allowing them to catch their breath. I heard yelling and slamming of fists banging against the outside door. Lexi turned to the source of the noise and cursed.

"They're coming," she yelled as she pressed her shield outwards and into Joe, searing his flesh as it touched him.

Joe instinctively backed away, giving Tristan an opening. He charged and jumped onto Joe and twisted his neck sharply until I heard the sickening pop and Joe's limp body fell to the floor. As Joe lay motionless a few feet away from me, my energy drained from him, transforming his huge mass back into the thin, lanky body he walked in with.

"We have to go now," Tristan ordered, gathering the others. I saw the light of my energy flow toward me, crawling along the floor until it reached my feet and shot up through my body. The pain was intense, and for the second time that night everything went black.

"Selena, wake up!" An angry voice yelled in my ear. I cringed and reluctantly opened my eyes to see Lexi straighten and stand before me, placing her hands on her hips. I was lying on the couch in the cottage. The side lamps were on, so it was still night. "You crazy bitch," she said.

"Whoa," I mumbled. "That's uncalled for." I sat up and the room spun.

"Is it?" She yelled, as Tristan and Genevieve walked into the room. "After all we talked about, after your failed attempt to teleport out of here, you have the nerve to leave anyway? You were reckless and stupid and endangered not only yourself but us as well."

"Did I miss the lashing?" Lachlan asked as he walked into the room eating a sandwich. Lexi shot him a glare.

"We were just starting," Tristan said.

"Well maybe she found out some information?" Lachlan offered.

"They have at least twenty witches working for them," I said, hopeful to get off the hook.

"Yeah we saw that," Lexi snapped.

"Look I was just-"

"No, you look," Tristan said. "We were lucky we didn't get hurt, or killed fighting those mammoth witches. You did nothing tonight except tip Crystal and Yuri off that we knew about their hideout."

"I wanted-"

"Selena, enough," Genevieve said quietly, but her words held her authority. "You cannot do this. We are a team. We have to work together. You going on your own will show Crystal and Yuri and their followers that we are not united. That's all they'll need to beat us. Do you understand how much power you gave them tonight?"

Crap. I hadn't thought about that. I supposed that was the problem at hand though.

"I'm sorry," I whispered, looking down at my hands.

"We'll see," Lexi said. "You're sleeping on the couch tonight. I don't want you in my room." She walked toward the stairs. "And just so you know, I placed a spell so that if you so much as crack a window, I'll know about it." Her heavy footfalls stomped up the stairs followed by the slamming of her door.

"I'm going to bed too," Genevieve said, sounding tired. She headed upstairs with Lachlan following.

"Sorry, lass," he said, taking his sandwich upstairs

with him.

Tristan paced in front of me, opened his mouth to say something and then closed it. He looked me in the eye, shook his head and left me downstairs.

I pulled the throw blanket off the back of the couch and covered myself as I curled into a ball.

I really screwed up this time. I fell asleep with tears still wet on my cheeks, and then I had troubled dreams.

I saw the back of a man as he walked through an unfamiliar place, and then my perspective changed, as if I was seeing through his eyes. The metal door creaked on its hinges as the man swung it open. The dark tunnel that led to the stairs smelled of mold, and the dampness in the air was almost suffocating. His footsteps echoed in the confined space, and he sped up to get through this path faster. Finally reaching the stone stair way, he slowed. The stench wasn't as bad down there.

At the bottom of the three flights of steps, in the pit of the ground, was a hatch, one he had visited many times over the past twenty-six years. The lock clacked open, and he swung the hatch up. The dim glow from the lamp illuminated the opening. He slowly climbed down into the hole and found the rungs that trailed down one side. Reaching the ground, he followed the familiar path that lead to the familiar cell.

The old man was curled in the corner, the ragged clothes he wore, torn in various places. His hair had grown long and shaggy, as had his beard. He really was frail, a tiny little thing. The man stood outside the cell, the smell was ferocious.

"Oh, Artemis," he called, the voice sounded muffled in the haze of my dream. The old man's body tensed and he pushed himself farther against the wall. "Oh come now, I'm not going to hurt you, so long as you give me what I want."

"I have nothing for you," the old man rasped.

"I think you do. Tell me, where are they hiding the girl?"

"Don't you have seekers for that?" He retorted.

"My seekers have not been able to find her. Do you really think I would venture down here, that I would subject myself to your extraordinary stink if my seekers were able to find her? It seems that wherever she is has been hidden." He chuckled. "At least one of them must have some brains, because each of them has been hidden as well, individually. What do you think of that, old friend? Clever young things, hmm?" He paused, and when Artemis didn't respond, continued without mirth. "So I come to you. Tell me what I need to know," he said, stepping forward slowly to grip the cold iron bars, "and I won't have to come in there."

Artemis turned to face the man. His cheeks were sunken in, and his blue eyes were so light, they almost looked white, but they too were sunken. Age was finding this man fast.

"Friend?" He wheezed a laugh. "I won't help you anymore, so you might as well kill me."

The man clucked his tongue, "Now Artemis, that's no

way to behave. You know I won't kill you, but I will use those tools you enjoy so much until you tell me where the girl is," he yelled the last part and Artemis flinched.

Artemis stood and walked slowly toward the man. He stopped a few feet away and his body tensed. His eyes widened, and the color drained from his irises, turning them white.

In a strained voice he said, "Down the path into the old dark wood, follow the trail to the cabin that stood. One side trees, the other side not, you will find the one you sought." Artemis slouched and slowly dropped back to the floor.

"Thank you. I will make sure you receive a fine supper tonight." The man turned to leave, and the old man wheezed his laugh again. "Is there something else you want to share?" The man inquired.

"No, nothing at all, *friend*." He continued laughing. The man brushed off his madness and headed out of the hole, up the stone steps, through the stinking rotting tunnel and out into the fresh air. I was back in the cell with the old man, seemingly invisible.

"Ah, Selena, Selena, he comes for you," The old man said quietly to the stone walls around him. He watched a cockroach hobble by. "But you will know, oh yes you will. You will not be unprepared, I will see to it." He laughed his wheezing laugh. He picked the cockroach up, watching its legs move frantically, searching for ground, trying to flee. He bit off the head of the insect and chewed merrily. "A fine supper indeed." He laughed, and then he turned and looked right at me.

17. WARNING

I bolted up and almost fell off the couch. That was one of the weirdest dreams I ever had, even including Darien's. I felt like I had really been there, like I could smell the damp, stuffy cell and see each chip in the stone walls. It wasn't until I washed up that the dream faded to the back of my mind.

The rest of the morning was rough. Tristan hadn't spoken to me after his lecture last night, and I was feeling terrible and humiliated. No one brought it up at breakfast; everyone just acted normal, which made me feel worse.

"Listen, I want to apologize," I started, fidgeting with my fingers. "I really didn't mean to hurt or disrespect any of you, and I am really grateful that you all came to help me out. I'm sorry I put you in that position." The words tumbled in a torrent off my tongue before I could lose the nerve to say them.

"It's all good," Lachlan answered, throwing me a smile.

"No, it's not," Lexi said. "You screwed up."

"I did," I admitted.

"You almost got us killed," she threw back.

"Yes," I said. "And I'm sorry. I know I can't just say it, so I will try to make it up to you."

"Damn right," Lexi mumbled.

"I suppose there's nothing to be done for it now," Genevieve said on a sigh. Tristan stayed silent, not looking at me. I knew he was still mad at me, but he just needed time. Soon he would forgive me too. I hoped.

"So, what happened? How did you get past those witches?" I asked, nibbling on a muffin.

Lexi sighed. "Well, I came back downstairs, 'cause I noticed you hadn't gone to bed yet, and found the front door cracked open. Obviously we knew what you did, so Tristan teleported us one by one to the site." Lexi forked some eggs and chewed silently a moment. I tried waiting patiently but I shifted restlessly in my seat.

"Anyways," she continued the story and concluded with how Tristan teleported me unconscious to the house, and then went back for the rest of them.

"So, knowing how many witches there were gave us an edge, right?" I asked sheepishly. Lexi and Genevieve glared at me. "Too soon?"

"Selena," Tristan said, surprising me. "Let's go out back and do some training," he said in a monotone voice. "If you want to be tough and be able to take on witches by yourself, you need to practice more." He headed out to the back and I followed him. He was right; I needed to work harder, and something inside came to focus. I could be stronger, I could be better. I just had to try. He didn't go easy on me, and I was grateful. I suspected he was taking his anger out on me, and I welcomed it. Better his physical thrashing than a verbal one. Plus, I needed to be treated like everyone else, not special or weak.

He threw punches and I dodged them. He attacked and I blocked, I even landed a few punches and kicks of my own.

We sparred for over an hour, and by the time we came back in, we were both sweating. And Tristan was smiling.

"Why do you look so happy?" I asked him as we came inside the house. His smile faltered and then vanished altogether.

"I'm not happy. You just did really well. You didn't back down, you weren't scared, you didn't even flinch. What happened?"

"I don't know. I just didn't feel like holding back anymore. I wanted to be tough, so I was."

"See? All you needed was to believe in yourself. Imagine how much better you would be if you stopped doubting your true abilities." He chuckled, and then he looked at me, and his face became serious.

"I really am sorry," I said, touching his arm lightly.

He nodded, "I know."

After showering and changing, we joined the others in the living room. I was feeling upbeat and energized. A little sparring was just what I needed to start feeling tougher and even more productive. Genevieve finished unloading the latest batch of groceries in the kitchen and came to the living room.

I went to sit on the couch beside Lexi when the room swayed. I teetered a moment, and then everything came back into focus.

"You okay?" Tristan was watching me.

"Yeah, I just had a dizzy spell," I answered, sitting down. Lexi looked me over as well.

"You should drink something. You might be dehydrated." Tristan went to the kitchen and came back a moment later with a glass of cold water. I took the glass and gulped down the cool liquid.

"Thanks, that must have been it." I smiled, feeling refreshed.

"So the plan is still in place for tomorrow," Lexi started, getting everyone's attention. "Now that we know what we're up against we can be prepared. Operation Smack-Down is commencing."

"Smack-Down? Couldn't you think of something more original?" Tristan teased.

"Like what? Operation get the bad guys?" Lexi responded sarcastically.

Tristan shrugged.

"This isn't a joke, Lexi," Genevieve said. "These witches tortured Selena, and you saw what we were up against last night."

Lexi slouched. "You're right," she said in a somber tone.

"Will they still be there?" Lachlan asked, and everyone turned to look at me. I shrank in my seat.

"We don't know," Tristan said.

"I can teleport us to wherever they are," I offered.

"I guess," Lexi said. "Without knowing the details of how many people we will be up against now, or where we're going to end up, it gives them the upper hand." Again, everyone turned to look at me. I sighed, and Lexi continued. "So I guess there isn't a whole lot we can do to prepare, except to make sure we are all on our game.

"Practice your most effective spells. Lachlan you need to practice with fire, not just fireballs but every extension of the element. Tristan wind and focus on earth, you excel with that. Genevieve suffocation with water, and the freeze spell was really cool. Try to expand your offensive spells as well as blocks and shields. Focus on the abilities you specialize in, and center yourselves – we can't lose focus. Make sure you know what attacks you can and will do that will defeat the opponent."

"When you say defeat…" I said.

"Kill, Selena," Lexi answered, and I swallowed hard.

"Is there no other way?" I hated Crystal and Yuri, and I wanted them to suffer, but I couldn't imagine killing them.

"We could torture them for information," Tristan said, a spark in his eye. "Find out where Darien is."

"Or we can call the Charge," I said. "Tell them what we know about their hideout."

"What hideout?" Lachlan asked.

"I don't know," Lexi said. "If we fail and they escape,

they *will* come back for us. We have to kill them or it will never be over."

"You do realize Darien probably has like fifty other people working for him, right?" I countered. "Even if we kill Yuri and Crystal, there will be so many others coming after us."

"That's why we need to get to the source," Tristan said. "Let's go after Darien and stop him, and in doing so, stop his followers."

"You're right," Lexi told Tristan. "We know that Yuri and Crystal are after us right now. They are working for Darien and they won't stop until they get us. So, we need to deal with the immediate threat first, get information from them and then we go after Darien. It would be best not to get the Charge involved in this yet. They won't let us get the information we need, the way we need to get it. Not to mention the potential mole in their unit."

"Not to mention we don't have much to tell 'em," Lachlan threw in. I shot him a look and he smiled at me.

I looked at Lexi and saw her with fresh eyes. I was surprised to see her stepping up and taking charge like this, and I was proud. Lexi smiled at me, and her features became distorted. I blinked and shook my head, trying to right my vision, but everything swayed.

"What's wrong?" Tristan asked getting to his feet.

"I'm not sure," I answered. "I just can't seem to—"

Don't fight it. I heard an unfamiliar voice in my head. *Important.*

"What's important?" I asked.

"Huh?" I heard Lexi mumble. Tristan took my arm and turned me to face him, but my vision doubled.

He's coming, the voice said. *You must be ready.* I could no longer hear or see anyone around me. My vision faded into black and then, before my eyes I saw an image of the back of a man I didn't recognize, standing in a small room. The walls were completely white and bare, the one table bare as well save for the two chairs surrounding it. He spoke with someone, but I couldn't see who, just short, black, spikey hair.

"Find the cabin that's in the Old Wood and bring her to me. It would be better that you die there than to come back without her." The man said, his voice muffled.

"We'll take care of it." I heard a familiar female voice. Shivers ran up my spine as Crystal's face came into view.

"Take reinforcements. Failure is not an option," the man added. "Leave tonight."

The image faded into black. *He comes for you. You must fight,* the voice said.

"Selena?" My eyes came back into focus and I saw Tristan shaking me.

"They're coming," I gasped; it felt like the air had been sucked out of my lungs.

"Who?" Genevieve asked.

"Crystal and Yuri. They know where we are, and they're bringing back-up."

"That's impossible. I put a spell on this house; no one can find us." Lexi panicked.

"Well obviously they did," I answered. I stood up to

shake off the effects of… whatever it was that just happened.

"How do you know this? What happened?" Lachlan asked.

"Is she psychic?" Genevieve asked.

I paced in front of them. "I have no idea. One second I was fine, the next second I heard some voice telling me that he's coming, and I saw some man tell Crystal to come to the cabin in the old wood with reinforcements. Tonight."

"How's that possible?" Lachlan spoke up.

"I'm not sure," Genevieve answered. "If she were psychic she would just have the vision, no voices usually. Then again, Selena is a special case."

"No, I felt like someone was sending me a warning. I'm pretty sure it wasn't me."

"How do we know this vision can be trusted?" Lexi asked.

"We can't afford the risk of ignoring it. It felt too real," I commented.

"But who could do that?" Lexi asked.

"Never mind," I stormed. "They're coming for me tonight. We need to be prepared. Lexi, reinforce all the seals on the house. If they feel what I felt last night, they won't get very far. Lachlan, I want you to stand guard at the back of the house, and those who don't teleport into Lexi's security, you can take out. Genevieve you will cover the front. Is there an attic or any other way someone might be able to get in?"

"There is an attic, but the only way in is through the

stairs inside the house. There is no outside access." Genevieve answered.

"All right," I continued. "Tristan and Lexi, you cover the upstairs floor. And remember, try to keep them alive."

"And where will you be?" Tristan asked.

"Once I know where they're coming from, I will go there. Until then, I'll be right here. Waiting." I paced viciously in the center of the room.

"And she doesn't think she has strong character?" I heard Lachlan whisper to Tristan who chuckled and shrugged. I smiled in spite of myself. Then my smile vanished when I realized that I would be seeing Crystal and Yuri in the very near future. My stomach flipped, and I started to sweat.

"Breathe, Selena," Tristan said.

"Huh?" My heart was racing.

"Breathe," Tristan said. "You will be fine. We're all here and we won't let them get anywhere near you. Actually, I think it would be better if I stayed with you here."

I shook my head, "You need to cover the top floor. I'm surrounded with protection here, and I should be able to take care of myself with my magic," I answered.

"Selena, it would make more sense if we all stayed together," Tristan argued. "There aren't many of us. One person guarding a side of the house could be dangerous."

"Fine," I huffed. So much for my leadership skills.

"What do we do until tonight?" Lexi asked. I was tempted to say 'try not to lose our freaking minds!' but I held back.

"Rest, eat and make sure we're ready and energized," Tristan said. "Also we can practice our magic like you suggested, Lex." Tristan answered. That plan sounded much better than what I had in mind.

"Selena," Lexi said. "Maybe we should try to teach you to manifest the elements to better protect yourself."

Right, we were supposed to do that before my apartment got demolished.

"Sure," I said eagerly, needing the distraction. "I guess it was a good thing we took out Super Joe, huh? One less witch to worry about." I received blank stares. "Still too soon?" I shrugged.

Even with that new power to learn, the next few hours were the longest hours of my life.

18. AMBUSH

Night came eventually and we stayed close together in the living room. All we could do was wait and hope that this wasn't some kind of trick.

I paced. I knew they would be coming soon. They had to be. There was no way I imagined what I saw. We had been waiting for hours, trying to always be alert and on guard. I didn't know who sent me the warning or why, but I was damned if I would give up the opportunity to protect myself and my friends.

I had long since finished practicing elemental magic and felt comfortable enough to use it if the situation called for it.

It was just past midnight when it happened; it was completely still and quiet, until the windows shattered throughout the entire house and the alarms went off, sending my adrenaline pumping. This was it, the moment we'd been waiting for.

Witches were everywhere, covered in black, climbing through the windows and breaking down the doors. They wore ski masks and were indistinguishable from each other.

Two witches, covered from head to toe in black, fell to the floor dazed, having collided with Lexi's protective spell.

"There's our teleports," she said as she flung one of the other witches away with a wind spell.

Three other witches crashed in through the windows in front of Lexi, but she was already crouched, ready to spring. Lexi crossed her arms over her chest, and as she spread them open, a jolt escaped her arms sending two of the men flying into the front wall.

Genevieve quickly swirled her fingers in the air. A globe of water materialized and grew larger creating a barrier between her and her attacker. Pushing with her mind, the water enveloped the man and suspended him in the air, where Genevieve left him to drown. Another two witches leapt through the window, but before they had a chance to gain their bearings Lexi landed a punch on one of them before shooting electric sparks from her fingers, zapping him unconscious. Genevieve swept her hand and the other man flew against the wall, landing on the floor.

A few witches ran down the stairs from the top floor while four intruders covered in black broke down the back door, shattering it into tiny fragments of wood. Tristan let out a war cry as he charged the first person. Pushing his magic aside, he punched the man square in the face, knocking him unconscious.

I raised my arms above my head summoning air to me, and was relieved when it obeyed. I commanded a fierce wind that started to swirl fiercely around me, whisking up the debris and glass from the floor. The wind spun, raising my hair and I pushed out with my mind, and ten witches were thrown away from my friends. My group gathered to me and stood back to back in a circle.

An endless stream of witches poured through every broken window or open door, like cockroaches running out of holes in the wall.

"Selena, you have to try to kill or incapacitate them, not just push them away. They will keep coming!" Lexi shouted over the alarm, and then she decided to finally silence it. I thought about Lexi's advice, but I hated the idea of killing anyone.

"What about Crystal and Yuri? I can't tell where they are!"

"That doesn't matter anymore. There are too many of them."

"I can't do it," I yelled, flinging two witches away.

"You have to," Lexi yelled back, stopping a charging witch by casting an electric shock spell. He jerked as the current shot through his body, and fell to the ground dead, smoke curling from his scorched outfit.

Lachlan snickered as he threw a fire ball at two of the intruders, setting them ablaze. They screamed and ran outside through the broken door. One flailed his arms, swinging wildly at the flames, the other dropped to the ground rolling, trying to put out his enflamed body.

Lexi was right; they kept coming, and they were getting closer. I had to do my part.

I focused all my energy, gathering all my power into a ball that grew larger and larger inside of me.

Until it exploded.

I heard screams and saw the witch's bodies burn. Their flesh bubbled and seared from the inside out, turning to ash before my eyes. Then, just as suddenly, it was deathly quiet. I looked around and saw my group still standing in a circle, and all around us, the ashes of those I had killed, drifting like snow to settle in our hair and on our clothes. The smell of burnt flesh reminded me of cooked meat, tainting the air and permeating my senses.

I couldn't breathe. I tried, gasping, but it was like my lungs were completely deflated and wouldn't allow any air in.

"Selena, it's okay." Tristan held my shoulders. "Breathe, Selena," he said. "Relax and breathe. It's over."

Finally I took a shaky breath, and then another, but all I could manage were quick, shallow breaths. My head swam, and I felt my knees buckle.

I fell to the floor. I killed all those people. I imagined them rushing home to their families and picking up their kids after completing a job they hated, just to pay the bills.

"You did what you had to do," Lexi said, as if she could read my thoughts. She knelt in front of me. I still couldn't believe it.

"Look at her aura," I heard Lachlan whisper to Genevieve, both staring at me wide-eyed. Who cares?

The silence didn't last long though. There were people shuffling outside, and whispering.

I rose to my feet, realizing that I didn't have the time or luxury to wallow. I focused on the noise around me. I signaled for Tristan and Lexi to peek outside and see how many people were out there. I felt like a sergeant in charge of my troops.

They crept to the windows, keeping their bodies pressed up against the walls and out of sight. Lexi squinted outside, then turned to me raising four fingers. Tristan, on the opposite side of the house, raised five fingers.

Damn, we were still very outnumbered.

Tristan and Lexi gathered around me, spells sparking from their fingers as they waited for the next round to begin.

The witches crept through the broken doors, trying to be quiet, but we were ready for them.

Lexi threw her shock spell at two witches, zapping them and sending them twitching to the floor. Tristan raised the earth from the ground outside and the rocks shot through the windows, pelting three of the witches.

Genevieve forced a strong wind to fling one intruder away and through the wall, while Lachlan physically picked up another and threw him through the wall. He spun quickly, grabbing the neck of another witch and snapping it. I stared, transfixed until a witch approached me. He was over six feet tall and huge.

Matthew

He seemed to be studying me, trying to figure out a way to incapacitate me, but he wasn't out to kill me. I had to make sure he didn't touch me this time.

The witches Tristan and Genevieve had fought regained their composure and retaliated with their own spells; wind and fire spread around us. We were now evenly numbered, and each had our own witch to... defeat.

I backed away from my attacker, hoping to give myself time to think. I didn't want to kill him either. I tried to create a water barrier, but all I managed to do was create a puddle that I nearly slipped on. I tried to create a fire ball to throw at him, but nothing came. I wasn't sure why my powers weren't cooperating, and I panicked. It wasn't Matthew; he had to touch me to block my powers. I had to resort back to basics.

As he charged at me I punched him in the stomach, and he buckled over. I grabbed his head and thrust my knee into his face. He staggered back, and I looked to my friends who were still engaged in their own fights.

Like me, Lachlan had resorted to hand-to-hand combat. Lexi created a sphere shield, pressed it against the intruder, and disintegrated her. Genevieve cast a spell I couldn't see, and her attacker fell to the ground motionless. Before I could look at Tristan, the huge witch tackled me to the ground and elbowed me in the face.

I blacked out for a split second, and when I came to, Tristan had thrown Matthew off me, grabbing him by the back of his collar. Tristan spun him around and elbowed him in the face... clearly tit for tat. Then he cast a spell I couldn't see, which I assumed was the same spell Genevieve cast moments before, because Matthew fell to the ground in a heap of black.

Lexi helped me to my feet.

"Are there any more?" I heard Genevieve whisper. We all stood silently, trying to listen for any sign that there were others, but only silence followed. Slowly we broke our circle and started searching the house. Lachlan and Tristan checked the grounds outside, while the rest of us checked the interior.

After a few minutes, we regrouped in the living room and confirmed that we were alone once more.

"What a mess," Genevieve said, shaking her head slowly as she took in what was once her home.

"Lexi, can you fix some of this?" I asked. She nodded her head and started the repair process.

"I'll take care of the bodies," Lachlan offered, fire already springing from his hands. I had to look away as he left to cremate the rest of the corpses.

"A lot of this wasn't magic, so I can't fix it all," Lexi said after she attempted to repair some of the damage. The ashes of the bodies were now gone thanks to a wind spell Lexi cast and some of the holes had been repaired, but it was nowhere near perfect. There was broken glass and plaster everywhere, huge holes in the walls, broken pictures and knick-knacks scattered across the floor.

"We can't stay here. We need a place that's in one piece where we can be safe," Tristan said as he studied the remains of the house. Everyone nodded in agreement. I headed toward the stairs.

"Where are you going?" Lexi asked.

"I just want to check something. I'll be back in a

minute." I hurried up the stairs before anyone could follow me. I wanted to try something without the others watching, just in case. The top floor also had broken glass everywhere and cracks in the walls. I closed my eyes and concentrated on mending the windows.

I imagined all the pieces coming together and sealing off as one pane of glass. I heard glass shifting on the floor, scraping quietly as it pulled itself together. I opened my eyes and saw the tiny shards re-attaching themselves in the window frame. In a flash it was all back together. I let out a triumphant breath, glad that my powers were cooperating this time, and I started working on the walls. Slowly it was all mended, and the entire top floor looked like it had never been touched.

I swallowed hard and nodded before deciding to go downstairs to mend the rest of the house. I turned and saw Lexi standing at the top of the stairs.

"Whoa," she said, taking in the area I had just repaired.

"I know," I answered awkwardly. I hadn't wanted anyone witnessing that, but I guess it didn't matter since I was about to fix the downstairs in front of everyone.

"I can distract them if you want," Lexi offered, as if reading my thoughts. Then again, maybe she had.

"That would be great actually."

Lexi nodded, took one more look around and headed down the stairs. "Guys, can we check the outside of the house one more time? Girls check one side, boys the other? I'm feeling uneasy. Could there be another group coming?"

I heard her tell everyone downstairs. I heard their muffled responses and waited until they had all gone outside.

I made sure to hurry so that I could work before they came back inside. I ran down the stairs and into the living room where I could see the extent of the damage throughout the whole house.

Again I imagined the glass and walls repairing themselves and I watched as all the little specs of glass and debris shifted and came together into one solid piece of glass. The walls mended themselves, the knick-knack shards rose, attached, and righted themselves on the tables. It was amazing to see everything back together, and I had to stop myself from laughing out loud.

I heard shuffling as everyone approached the front door. I wanted to hide, to be honest. I didn't want everyone knowing I fixed the house, even if they didn't see me do it, but I just couldn't get away in time.

Genevieve stopped short as she reached the front door, her eyes widened in amazement as she took it all in. The others came in behind her and looked around.

Then everyone looked at me. I froze. Genevieve rushed toward me and threw her arms around me.

"Thank you!" She exclaimed happily.

"No problem?" I answered, though it sounded more like a question. The others started chattering as they looked around. I was starting to feel uncomfortable, and wished I could disappear.

"Selena?" Tristan asked panicked.

"Yeah?" I answered in a question, scanning the room

for the source of his panic. Why was he acting so weird?

"No way," Lexi chirped. I looked around trying to see what had her so excited, but I couldn't see anything.

"Unbelievable. Do you know anyone else who can do that?" Genevieve asked the others.

"Guys, really it's no big deal. I just cleaned the room." Now I was feeling really, really, uncomfortable.

"No, Selena, it's not that," Lexi started. "Look at your hands."

I lifted my hands up to my face and saw... nothing.

There was nothing there.

I started to panic, "Oh my God! Where are my hands? What happened?" I was borderline hyperventilating. The others didn't seem concerned though, and that was confusing the hell out of me.

"Selena, calm down. You're invisible," Tristan said as calmly as possible. It didn't help.

"I'm WHAT?" I yelled. I ran to the bathroom to see my reflection. I didn't have one. Even my clothes were invisible. "How do I fix it?" My heart was beating in my throat from fear.

"Probably the same way you did it in the first place," Lexi answered as she came into the bathroom.

"I don't know how. I just thought it."

"So think that you want to be visible. And mean it."

"Oh, I mean it, believe me." I willed myself into being and in the mirror I saw myself materialize. I let out a long sigh of relief.

"That is so cool!" Lexi said excitedly. I shook my

head, and after a moment of gathering myself, headed back into the living room.

The rest of the group was looking at me. Tristan walked to me and placed his hand on my waist. "It's nice to see you again." He smiled, and my heart picked up a beat until he quickly moved his hand away. Ugh, here we go.

The others laughed; some sincerely, others nervously. It felt like they were scared of me. I couldn't blame them, I was scared of me. I had no idea what I was capable of, or what could happen just with my thoughts. It was very dangerous.

"What happened to Yuri and Crystal?" I asked, trying to change the subject from my new abilities. The others seemed grateful for the change.

"What do you mean?" Lexi asked.

"I didn't see them. I know they were sent here, but I couldn't tell where they were. Did they get away or were they... incinerated?" I asked.

"There's no way to know for sure," Tristan said. I nodded, knowing he was right, but I wished I could have gotten some kind of confirmation one way or the other.

"Darien knows where we are now, as well as Yuri and Crystal if they're still out there. We should probably still move somewhere else," Lexi said.

"He found us here; he will find us wherever we go," Tristan answered. "But he knows now that we can defend ourselves. I'm sure he'll think twice before he sends another group. And if he does, or Crystal and Yuri show up, we'll deal with it again."

"It'll be fine. Don't worry." Genevieve smiled at me. "Now I think everyone should get some rest. It's very late."

"I'm going to reseal the house and set the alarms." Lexi said, already getting to work. I practically ran upstairs and into bed. Adrenaline was the only thing fueling me, but more importantly, I wanted an excuse to get away from everyone's staring.

"That was really cool what you did," Tristan said, following me into the room.

"Which part? Cleaning the house, going invisible or killing dozens of witches?" I asked sarcastically.

"All of it actually. Don't feel bad. I know it's easier said than done, but you did what you had to do. You saved us all," he said. I tried to take comfort in that, but I was still unnerved. I was a murderer. Even my thoughts were weapons. I could sugar coat it all I wanted, but I killed people tonight. My stomach flipped uneasily.

"Maybe we should leave. I mean why stay here now that they know where we are? Let's go back home."

Tristan looked at me and studied my face. "We can't, Selena. We have to finish this. You know that. If we run, we will always be running."

I knew he was right, but I was hoping that somehow he would just tell me to grab my things and go back to my place.

"When I tried to cast a water and fire spell at that witch, it didn't work. Do you know why?" I asked, worried about the unreliability of my powers.

"I can guess," he started. "When you used that first

spell to ki— burn the witches, you used a lot of energy. I think you were just drained."

"But I was able to fix the house after, how did I have enough strength for that?"

"Elemental magic requires a lot of power to control, other spells don't. I'm sure you'll be able to cast those spells tomorrow, after you've rested."

I nodded and pulled the covers up. Tristan opened his mouth to say something, but left the room instead.

It took a while for me to get over my conscience and my uneasiness and allow myself to relax, but I finally managed. And the sleep was surprisingly blissful.

The dream I had was strange though.

A man stood with his back to me, facing Darien.

"What do you mean? There was no way they could have been prepared. Where is Crystal?" Darien yelled, but his voice in my dream state was muffled.

"I-I don't know," a witch beside them said, shaking in fear, "there was too much going on, it's hard to say if they made it out alive or not."

"Find them and bring them to me. If they aren't dead already, they will be," Darien ordered. The witch nodded and ran out.

"How did they know?" The man asked.

"It's impossible."

The man shrugged. "We'll get them eventually. We just need to be patient and smart."

"Yuri and Crystal better be dead," Darien said.

"You know, even if they're alive, none of the other

witches will be strong enough to bring them back to you," the man said.

"I know, but it makes me feel better to threaten them, and it doesn't hurt to try."

"How could they beat so many men?"

"Selena," Darien answered.

The man flipped the table over and stormed off in a rage.

Far away, through the dark, damp tunnel, down the three flights of stone steps, down the hole in the ground, in the cell that had been locked for twenty-six years, an old man laughed his wheezing laugh.

I woke up feeling un-rested and confused. I looked over at the clock on my cell and saw it was still the middle of the night. I rolled over, threw my pillow over my head and fell back asleep, immediately forgetting the dream.

19. MY LIFE IN RUINS

"Selena," a voice whispered by my ear. I groaned and swiped my hand at the air beside my head to clear the noise.

"Selena, wake up."

I woke up to see Tristan's green eyes gleaming right in front of me. He was kneeling beside my bed, a mug of coffee in one hand, the other gently shaking me.

"Is something wrong?" I asked, turning to sit up.

"No," he whispered, a ghost of a smile on his lips. "I just wanted to show you something. Come on, get dressed." He placed the coffee on the night stand and left the room. The smell wafted toward me, bringing my senses to high alert. I washed up quickly, not wanting my coffee to get cold, but I couldn't drink it until my teeth were brushed.

I got dressed and took my mug downstairs where Tristan sat in the living room with his own coffee in hand.

"What's up?" I asked, looking around to see what Tristan wanted to show me.

Everyone else was still asleep, and I could feel that it

was much earlier than I usually woke up.

"Finish your coffee," he said.

"Okay," I said, drawing the syllables out in exasperation. I sat on the couch and practically gulped my now cool coffee. After emptying the mug's contents in four swigs, I made a show of putting it down. "Ok, what is it?"

Tristan chuckled, "You're very impatient."

"Yeah," I quickly agreed, almost bouncing in my seat. I didn't have the slightest idea what Tristan was up to, but I could sense it was something even he was excited about. I felt like a kid on Christmas, knowing I was going to get something, but not knowing what. The anticipation killed me.

"Grab a coat," he said as he stood and headed toward the door. I rushed to Genevieve's coat closet and grabbed a sweater I hoped she wouldn't miss. It was a soft, beige cashmere coat with wooden toggles that latched down the middle. It complemented my boot-cut jeans and blue blouse. Looking at Tristan I saw that he only wore jeans and a black t-shirt.

"Won't you be cold?" I asked.

"Nah," he answered.

"Okay, where are we going?" I asked as we walked out of the house. "And should we tell the others we're leaving?"

"Don't worry, it's taken care of."

"Okay," I repeated yet again.

We walked outside and were greeted by the rising sun. The air was cool and refreshing and I inhaled a deep breath, letting its freshness fill my lungs.

"Where are we going?" I asked again.

Tristan smiled and extended his hand. "Let me show you."

I took his hand and we teleported, invisible forces pushing and pulling and twisting us until our feet hit ground.

When I was able to focus on the scenery around me, I let out a small gasp. Tristan looked at me, studying my reaction. Blue skies stretched above us as the rising sun reached its peak. We were on top of a hill, the valley below us undisturbed greenery, an expanse of land that seemed to have been untainted by man.

Trees lined the clearing in front of us, which held the broken remains of what once must have been a beautiful architectural structure. It looked like it could have been a castle at one point, or even something from Mayan times, but it was hard to know for sure what it used to be.

Before me now was a jumble of broken stones and half erected pillars, like a jigsaw puzzle without all the pieces. Between the large stone remains, grass grew in sporadic clumps claiming this unclaimed territory. A stone wall with numerous archways stood, though it was not complete; both ends were crumbling and vines grew up and around the stone. In the center of the remains, there was a circular piece of stone that could have been a beautiful marble in its day. It sat covered in dirt, and in the center of the floor, the stone was shattered where a large, blue tree grew from its core. The trunk was a sapphire blue, and its turquoise branches reached for the heavens with leafless arms.

Only yards away and running parallel to the broken shards was a beautiful waterfall complete with sparkling, rushing water and a rainbow.

It was breathtaking, and heartbreaking.

"I thought this might take your mind off things," Tristan said, breaking my serene trance.

"Where are we?" I asked in a whisper.

"Aracali Ruins," Tristan said just as quietly.

I took a tentative step forward and a squirrel darted out from behind one of the stones and scurried up a tree.

"It used to be a palace, made up of the rarest stone, a stone only witches could get. It's an interesting story. Would you like to hear it?" Tristan asked, taking in the view.

"I really would," I answered. Tristan smiled and ushered me to a protruding piece of stone that we used as a bench. I felt the cold of the stone seep through my jeans and into my skin. I pulled Genevieve's sweater tighter around me. Then I felt the stone heat beneath me, thriving off my energy and I felt connected to it, as if we were one.

Tristan took a deep breath before beginning. "The stone was formed by many witches thousands of years ago. It was built to sustain a witch's life, keeping them ageless and free of illnesses. When it was intact, it would shine an iridescent rainbow of colors. As the witches lived off the stone, the stone too lived off them, reusing and regenerating their energy and preventing them from aging.

"Many witch tribes heard of this stone and wanted it for themselves or their societies, and many wars were fought over it. The people of Aracali always prevailed, keeping their palace safe. There weren't many witches living here, so they were all able to live comfortably in the palace. Although they had crops and livestock protected within its walls, the stone would not have been enough to sustain a large town or city, and other witches failed to acknowledge that.

"The princess of Aracali, Larissa, was a beautiful woman with red hair and green eyes. She was said to be a kind and fair woman. One day Larissa was in the forest collecting herbs for a spell, when a large braktus attacked her."

"A what?" I interrupted.

"Oh, sorry, I forgot you didn't grow up in the Hidden City," Tristan said. Again with the Hidden City, I was extremely curious to know what this place was. "A braktus is a... well, let's call it a dog for lack of a better word, with three heads, six legs and two tails."

"Ew, that's disturbing."

"It is. So she was attacked by a braktus, and she tried to fend him off, but she couldn't. She screamed as the braktus opened its maw."

"Did she die?" I asked.

Tristan chuckled. "Selena, if you'd stop interrupting, you'd find out."

"Fine, sorry," I mumbled.

"Anyways," Tristan continued, smiling. "As the

braktus opened one of its mouths to eat her, a man charged out of the forest and cast a spell that killed the beast."

"Why didn't Larissa cast the spell herself?" I asked.

Tristan sighed. "When this happened, thousands of years ago, they believed that royalty should never have to use their magic. They were taught to perform rituals and certain spells, but not much else."

"So this hero guy was… lower class then?" I asked.

"Exactly. Now obviously Larissa was smitten with her hero-"

"Why is that obvious?"

"Selena, do you want to hear the story or not?" Tristan huffed, and I repressed a laugh.

"Okay, sorry, sorry."

"And don't try to tell me you don't like a hero," he threw in, eyeing me, before he continued with the story. "So she was attracted to this man who introduced himself as Teague from the town of Portola. Since he was lower class as you called it, they couldn't be together, so they would meet in secret during the night. They married in secret as well, and that night Larissa snuck Teague into her chambers in the palace. They made love and fell asleep in each other's arms. However, when Larissa woke, Teague was not by her side. She searched everywhere for him but couldn't find him.

"Then she heard yelling and fighting and felt the remnants of magic. She rushed to the entrance of the palace and found Teague lying in a pool of blood on the floor. She screamed and rushed to his side, but he was already dead.

"Larissa looked up and saw her father standing above her dead husband.

"'I found him lurking about as the Portola army invaded. He snuck them in,' her father said, unknowing why his daughter reacted in such a strong way. Larissa couldn't believe it. Her father left to gather his own army to defend their home while Larissa knelt over Teague, tears streaming down her face and the war broke loose.

"Larissa refused to believe that Teague would betray her and her city. When she finally rose, the army had made its way through the palace walls and was slaughtering her people. She took it all in, Teague's blood soaking her hands and her nightgown, her people's screams and bodies all around her, and the Portola coming to kill her and end the Aracali bloodline. She took her own life, falling on her lover's sword. Witches from Aracali fought against those trying to take their livelihood. The war raged for five days, and the battle proved too much for the town of Aracali and the stone walls that preserved it. The small palace crumbled under the strength of the Portola, leaving rivers of blood in the wake of the destruction.

"It's said that Larissa's and Teague's spirits reunited in death and merged into that tree." Tristan pointed to the blue oak in the center of the ruins. "Teague, the trunk, stable, strong and sure, and Larissa, the branches, reaching out to those around her, providing hope. Once a year, for one day only, that tree blooms white flowers. Those flowers bloom and wilt, always on the day that Aracali was destroyed."

"So Teague was a traitor?" I asked.

"No one knows for sure."

I thought about it for a moment, "Wow, that is a cool story."

He nodded. "My mom used to tell me that story when I was a kid. She even brought me and-" Tristan paused, "brought me here once."

"Your mom must have been awesome." I tried to picture Tristan as a small boy, but I couldn't manage it.

Tristan smiled tightly.

"Can we visit Portola or the other tribal towns?" I asked, sensing Tristan didn't want to talk about his personal life.

"The tribal towns are all ruins. As human civilization spread, all of the great tribes that hadn't been killed off by endless warring either assimilated into human society or settled in the Hidden City. The only way we can live peacefully with humans is if they think we are humans."

"That's sad," I said, "But it makes sense I guess. How can this place still exist after all this time?"

"There's still magic here. I'm sure you can feel it." I could. The stone felt alive beneath me. "It preserves this place."

"Why couldn't the other witches make their own stone?"

"It required a very strong, very specific type of magic that only the Elders of Aracali possessed. It was passed down through the bloodlines, but very few had the gift. It died with the Elders."

"Is it true? About the spirit tree?" I asked, staring at the mystical blue branches.

"What do you think?" Tristan countered.

"I think anything is possible." I looked at Tristan, and he smiled.

"Me too."

"How long were we gone for?" I asked Tristan as we landed outside of the half-way house. The sun was long gone, the stars shining brightly in its place. I could have sworn we were only gone for an hour or two.

"Time passes a little differently there…I think it's because there is still some remnants of magic infused in those stones. It seems to stop or at least slow time, but no one knows why."

"Oh," I said. "Thanks for taking me."

"I'm glad you liked it." Tristan reached for my hand, but stopped as he spun his head quickly to the area behind me. I turned to see what had gotten his attention.

"What?" I asked, after a moment.

Tristan shook his head, "Just seeing shadows. Come on." He led me inside the house where the others had just finished dinner and were cleaning up.

"Did you two have a nice time?" Lexi sing-songed.

Tristan huffed.

"Yeah, it was really cool," I said. "Have you ever been there?"

"No," Lexi answered for everyone. "It's almost imp-ossible to get there without teleporting and *someone*," Lexi dragged the word out, "won't take me."

"I told you I'd take you another time," Tristan said. "Selena really needed to get her mind off things."

"Yeah, yeah, yeah, Selena, Selena, Selena," Lexi whined, but she shot me a smile.

"I have actually been there before," Genevieve said, giving Lexi a 'don't speak for me' look.

"Isn't it just so…" I searched for the right word.

"Tragic?" Genevieve supplied.

"Yes, but I was also thinking more spiritual," I sighed feeling very content.

Tristan and I sat at the table, and Genevieve reopened the containers of chicken and vegetables for us. "Hey," she said as Tristan and I filled our plates, "Lexi told me about that psychic in Sedona."

"Yeah, that was weird. Her words still creep me out," I said.

"Well I was wondering if I could see the hematite." She asked.

"Sure," I said, walking to my purse and finding the magnetic stone. I handed it to Genevieve. "Lexi said it wasn't infused with anything."

"That psychic was right though," Lexi said. "She told you pain was in your future and you got… tortured right after that."

I cringed, "I guess she knew what she was talking about."

"Let me see." Genevieve closed her eyes, and didn't speak for several moments. I looked at Tristan, Lexi and

Lachlan who all watched Genevieve. Finally she spoke up. "It's not infused with a purpose, but there is a spell on it."

"What spell?" Lexi and I asked in unison.

"It's a spell that wards off negativity," Genevieve said.

"Yeah, that's what the psychic told us too," I confirmed.

"It doesn't repel negative people," Genevieve explained. "It repels negative thoughts. It may have been helping you deal with all of this, helping you stay positive so you can be strong and get through it, and maybe even help you deal with the aftereffects of the trauma you've endured."

"I'm not so sure about that," I said. "I mean I did feel negative when I went after Crystal and Yuri on my own – it was my self-pity thinking that got me caught in Lexi's spell, remember?"

"That may be," Genevieve said, "but I am quite certain that things would have been much worse had you not kept this."

"Huh, well next time I go to Sedona I'll be sure to thank that lady." Genevieve handed me the stone, and I placed it back in my purse. I had no idea if it worked, but it wouldn't hurt to keep my thoughts more positive. Tristan and I ate quietly and cleaned after ourselves.

Suddenly I felt as if time had finally caught up with me. I yawned, exhausted, and hauled myself up to bed with a mumbled "Good night." It was the shortest day of my life.

20. REVENGE IS A DISH
BEST SERVED COLD

"I'm going home," I said. "I need more clothes, and I miss my bed."

"You're apartment is uninhabitable," Tristan said.

"I can make it… habitable." I wiggled my fingers and smiled.

"I hope you're not leaving because you're uncomfortable here," Genevieve said, concern coloring her tone.

"Oh, no, it's not that. I just really miss my place," I said. Genevieve looked sad anyway.

"I don't blame her," Lachlan answered.

Won't you even stay until your friends are out of danger? I heard a voice say inside my head.

I shook my head to clear it.

Listen to me! The voice hissed.

"Who..?" I asked, panic creeping within me.

I have warned you before; you must heed my warning now.

"Danger?" I asked, and Tristan sat up straight.

From those you thought were a threat no more.

"Crystal and Yuri?" I asked, body tense with anticipation.

"Well, it's been a few days," Lexi said, oblivious to the voice inside my head. "I'm assuming they died with the others."

"No," I shook my head at Lexi. "Not you."

They are not dead; they have been watching you.

"Who are you talking to, Selena?" Lexi asked.

"What?" I asked the voice, but Lexi thought I was talking to her.

"Who are you talking to?" She repeated.

"Shh," I hissed at Lexi. I could feel the others staring at me in confusion. "They're not-" I started.

No, they are not dead. They've even been spotted by your protector.

Then it dawned on me. Yesterday when Tristan thought he saw something. My stomach dropped and my heart rate raced. They had gotten so close to us.

"Where?" I whispered.

They aren't here at present, but they remain close. They are watching and preparing for the moment you will be vulnerable. Only your strength in numbers is keeping them at bay.

"What do we do?" I asked.

You must hunt them. Then you can defeat them on your own terms. You will find them in the woods, two miles to the northeast tonight at sunset. I believe that would be the ideal time to kill them.

Bile rose in the back of my throat. They weren't dead, but they would be.

"This could be a trick," Genevieve said.

"It could," I conceded, "but I recognized his voice. Whoever this is warned us they were coming in the first place. I think we need to trust him again."

"I want to kill them with my bare hands," Tristan snarled as he paced the living room. I was surprised he was willing to believe the message so easily when the others had been doubtful.

"I can agree with that," Lachlan said.

"So, how do we do this?" I asked, watching Tristan as he walked back and forth.

"We surround them," Tristan said. "We come at them from all around and close in on them. When we get close enough, we jump them, tie them up, drag them back here and take care of them. We should lay out some kind of tarp, so we don't get blood on Genevieve's floor."

I hated to admit it, but he was scaring me. He was so angry it was almost tangible.

I wanted them hurt, so part of me shared Tristan's rage, but the other part was queasy at the idea of killing two more people – no matter how bad they were.

"Calm down, lad. We'll get 'em," Lachlan said.

"Do we have to bring them in here?" Genevieve asked. "There's been enough bloodshed here already."

I felt so bad for her. Who knew what kind of fears or nightmares she had been having lately? Knowing that her home, her sanctuary had been threatened, and was still not safe would be unbearable.

Genevieve's words seemed to calm Tristan down. He stopped pacing and ran a hand through his hair.

"I'm sorry. You don't need any more stress, so I'll take care of them by myself. No need for you all to be involved," Tristan said.

"Like Hell you will!" I stood abruptly. "There is no way you will deal with them alone. You will be outnumbered, and there's no reason to put yourself in that situation. There are so many of us here."

"Yeah, and I want my share of revenge," Lexi said. "They took me too."

"Fine, Lexi and I will take them out," Tristan amended.

"I know you're not going to leave me out of this," I spoke through clenched teeth. "If there's anyone that deserves to get Yuri and Crystal, it's me."

"And there's no way you're going without me," Lachlan added.

"Fine, we will handle it. Genevieve can stay here. She needs some peace and quiet. We'll deal with them outside," Tristan said.

Lachlan sat beside Genevieve, and she shook her head.

"No, I will come too. I will get my peace when I know the threat is over," she said.

"Are we still going to try to get information out of them?" I asked.

"If we can," Tristan answered. "If they don't talk, we'll kill them.

I was suddenly very nervous. I mean sure, I could talk the talk of wanting vengeance, but could I walk the walk? Would I be able to kill them? My stomach churned with the thought. If I didn't kill them, they would keep coming after us, so there really wasn't a choice but... could I do it? I killed the horde of witches who ambushed this house. Was that any different?

Sunset was just a few hours away, and my nerves were shot. Genevieve went to the kitchen to make dinner, but I couldn't even think about eating.

"Dinner's ready," Genevieve called a while later.

We all shuffled into the kitchen, following the smell of spaghetti with meatballs on the table. Beside them garlic bread steamed from beneath a kitchen towel. The smell was enticing, but I couldn't bring myself to eat anything.

"I'm not all that hungry," I said. Tristan shot me a disapproving glance, but I just smiled at him.

The other's filled their plates, clearly not feeling the same aversion I was. Was it bad to have such a heavy dinner before an ambush? I didn't know if there was a protocol, but a feast before an attack seemed weird to me. How did they still have their appetites? Were they so desensitized that the thought of hunting people didn't affect them?

"Just eat something, please," Lexi said.

"Fine." I took a piece of bread and went to the living room.

I sat in the arm chair and nibbled on my bread. I tried to

mentally prepare myself, but I had a feeling that if we got through this, I would be even more traumatized.

The clanking of dishes in the kitchen brought me back to reality, and I finished the last piece of my bread.

"That was really good, Geni, thanks," Lexi said. The others murmured in agreement, and I heard the faucet turn on. I went to the kitchen and pushed Genevieve away from the sink.

"Hey," she said, shocked.

"You shopped and cooked, let me clean," I offered, not really giving her a chance to argue. I needed the mundane task to distract me, and it really wasn't fair that Genevieve did everything for the rest of us.

"It's not a problem," she said. "I can clean."

"Look, I'm sorry I haven't really been helping out, and I would like to change that now. So please go sit down and relax, will you?" I scrubbed a dish, keeping my eyes averted, hoping she would just go. It worked.

"Thank you," she said as she went into the living room. I focused all my little brain cells on scrubbing the plates clean. Making sure I didn't miss a thing kept my mind busy with images of food rather than... I gulped at the thought. Damn. Scrub, Selena, scrub!

Unfortunately there were only so many dishes to wash, so once I finished, I dried each plate into a streak-free shine. Then I put them away. After I wiped down the table and placed the centerpiece back in the middle, I wiped down the counters.

Then I had nothing left to do but think.

Balls.

Tristan stepped behind me, "You okay?" He whispered in my ear.

My heart beat raced. "Yeah, fine."

"You sure? Cause you've been cleaning like a mad woman. I've never seen someone so dedicated to cleaning dishes." He chuckled in my ear, and my heart skipped a beat.

I turned to face him. He stood so close I could feel the heat from his body caress me. I looked into his eyes and saw him struggle. He clenched his jaw, and I could tell he was trying to decide if he should step away.

"Say something," a voice whispered from outside the kitchen.

"No, you say something," another voice said.

The first person cleared their throat, "Um, Selena," they started. The sound penetrated the haze in my mind, and I recognized Lexi's voice. I reluctantly looked away from Tristan, and he stepped away from me.

"Yeah," I answered shortly.

"The sun's starting to set," she said.

Oh.

"I've been trying very hard not to think about that."

Lexi stood next to Lachlan in the entrance of the kitchen and leaned against the doorframe casually.

"Yeah, I get that," she whispered.

"I guess we should be going then," Tristan said quietly.

"Yeah, I guess so," I reluctantly agreed.

I pictured ambushing Crystal and Yuri and almost felt

sorry for them. Almost. Then I remembered Yuri's expressionless face as he crushed my body. I remembered Crystal's evil cackle as she sliced through my flesh.

No, I didn't feel bad for them. I was ready to see them get what they deserved. I looked at Tristan, and his face seemed to harden. I could tell he was getting himself in the right mindset for the task. I could see it happening, his mind shutting off, as he opened one of the drawers and, after looking through it a moment, took out scissors.

"There's not much here," he said under his breath. He went upstairs and returned with a bundle wrapped in cloth. He laid it on the table and unrolled it, revealing a line of fighting knives. I swallowed hard.

"Who wants what?" Tristan asked, holding the weapons out. I shook my head. If I took one of those, it would just make this feel too real. I was having a hard enough time as it was.

"I already have my weapon of choice." Lexi smiled, sparks shooting from her fingers. Lachlan stepped inside the kitchen and assessed his options when Genevieve walked in. She walked to Tristan and took the smallest blade.

Concern was evident on Lachlan's face, but he shook it off and took a knife that would have suited Michael Myers. Tristan grabbed a medium-sized knife, tossing it expertly in the air.

"Those are quite the selection," I said, trying to lighten the mood.

"Yeah, but they each have their purpose." Tristan answered. "I brought these knives from home. They will get the job done." He smiled as he pocketed the scissors, "And so will these if we want them to talk."

Oh God, this was not going to be good. I let out a groan.

Tristan spun to face me, "Hey, are you going to be okay?" He asked, his green eyes piercing mine.

"I think so." My head was spinning though.

"You don't have to do this, you know. I will take care of it for you." His words weren't really comforting. It was him I was more scared of right now.

"I can do this." I nodded, and the more I thought it, the stronger my resolve became. I would make sure they paid for what they did to me.

The five of us left through the front door and headed northeast as the voice had instructed. My heart was beating erratically and my stomach was doing somersaults. I wanted to send up a silent prayer for this to work out, but I couldn't. How could I ask God to help us capture and torture people? I pushed the thought aside; I didn't have room for a conscience tonight. I would just have to ask for forgiveness later - assuming I survived this.

I gathered the group, and we teleported half a mile away from where Crystal and Yuri were supposed to be.

Lachlan and Genevieve walked closely, their hands brushing as they swayed. I was walking closely to Tristan, and to be honest, I didn't even long to hold his hand just then. Lexi walked on the other side of Tristan.

We walked almost the whole distance, and then crept in

silence the last few hundred feet before we heard muttered conversation. We all froze at the same time, and then we ducked behind the trees. I repressed a shudder. Yuri, with his bald head and psychopathic expression stood at the edge of a small clearing. A glow from the small fire lit his features as he searched the area. Crystal stood next to him, her black and blue hair spiked in shambles, her gap-toothed mouth twisted in a sneer.

I almost hyperventilated and squeezed my eyes shut in an attempt to calm my breathing. I could do this. I could do this…

A twig snapped and my eyes shot open. Was that us? Or them? I stood very still, holding my breath, scared that they would see us. They didn't make any move to search the area, so I assumed they had made the noise. I looked at my comrades and nodded.

We split up, each going in a different direction around the clearing and closing in. We made a circle around their meager campsite. It was merely a log used as a bench, a small, newly made fire, a couple bags of food and other things I couldn't make out.

It wasn't until we were ten feet away that Crystal noticed our approach. She stood abruptly, and Yuri followed suit. We were already closing in on them.

Crystal's head darted around, trying to keep each of us in her line of vision. Yuri stood completely still. Only his eyes moved as he looked Tristan and I over.

"Well, look what we have here," Crystal sneered. "How did you know? Or is Selena psychic now?" She asked smugly.

"We have our ways," Tristan answered. As we got closer I was able to see the other things they had with them in the bags, the 'tools' of their trade: knives, clamps, pliers, and other things that I never wanted to see put to use. They brought these to use on us, so why was I still hesitant to return the gesture?

"We came to warn you and… and join you," Crystal said.

"Right, I'm sure you've seen the error of your ways and come to redeem yourself… with your torture devices and all." Tristan lifted a large bolt cutter from one of the bags, clearly more satisfied with that than the scissors.

"Believe us, or don't believe us-" Crystal started, but I didn't wait for her to finish.

"Alright," I said. "Then tell us, where is Darien and what has he been up to?"

"You mean you don't know?" Crystal retorted.

"We can find out." Lexi smirked, taking one step forward. "We have some business to settle. I think I'll play with you first," she said, looking at Crystal.

Crystal flicked her wrists in an attempt to cast a spell, but Lexi's fingers lashed out, and an electric current shot forward, hitting Crystal right in the chest. Crystal jerked from the shock. Yuri rushed forward to stand between Crystal and Lexi's sparking fingers, but Tristan thrust his arm out sending a fierce wind to push him back.

I didn't like this. I don't mind fighting people, but it was unsettling when they were ambushed and outnumbered. I couldn't do it.

Just as I had the thought, Crystal blocked Lexi's attack. She pushed her hands out, and a strong gust of wind lifted Lexi and flung her into a tree.

"Lexi!" Genevieve called as she rushed forward to make sure she was alright, leaving the circle open.

Yuri ran for the gap, but Tristan leapt forward and pushed him back. Yuri's eyes were black as coal. He swung his arms, and Tristan flew backward. Well so much for outnumbered.

I created a ring of fire on the ground around Crystal and Yuri to keep them in place. Crystal tried to run through it, then used the wind to lift herself over it, but the flames jumped higher, forcing her back. Crystal hissed at me as Tristan, Lexi and Genevieve closed the circle again. Suddenly Crystal stood up straight and smiled.

Her eyes darted behind me, and I turned to see a man step out from behind a tree, then another, and then two women.

"You didn't think you killed all of us, did you?" Crystal asked smugly. "Now, you know we can't go back empty handed."

Yuri's mouth twitched... was that a smile?

The others came at us from the trees. Now this was a fair fight. They charged us, and Lachlan, Genevieve and Lexi stepped toward their opponents. Lachlan threw fireballs at two of the witches, Lexi shot sparks from her fingers at the woman, and Genevieve blasted an icicle spell, knocking a man backward as he charged at her. That left

Crystal and Yuri for me and Tristan.

I nodded to Tristan and saw him smile. I removed the ring of fire and charged Crystal. Not bothering with spells, I slammed my fist into her face. She fell backward, letting out a shocked curse.

Tristan ran toward Yuri, lowered his shoulder, and plowed into his chest, flinging him backward. Tristan pounced, straddling Yuri and punching him repeatedly in the face. The thought crossed my mind to stop him, but what was the point? We were going to kill them anyway.

Crystal stood and walked slowly toward me, blood streaming freely from her nose. I felt a great swell of satisfaction. She flicked her wrists, and I stumbled backward, almost losing my footing. I didn't want to use magic. Maybe because it was so amazingly satisfying to feel my fist land in her face – to have that kind of contact, or maybe it was because the last two times I saw her, I couldn't use magic, and there was some sentiment in that. All I know is that I wanted to spill more of her blood, and I wanted my hands to do the damage.

She raised her arms, the dirt swirling around her feet rising with them, and she pelted me with it. I threw my arms up and blocked it. Huh. I didn't know I could do that. She cast a spell to push me away, and again I blocked it, eliciting a shriek of frustration. I laughed.

I looked to see that Tristan had his fist poised to strike Yuri again, only Yuri jerked suddenly and got to his feet, his eye swollen shut. It looked good on him.

Lachlan was still shooting fireballs at the two witches

who were blocking them, but not before getting their skin singed. Lexi leaped onto the back of the witch she fought and knocked her to the ground. Genevieve countered her attacker's fire spell with water, dousing the flames before they could reach her. I could end this in a matter of seconds. I could kill them all.

Before I could think it through, Crystal charged at me, a piercing war cry escaping her thin lips. I waited for her to reach me, and then I opened my hand and slammed my open palm into her mouth. Her lip ring caught on my finger and tore out of her flesh as she fell backward.

She screamed in pain and fury as blood gushed from her split lip. Tristan turned to see what had happened, and a look of pride crossed his face. He quickly turned back to Yuri just in time to deflect a shock spell. Tristan charged, slamming his elbow into Yuri's face. As Yuri fell Tristan grabbed his head and slammed it repeatedly into the ground. Crystal stood and faced me. Her eyes blazed with fury, her hair was disheveled, and blood gushed from her nose and mouth, creating a stream down her neck and onto the front of her shirt.

I ran to the bag of tools on the floor and grabbed what looked like an ice pick. I had a few debts to repay Crystal. I cast a spell sending her flying backward, and landing paralyzed on the ground. She stared at me with helpless fury. I jammed the ice pick into the front of her thigh and dragged it downward to her knee. It was surprisingly sharp and sliced through her flesh like butter.

The sound she made, with such anguish, froze my

insides, snapping me out of my bloodlust.

What was I doing? I moved quickly away from Crystal, but I didn't remove my spell. I needed her to stay put. Lachlan threw the large knife at one of his opponents and the blade landed squarely in the man's chest, sending him to the ground permanently. He spun quickly toward the woman and slammed a fireball into her chest, leaving her charred remains smoking on the ground next to her friend.

He ran to Genevieve in time to see her fingers lash out and the man's neck snapped instantly.

Lachlan then sprinted to Lexi and shot sparks from his fingers at her attacker. Lexi shot shock spells of her own at the witch. The witch tried blocking the assault, but was too slow to block in both directions. She too went down.

Tristan had taken the bolt cutters out and held them over one of Yuri's fingers, Crystal lay in front of me whimpering, and although I wanted to feel bad for her, I couldn't. She deserved what she got; I just didn't think I could be the one to give it to her. I forced her into an upright position so that she could see Tristan and what he was going to do to her Yuri.

"You should have killed me when you had the chance," Tristan snarled, "You fucked up." He squeezed the bolt cutters and Yuri wailed in excruciation. I didn't want to look, and yet I couldn't look away. Yuri's finger snapped clean off, and blood spurted from the stump. Crystal cried out in response to her lover's pain - that was my vengeance for what Tristan had to endure.

My stomach heaved reflexively, but I didn't throw up.

Yuri held his bloodied hand and screamed in pain.

"Tell us where Darien is, and what his plans are for Selena," Tristan told Crystal. "Or I'll take Yuri apart piece by piece." He jerked Yuri's hand back into his own and pressed the bolt cutters over another finger.

"I—I don't know anything," Crystal stammered.

"Wrong answer," Tristan said, squeezing the bolt cutters and slicing off another finger. Yuri's scream was garbled as he pressed his hand to his chest. I couldn't stand to see the torture anymore. I turned to Crystal instead.

"I swear! We were only hired to get you, nothing more." Crystal's eyes blazed, and the wind swirled around me, threatening to push me away, but I blocked her attack.

Filled with shame, I decided this had to end now.

I imagined my ball of destruction, allowing it to grow with whatever anger I had left and I unleashed it on Crystal and Yuri.

They shrieked and writhed in pain as they burned from the core of their being. Their skin blistered and boiled, then blackened, emitting that cooked meat smell. Finally their bodies settled, steam streaming from their flesh before it turned completely into ash.

I dropped to my knees and placed my head in my hands. How had this happened? I was so scared, so sure I couldn't hurt them, and I had nearly turned into them.

"Selena," Tristan started as he walked toward me. He placed his hand on my shoulder, but I jerked away. "I'm sorry," he mumbled and took a step back. Could I really judge him when what I did was so much worse? No, but I was just too disturbed, too raw with the image of his hatred and rage that I couldn't have him touch me just yet. And I didn't think I deserved to be touched either.

"Come on. Let's go back to the house," Lexi said behind me. She put her hands under my arms to help me up, but I jerked away from her too.

"Just leave me," I whispered. The tears streamed hot and silent down my face.

Tristan and Lexi backed off, but I could tell they were trying to decide what to do.

Lachlan went to the other four corpses and set their bodies ablaze, making sure there was no evidence to be found, and Genevieve drowned the ashes into the earth and extinguished their campfire.

Tristan took the ice pick from the ashes and buried it with their tools deep in the ground, even though we were pretty sure no one would look for Yuri and Crystal, especially not here.

Finally we all just stood watching the area that had been a battlefield only a short while ago. My body shook uncontrollably as I thought of what had just transpired. What was I becoming?

I suddenly couldn't stand to be there one more minute. I turned and ran back in the direction we came from.

"Selena," I heard Tristan call after me, but I didn't stop. I couldn't. I ran hard and fast until my legs ached and my lungs burned. My vision was blurred by the tears in my eyes, and I ran into a few low branches, scratching my skin.

I kept running, not sure where I wanted to go. The

house seemed too quiet, too ordinary after what I had done. But where else could I go? I turned abruptly and ran south through the woods. I kept going, burning off the shame and guilt as my legs pumped me forward.

I heard water flowing ahead of me, and I ran toward the sound. I reached a clearing, and there I saw the source of the noise. There was a small creek running parallel to the woods. The moonlight sparkled on the ankle-deep water, revealing every single stone below the surface. I felt a sense of calm I couldn't explain.

I knelt at the water's edge and put my hands in. The water was cool, but not cold. I grabbed a handful and splashed the water on my face. It was refreshingly sobering, giving me the sense that I had been dreaming, but was now awake.

I tentatively drank the water and was surprised by how good it tasted. No water in Arizona could ever compare. I drank a few handfuls and felt my tension ease. I sat cross-legged on the ground and watched as the water swept past around the larger rocks that sporadically jutted from the water's surface.

I felt wrong. There was something in my gut telling me I had done a bad thing, making my stomach flip with guilt. I had somehow managed to ignore what I had done to the other witches, able to convince myself it was necessary. Now those deaths caught up with me, adding to my grief. My heart raced with shame, and I held back a sob.

I twisted my mother's ring around my finger and was immersed in its beauty. The water reflected dimly off the sapphire stone, making it seem to be in motion. I became mesmerized by the stone, wondering what magical attributes it could possibly have. My eyes unfocused as the stone lured me into its depths.

My mother's words rang clearly in my ears: *'I have left you my ring, in hopes that it brings you comfort during hard times, as it has done for me.'*

Her words swirled around me and engulfed me, sucking me deeper and deeper into the stone. I could no longer see what was around me, could no longer hear the birds chirping, or the water rushing by.

It was as if I had fallen into a deep, vivid dream, but I had no sense of what was happening or where I was.

"Selena," A familiar voice whispered. I looked up and saw that I was alone in a room. There were no windows, all the walls were white, and there was just one plain metal door.

"Don't be afraid." I heard. When I looked around to see who had spoken, there was no one there. "Watch."

The room became immersed in darkness, and one of the walls lit up brilliantly. A few scattered images appeared on it, one after the other, until it settled on one I recognized. I saw Tristan and I watching as Crystal and Yuri burned, and then the images seemed to move backwards.

Crystal and Yuri were dead, and then they weren't. As it continued in reverse, I saw them lurking around our house, only I saw it from their perspective. Then it played forward, showing Tristan look suddenly in their direction as they caught his attention.

The image rushed further back to the day they had captured us then played forward again. I hung from my wrists in pain, while Crystal and Yuri relished in it. I saw Crystal and Yuri break the spell on Tristan's house to teleport in and take him and Lexi.

Then I saw as they received a call, jotting down my name and whereabouts on a pad of paper. More images flew by, faster and faster. I saw their victims tortured through the eyes of the monsters, saw them begging for mercy, begging to either be released or killed, so they wouldn't have to endure any more.

Crystal and Yuri only laughed and continued with their sick enjoyment. More victims, so many my head spun.

Then the images changed completely and I saw the day the group of witches attacked the half way house. Again it went backwards. I saw the people I killed, and then saw them alive. Then it played forward as I saw them lurk around our house, planning to attack.

Time went further back, and I saw them in a room with Darien, Crystal and Yuri. All planning. All wanting us dead. I saw their faces sneering angrily.

And yes, I saw the ones who had families, their husbands, wives, and children who waited for them to come home, but they never did. My heart ached at the thought, until I saw other people they had been hired to kill. I saw the ambushes and the unsuspecting victims that succumbed to their evil, and their families, who were broken.

Then the images flickered and started to fast forward

before settling on the image of a man coming home late at night. As he unlocks his front door, Crystal and Yuri grab him from behind, but instead of taking him, their bodies burn and blaze from the inside and they turn to ash without the man even seeing them. Then the images speed past and stop as a young girl appears carrying school books and walk-ing home. The image shows her parents getting dinner ready as Crystal and Yuri teleport into their home and grab the parents to teleport them out. Again, they turn to ash before they reach the parents, who carry on cooking unaware.

Complete darkness suddenly engulfed the room.

"Do not feel guilt. You killed evil witches, and had you not, they would have killed you and your friends before moving on to other innocents. That little girl will grow up with parents because of you. That man and the girl's parents were only a few of the many lives you have saved tonight."

"Who are you?" I asked, the familiar voice tickling my memory.

"Know that you are destined for great things, and that all who oppose you, all those you may have to kill, will all be deserving. Do not feel remorse. Not for this, baby girl."

My breath caught in my throat. I did know this voice.

"Mom?" I asked over the lump in my throat.

"I love you, Selena," she whispered.

21. LEAVING

"Mom! Mom, I love you too," I whimpered.

"Selena." My eyes snapped open. Tristan stood above me. The dark forest behind him came into focus. "Are you okay?" He asked, his eyes intense with concern.

"Yes," I said. I was lying on the ground beside the creek.

"Oh, thank God. You scared me," he said as he lifted me to my feet. "Were you sleeping?" Confusion was written all over Tristan's beautiful face.

"I'm not really sure."

"Why did you take off like that? I was worried I wouldn't find you."

"Sorry, I just needed to... get some perspective I guess."

Tristan pulled me into a fierce hug, and I let him. I no longer felt guilty for what either of us had done.

"What happened?" He asked.

"I think I just found out what the ring can do," I said with a small smile.

"Really? What is it?" He asked with genuine interest.

"Well I think it takes your worries and spins it, putting it in perspective so you will feel better, more comfortable about it. So, the ring, and I guess my mom, made me feel better."

"Your mom?"

"Yeah, well I heard her voice. She was consoling me."

"Huh, that's pretty cool," he said contemplating my words. "Were you…are you…mad at me?" He asked hesitantly after a moment.

"I'm not mad at you. Why?"

"Well, you were acting kind of weird, and if you felt this bad about what you had done, what must you think of me? I mean I really lost control back there and I'm sorry." He let out a sigh and ran his hand through his hair.

"I'm not mad at you, Tristan. I was scared, a little, but not mad." I smiled up at him then.

He nodded and clenched his jaw. We stood in silence for a few minutes.

"Come on, we should get back. Everyone else is already at the house." He held his hand out and I took it. We walked back, the crickets croaking the only sound.

My body was suddenly heavy, all that fighting and running and adrenaline had taken its toll. I hadn't realized how far I had run until we had been walking for half an hour and I still couldn't see the house.

"Thank you," I said when the lights of the cottage shone through the trees ahead.

"For what?" Tristan asked.

"For caring so much that you went crazy to exact my revenge," I said teasingly, even though my words rang true.

"I will go crazy for you any day," he teased back smiling. My heart skipped a beat, and I wished I knew what he was thinking. Having this light conversation made me feel that much better. A weight lifted off my chest and I realized that, up until that moment, I was still a little uneasy about Tristan. Huh.

We entered the house through the front door, and Genevieve greeted us with a hug.

"I was so worried about you," she whispered in my ear as she held me tight. I was overwhelmed by her concern. "It took you so long to come home."

Home. This wasn't home, not to me, and nothing I did would make me forget that. I wanted so badly to be home. My home.

I hugged her back tightly, feeling she deserved to know that I cared about her too.

"Thank you, but really, we're fine. It's over – well this part is anyways," I said, releasing her. "I think I will go to bed now. I'm pretty beat." I looked at the others and saw that they were nodding their heads. I was sure they were feeling the same way.

I made my way slowly up the stairs, my sore muscles protesting with each step. I showered quickly, watching as Crystal's blood washed off me to dilute in the water in a light red trail down the drain, and when I dressed, I pulled a sweater on. There was a chill coursing through my body that I just couldn't shake.

I crawled into bed and immediately sank into the soft mattress. This had to have been the longest day of my life.

Just as I was about to reach sweet oblivion, there was a knock on the door.

"Yeah," I mumbled.

The door opened and Tristan walked in. He stood by the bed uncertainly.

"I'm sorry, it's late. I just have to say something." He rocked on his heels.

"Sure, what's up?"

"I know I haven't been honest with you," he said, running a hand through his hair. "Or, well I guess I should say I haven't been honest with myself."

I sat up in bed, "What do you mean?"

"You know I care about you," he started. "And I keep telling you that we need boundaries, even though I sometimes cross them. The thing is we do need boundaries." He held my face in his hands and caressed my cheek with his thumb.

"No, we don't," I whispered. I saw agony flash in his eyes and then he brought his lips down to mine. He kissed me, so softly, yet I could feel pain in that one kiss, confusing me. He stepped back quickly and shook his head.

"From now on, I will only protect you. I won't act in an unprofessional manner. This I promise you." He clenched his jaw and gazed at me as if this promise was a good thing.

Oh.

An ache formed in my chest and I bit my lip to keep my emotions in check.

"If that's how you feel, I can respect that."

He nodded, and left the room.

I released the weak hold I had on my emotions and cried. I cried for the lost love, and then the lost lives and by the time I cried myself out I was feeling acceptance.

The door opened a short while later and I hastily wiped my tears away as Lexi came into the room.

"What a day," she said.

"Yeah, what a day," I whispered.

The next morning I awoke, and headed downstairs after washing up. I saw my small luggage and Lexi's bag sitting by the door. Relief flooded through me as I realized we were going home. I walked into the kitchen for some coffee and saw Tristan sitting at the table by himself, a muffin lay untouched in front of him. He looked up and I hesitated a moment. I wondered where Lachlan and Genevieve were until I noticed the time. It was very early.

I nodded in greeting, trying to be "professional" and hide my irritation.

"I take it we're leaving today?" I asked.

"Yeah, you just need to throw the last minute items in your bag."

"Good."

"Did you sleep well?" He asked.

"Yeah, actually I did." I answered, reaching for a mug. I winced in pain.

"You okay?" He asked, assessing me.

"Yeah, I'm just sore," I answered.

"You should be. You went all mad woman on Crystal last night. Though I have to admit," he paused for a moment, "I'm proud."

"You are? Why?" I asked.

"You fought her with almost no magic. You beat her with your bare fists. My training paid off. I'm damn proud." He beamed. How easy it was for him to slip into protector mode. I almost forgot he had kissed me the night before. Almost.

"It did feel really good," I admitted. I took my coffee and walked out of the kitchen, not wanting to hang out with Tristan when my feelings were so out of whack.

I could feel him watching me as I left, but I didn't care. I went upstairs and sat on the bed with my coffee. Lexi was still asleep, so I made sure not to make any noise or sudden movements.

I'm not sure how long I stayed there before the smell of breakfast wafted up the stairs, and my stomach growled. Since I had skipped dinner the night before, I was pretty famished.

I jumped out of bed and regretted the sudden movement immediately. It was going to take a while for my muscles to settle. I wondered if I could heal them, but decided it wasn't anything I couldn't handle. Lexi woke up with the movement.

"Come eat," I said eagerly. I was so excited for food it was comical.

I rushed down the stairs – well I tried to rush, but it hurt - just in time to see Genevieve laying out the feast. Lachlan was already up and sitting at the table, and Tristan leaned against the counter. I grabbed a plate and threw bacon, eggs, pancakes, and a muffin on it. Genevieve had outdone herself again. Lexi came down and started making her plate.

I went to the living room and devoured my food in less than five minutes. By the time I went to the kitchen to wash my dish, the others were just starting to eat. Lexi eyed me mid-bite.

"Hungry?" She teased.

"I was." I tapped my full stomach, and beamed a smile at Lexi. "Thanks, Gen. That was amazing!" I said. I was definitely in a better mood now that I was full.

I left the others to eat and walked out the door to the backyard. I sat on the patio table and absorbed the rays. Setting Tristan's emotional handicap aside, I was feeling okay, but I couldn't ignore the nagging question in the back of my mind: Now that Crystal and Yuri were out of the way, what did we do?

Should we be proactive and go after Darien before he came after me? What were the chances that we could beat this thing? My mind wandered, asking and dismissing questions. I lost track of time.

"What are you thinking so hard about?" Lexi asked as she came outside.

"Just trying to figure out what to do next," I answered honestly.

"Well, we need to keep training as your powers develop, and find out what Darien is up to," Lexi said matter-of-fact.

"Why do I get the feeling that something bad is going to happen?" I asked.

Because it is, that familiar male voice said inside my head.

Damn.

298

DON'T MISS THE SEQUEL TO
UNINVITED!

FOLLOW SELENA AS THE STORY
CONTINUES IN

UNFORGIVABLE

Carol Rayyan is an avid reader of Fantasy and Paranormal Romance who decided to write her own trilogy, and create her own magical world. She grew up in Brampton, Ontario Canada but now lives with her husband Isa, and dog Chewbacca in Scottsdale, Arizona, where she is currently working on her next novel.

Questions or comments? Find her author page on Facebook.com

www.ingramcontent.com/pod-product-compliance
Lightning Source LLC
Chambersburg PA
CBHW020235180626
46810CB00006B/2207